Anonymous

Biographical Cyclopedia of Vanderburgh County, Indiana

Embracing biographies of many of the prominent men and families of the county

Anonymous

Biographical Cyclopedia of Vanderburgh County, Indiana
Embracing biographies of many of the prominent men and families of the county

ISBN/EAN: 9783337224110

Printed in Europe, USA, Canada, Australia, Japan

Cover: Foto ©Raphael Reischuk / pixelio.de

More available books at **www.hansebooks.com**

OF

VANDERBURGH COUNTY,

INDIANA.

EMBRACING BIOGRAPHIES OF MANY OF THE PROMINENT MEN

AND FAMILIES OF THE COUNTY.

PRESS OF THE KELLER PRINTING AND PUBLISHING CO
EVANSVILLE IND
1897

PREFACE.

"A book! O rare one!
Be not, as is our fangled world, a garment
Nobler than that it covers."

TO RECORD the lives of its people is the best history of a country. So said Macauley, the greatest of English historians; and one of America's most brilliant writers of this century has given expression to the same thought. This Biographical Cyclopedia of Vanderburgh County has been prepared in conformity with this idea. Rather than gather dry statistical matter from old and musty records that none would appreciate, I have gone direct to the people, the men and women who have, by their force of character, brought Vanderburgh County to a rank, in many respects, second to none among those comprising the great Hoosier State; and gleaned from them the story of the struggles and vicissitudes of their lives. No more interesting and instructive matter could be presented to an intelligent public. Complete sketches of many whose lives are worthy of imitation by generations yet to come will be found herein. It relates how many with meagre means and limited advantages, the environments of whom were of the simplest kind, have become great men and women, their influence extending throughout the land. It tells of men who have risen Phœnix-like from the humbler walks of life to eminence as statesmen, and whose names have been written in letters of shining gold and their forms lighted up by the sunshine of merited fame. It tells of those in every walk of life who have striven to succeed and records how success has usually crowned their efforts. It tells of many also who, seeking not the applause of the world, are satisfied with—they have done their best. It tells of how many in the pride of strength of young manhood, left the plow and anvil, the lawyer's office and the counting-room, left every trade and profession, and at their country's call went forth valiantly "to do or die" for the land which gave them birth, and to which, next to their God, their highest homage was due. This book will be loved and appreciated by generations yet to come, preserved as a sacred and precious treasure, and a priceless souvenir of those who contributed their lives and means in the interest of humanity, civilization and progress.

THE AUTHOR.

BIOGRAPHICAL CYCLOPEDIA

OF

VANDERBURGH COUNTY, INDIANA.

HON. F. W. COOK.

FREDERICK WASHINGTON COOK was born at Washington, District of Columbia, February 1, 1832, and when yet quite young he removed with his parents to Port Deposit, Cecil county, Maryland. After a residence of about three years at that place, they removed to Cincinnati, Ohio, and in 1836 to Evansville. In 1837 the stepfather of Mr. Cook, Jacob Rice, and Fred. Kroener bought property in Lamasco, near the terminus of the Wabash and Erie canal, which was then in course of construction, and in the same year built what was later known as the "Old Brewery" —the first brewery built in Southern Indiana.

Mr. Cook was educated in Evansville, also attending the Anderson Collegiate Institute at New Albany, Indiana. His first business engagement was with Mr. L. W. Heberd, who was in the dry goods business on Main street, with whom Mr. Cook remained for two years, until the death of his brother, when he was taken home by his parents to learn the brewing business. In 1853 Mr. Cook, in conjunction with Louis Rice, a brother of his stepfather, built the City Brewery—where the F. W. Cook Brewing Co., of to-day stands —the premises then being a corn field. When they began business the cash capital of the firm was $330.00, Louis Rice having accumulated $165.00, and Mr. Cook's father advancing him an equal amount. Louis Rice attended to the brewing department and Mr. Cook to business and financial department. In 1857 Louis Rice sold his interest in the brewery to Jacob Rice for $3,500. The new firm commenced at once the erection of a lager beer cellar and in 1858 made the first lager beer in Southern Indiana; also in that year an extensive malt house was added to the brewery property.

Mr. Cook was elected councilman for the Fifth ward in April, 1856, and for the Eighth ward in April, 1863, being re-elected in April, 1864, but resigned in the fall of that year, having been elected as representative from Vanderburgh county to the legislature of Indiana. In this capacity he served during the called session of 1864, and also during the regular session of 1864-65. After his return home, in 1867, the people again showed their appreciation by electing him to the city council from the Fourth ward, and it may be said of him that both in the city council and legislature his public services have been satisfactory to his constituents and have been performed with great credit to himself. In 1856 Mr. Cook was married to Miss Louise Hild, of Louisville, Kentucky, who died in February, 1877. He was again married to Miss Jennie Himeline, of Kelley's Island, Ohio, in November, 1879, who died in January, 1885.

Mr. Rice, the step-father and partner of Mr. Cook, met with an accident in April, 1872, and died on the 3d of May following from the injuries received, and Mrs. Rice, his mother, died on the 6th day of November, 1878, leaving Mr. Cook the sole heir to the City Brewery. The business was continued under the old firm name of Cook & Rice until 1885, when it was incorporated, with F. W. Cook as president, under the laws of the State of Indiana as the F. W. Cook Brewing Co., which name is not only identified with the growth of Evansville, but known far and wide in the southern and eastern states. On December 3, 1891, the brew house and offices of the F. W. Cook Brewing Co., were destroyed by fire. Hardly had the smoke cleared away and the ashes cooled before arrangements for a modern building were being perfected. The offices of the Brewing Company were temporarily removed to 706 Main street. In March, 1893, the new brew house—one of the most modern and perfectly arranged brew houses in the United States—was completed and the offices were again moved to their commodious quarters in the new building. The construction of this magnificent and imposing brew house, with a capacity of 300,000 barrels annually, is an evidence on the part of Mr. Cook of his confidence in the future of Evansville.

It is safe to say that there is no more energetic or ambitious man engaged in the manufacturing business than Mr. Cook. Few names are as well known as his, synonymous with advancement, only waiting an opportunity to meet any exigency. A prominent figure up to the last two years at the meetings of the National Brewers' Association, the wealthiest co-operative body in the world, his suggestions have always been listened to by that august body with the profoundest respect. Mr. Cook certainly deserves the great credit he has achieved, ranking as one of the wealth-iest men in Indiana. He is the architect of his own fortune and is to-day one of the representative citizens of Evansville. His pleasant face and his sympathetic nature are characteristic of the man. While devoting strict attention to busi-ness, Mr. Cook finds time to attend to the duties devolving upon him as pres-ident of the Evansville, Newburgh & Suburban Railway, also of the District Telegraph Co., and also of the F. W. Cook Investment Co. The latter con-cern has among its property Cook's Park, one of the finest summer resorts in the country, consisting of sixteen acres in the city limits and a club house. Mr. Cook is a director in the Citizen's National Bank, also in the Bank of Commerce, and in the Evansville In-surance Co. He is also interested in numerous other enterprises. From the above it is evident that Mr. Cook ranks as a citizen of great influence. Al-though sixty-five years of age, Mr. Cook possesses a splendid physical structure, and has before him a business career, which by its lustre and bril-liancy, must eclipse and dim by its brightness that which in the past has been so remarkable and pre-eminent His acts of charity and benevolence have been bestowed upon thousands. Equally liberal has he shown himself in all enterprises tending to benefit the general public and the welfare of the city of Evansville.

F. W. Cook belongs to that class of men to whom is chiefly due the creation of our industries and the building up of our cities. They are men that, having climbed to a higher level than the great majority of their fellow men, they become objects of universal interest, and the history of their business career becomes of espec-ial interest to young men who have yet to make their fortune. To one strug-gling to gain a foothold in the business world there is no such incentive to effort as the knowledge that another with whom he is brought into daily contact has met and triumphed over obstacles greater than those with which he him-self has to contend. There is some-thing to challenge admiration in the combination of faculties forming the character of a man who starts in life without the great advantages of wealth and literally carves out his own fortune, makes for himself a position and a name respected and honored in his commun-ity. He is the great man who has gained a mastery over himself and learned to rely upon himself, finding in his own person the qualities and charac-teristics essential to great achievements; who possesses ambition to succeed by honorable means, courage to undertake what may be unpromising, will and pertinacity to overcome obstacles and surmount difficulties. These are nature's powers for conquest. Such a man entrenches and fortifies himself. At the same time his labors and enterprises are contributed to the prosperity of the community. He who builds and oper-ates railroads honestly, who plants in-dustries and operates them without oppression, is not less deserving of praise than the man who ministers unto the churches.

HENRY EDWARD COOK, vice pres ident of the F. W. Cook Brewing Co., and secretary and treasurer of the F. W. Cook Investment Co., was born in Evansville, February 20, 1864. His early mental training was obtained from the public schools of Evansville, and when sixteen years of age he entered the Bloomington State University, being the youngest member of the class of 1884. He went abroad in the fall of 1884 to complete his education, taking a course of four semesters—two years —at the famous Heidelberg University in Germany, applying himself particularly to the study of modern languages. He returned home in 1886 and for a year was engaged in familiarizing himself with the financial department of his father's brewery business. In the early part of 1887 he again crossed the Atlantic, spending twelve months in traveling through Germany, Austria, Switzerland, Bohemia, Italy, France and England. He returned to Evansville in 1888 and immediately assumed active duties in the office of the F. W. Cook Brewing Co., and in 1890 was chosen vice president of that institution. This was rather an important position for as young a man as Mr. Cook to fill, but he did it with grace and dignity. It was a tribute to his worth and ability, as a bright and competent business man. Further attestation of the confidence imposed in him was his selection as secretary and treasurer of the F. W. Cook Investment Co., in 1891. So far his career has been a brilliant one, and if we are to judge the future by the past, some flattering predictions might be made. Henry E. Cook possesses many of the traits and characteristics of his father; although quite a young man, he has the qualifications for his position in an eminent degree, and the record he is making will certainly prepare him for other trusts, that are sure to come to a man of his ability. He is popular with all classes, refined and courteous. Being a man of fine mind as well as appearance he naturally has clothed his position with a dignity, commanding the respect of all with whom he deals. Henry E. Cook is a warm friend and generous in his opposition; he is painstaking, conscientious and determined, thoroughly conversant with the duties and details of the interests in which he is engaged, with that quick comprehension to rely upon his own judgment in the disposition of affairs generally.

SAMUEL BAYARD,

PRESIDENT of the Old National Bank of Evansville, was born in Vincennes, Indiana.

John F. Bayard, the father, was a native of France, and came to America at an early day. He was a French soldier, and served with the first Napoleon at Waterloo. He married Miss Mary Ann Boneau, of Vincennes, and nine children issued from their union, the subject of this sketch being the first. Samuel Bayard received his mental training in the public and private schools of Vincennes. After graduating he started out to fight life's battles alone,

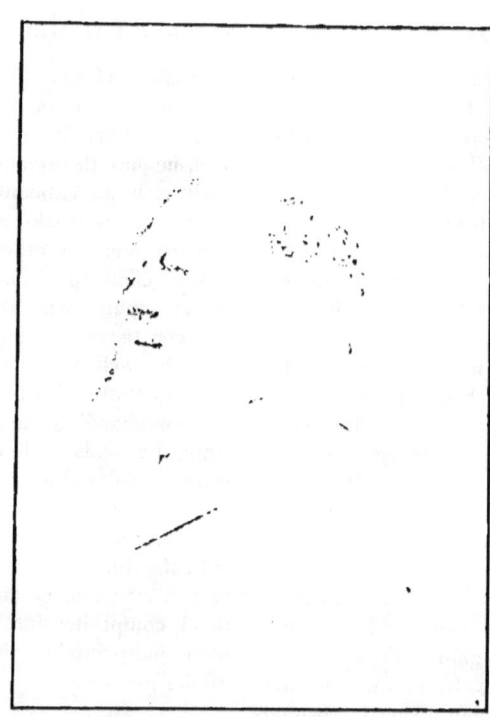

SAMUEL BAYARD.

and secured a position as deputy in the office of the clerk of the circuit court at Vincennes, where he remained for three years. In 1851 he resigned that position, and, coming to Evansville, entered the Evansville branch of the State Bank of Indiana, in the capacity of clerk. He was promoted to the position of teller two months later, and remained in that position until 1857, when, by a change in the banking system of the state, the affairs of the State Bank of Indiana were closed. Upon the organization of the Bank of the State of Indiana, Mr. Bayard was chosen cashier of the Evansville branch, and occupied that position until the advent of national banking, which was ushered in by congress during the war. The State Bank was then succeeded by the Evansville National Bank, and Mr. Bayard was appointed cashier. In 1867 he was elected vice president of that institution, and in that capacity, virtually had the management of the entire affairs of the bank. In 1876 he was elected president, and held the presidency of that bank and its successor, the "Old National Bank," which he organized, down to the present time. He has done more to strengthen the financial institutions of this section than has any other influence, and the reputation that the Old National Bank holds in the financial world, has done more to advertise Evansville, in the way it should be advertised, than any other thing in it. Its capital and surplus exceeds a million dollars. Samuel Bayard is a man of means and affairs, and his operations have not been confined alone to banking. In 1864 he assisted in organ-izing the firm of W. J. Lowry & Co., for the purpose of doing a banking business. He was one of the stockholders and mainly instrumental in organizing the German National Bank, which was succeeded by the German Bank of Evansville, and was a stockholder and member of the board of directors. In 1870 he was chosen a director of the Evansville, Carmi and Paducah R. R. Co., afterwards consolidated with the St. Louis and Southeastern, and finally became part of the Louisville and Nashville system. He was a director and also a member of the executive committee, which had charge of and controlled the management of the company's business. He served the Evansville and Terre Haute R. R. Co. as director, and was one of the six stockholders controlling an interest therein. He contributed liberally to the Evansville library association, being one of the citizens that formed that association. He served as its treasurer and afterwards as president. He was entrusted with the important commission of making the first selection of books for the library, and went to Cincinnati in person to purchase the books. For a quarter of a century Mr. Bayard has been a stockholder of the Evansville Gas Co., now the Evansville Gas and Electric Light Co., of which he is treasurer and the largest stockholder. He is an indefatigable worker in all the enterprises in which he is interested. His judgment is regarded as superior, and his advice sought by his colleagues. His prudence and conservatism lend unusual weight to his counsel in all monetary affairs. Mr. Bayard is one of the foremost financiers of this country, and his name has been prominently mentioned for secretary of the treasury of the United States. He is not a politician in the usual acceptance of the term, but by sheer force of character, has obtained a leading position in the ranks of the republican party, with which he affiliates. Although Mr. Bayard works as hard as he did three or four decades ago, giving many hours of his time each day to the various enterprises in which he is engaged, he still finds time to devote to his books in his magnificent library, and there finds delightful recreation. He has, perhaps, the largest library in the state, containing a large number of rare and valuable books, the systematic and careful collection of which has occupied many years. Samuel Bayard was united in marriage March 6, 1867, to Miss Mattie J. Orr, daughter of that prominent and influential citizen of Evansville, the late Samuel Orr.

Mrs. Bayard is an active and helpful member of the presbyterian church, prominent in charity work, and loved by all who know her. Mr. Bayard is not a member of the church, but attends upon the services of the Presbyterian church, and is very much interested in the organized efforts for the maintenance and propagation of Christianity. He is one of the most public spirited men in Evansville, and is identified with all public measures looking to the improvement of the city, and the advancement of society. It is known, moreover, among his neighbors, although he has sacredly guarded the fact as a secret, that he and his estimable wife are most generous in their donations to the cause of charity, and their liberality toward benevolent institutions is very great, having given something over $20,000 to the Young Men's Christian Association building fund alone, while their liberality to the worthy poor, in the way of private charity, approaches extravagance.

CAPT. JOHN GILBERT,

OF EVANSVILLE has for many years been one of the substantial and successful business men of the Ohio Valley. A native of Pennsylvania, he came west in 1836, at the age of eighteen years, and located in southern Illinois. For twenty-five years he was a country merchant, bartering the articles kept in a general store for all the products of a new country and selling comparatively few goods for cash. It required skill, tact, patience and sagacity to carry on a business of exchange safely and profitably at such a time, under such conditions. The man who was able to build up and hold a trade, and reach the markets with produce taken as the price of merchandise, was qualified for business on a large scale. He began at a time when it was necessary to float the products of the western settlements down the Ohio and Mississippi rivers on flat boats, to the markets of the south, of which New Orleans was chief. He continued to carry on commerce successfully, by steamboat, in the Ohio and Mississippi rivers during the period of the rebellion. At the present time

CAPT. JOHN GILBERT.

he is president and managing owner of a daily packet line carrying the United States mail between Evansville, Indiana, Paducah, Kentucky, and Cairo, Illinois, a route two hundred miles in length. He is president of the John Gilbert Dry Goods Co., one of the largest houses of its class in the Ohio Valley. His finanancial and commercial instinct and ability are further evidenced by his career as a banker. For many years he has been the senior partner in the firm of John Gilbert, Jr. & Co., a banking house at Golconda, Illinois, which has enjoyed the public confidence and a very profitable business patronage. In 1874 he became a director of the Merchant's National Bank of Evansville, and subsequently was appointed its vice president and manager, continuing in that relation until the expiration of the bank's charter in 1885, when it went into liquidation. Under his judicious management the bank was so prosperous that the final dividends exceeded the expectations of its shareholders and were therefore very gratifying. When the affairs of the Merchant's Bank had been satisfactorily closed he was elected a director of the Old National Bank of Evansville, and at the same time was chosen vice president. His official relations with this bank have continued unbroken to the present time. The young man of to-day imperfectly apprehends the broad and varied experience of a business life in the west, extending over a period of sixty years. Captain Gilbert is one of the remnant of old merchants that connect the ginseng and coonskin age of traffic with the cash

and discount system of the present, by continuity in the mercantile pursuit, which has been constantly progressive. His experience covers the frontier country store, which bartered calico, bullets and molasses for eggs, furs and beeswax; and it has covered all the intermediate period to the great department store of the present. It began before the chartering and equipment of common carriers, when every successful merchant in the new west provided his own means of transportation on the natural waterways to the commercial cities and the sea. It has continued until the consumption occasioned by the establishment of manufactories and the opening up of varied industries has enlarged the home maker, and the fast freight lines send their cars on side-tracks to every man's warehouse for his surplus. Captain Gilbert in his varied business experience and unbroken line of successes, is a conspicuous example of the best type of the pioneer merchant—one who has the capacity for expansion and growth equal to the development of the country and the progressive methods of business. He had the courage to manage a line of steamboats for commercial purposes. in the time of war, in the enemy's country, when danger from land batteries multiplied the ordinary risk of river navigation. He advanced continuously in merchandising from the small country store to the head and control of the largest dry goods house in the state of Indiana. He has achieved prominence as a banker by familiarity with the principles of finance and the prudential management of fiscal institu-

8 VANDERBURGH COUNTY BIOGRAPHIES.

tions. His wide influence as a citizen is the natural outgrowth of confidence in his ability, integrity and sound judgement, a confidence that is well-founded and has never been abused. A man of high moral character, beloved and highly respected by all who know him. He is a trustee of the "Home of the Friendless" and also of the "Orphan Asylum," two institutions whose good work cannot be overestimated. Captain Gilbert took charge of the former when it was in dire need of aid and by his liberal assistance placed the institution on a solid financial footing. He has been liberal in his support to the cause of religion and there is not an Evangelical denomination in Evansville that has not been benefitted by his subscriptions. By these and kindred actions he has endeared himself to the people of Evansville and made for him a name which will survive him many years, and his work and exemplary life will be held up as an example to future generations. A life history told plainly and simply need not be classed as uneventful. To be born, to marry, to become a parent and to die is but the common lot of man; but to start like the trickling rivulet from mountain mosses on the cliffside, to form misty cataracts and limpid pools in the descent, to broaden like a meandering brook and fertilize the fruitful fields, to become part of the broad breasted river which turns the whirling wheels of factories and great industries, and bears its white-winged commerce to the sea and yet retain the purity and gentleness of the mountain dew is not the heritage of every man.

To this man such a life has been—a life of usefulness, of gentleness, of grace and peace.

ABRAHAM M. OWEN, M. D.,

THE acknowledged leader in the active practice of his profession in the city of Evansville, and the most eminent and successful surgeon in Southern Indiana, is the son of Abraham B. Owen, M. D., a Virginian by birth, and in his day one of the most prominent and successful physicians in Kentucky. The elder Owen practiced his profession for several years in Louisville, but about 1843 removed to Madisonville, Hopkins county, Kentucky, where Dr. A. M. Owen was born March 19, 1849. The mantel of the father fell upon the son, for while a mere boy he evidenced a decided love for medical knowledge and an especial fondness for surgical science. He received his education in the academies of his native state and the university of Virginia, and began his preparatory course in medicine in the office of his father. It soon became evident to the father that his son needed advantages in the prosecution of his medical studies, not obtainable in his native town, and in 1865 he entered the office of that eminent physician and surgeon, Dr. Frank H. Hamilton, of New York. Completing his preparatory course he entered the Bellevue Hospital Medical College in 1866, from which he was graduated with honor in the class of 1870. His graduating thesis,

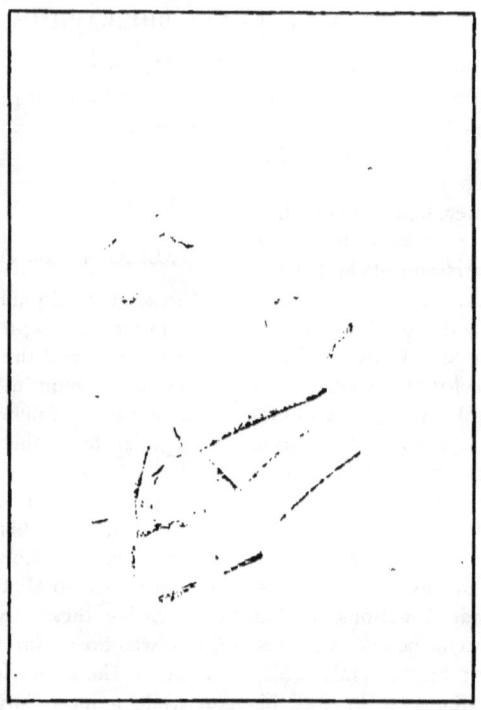

DR. A. M. OWEN.

"Tetanus," was ably prepared and did credit both to himself and college. Immediately after his graduation he came to Evansville and began the practice of his profession under rather adverse circumstances, but in a comparatively short time he found himself in the possession of a large and lucrative business. His success in surgery gave him an enviable reputation and his territory grew until now it embraces Southern Indiana, Northern Kentucky and Southwestern Illinois. He was the founder of the Evansville Hospital Medical College, of Evansville, and occupied the chair of surgery until his large and growing practice and his extensive business interests compelled him to tender his resignation. The heavy demands upon his time have prevented him from making any contributions to medical literature further than reports of some of his most important surgical cases. He established, and for three years was the editor and publisher of the Indiana Medical Reporter, afterwards known as the Western Medical Reporter, of Chicago. He is a prominent member of nearly all of the more important medical organizations of the country, notably among the number the International Medical Congress, the American Surgical Association, the Mississippi Valley Medical Association, the American Medical Association, the McDowell Medical Association, the Indiana State Medical Society and the Vanderburgh County Medical Society. Notwithstanding the magnitude of his general and surgical practice, Dr. Owen

has given due attention to matters of public import and has identified himself with all enterprises having for their object the advancement of the interests of the city of Evansville. He was one of the incorporators of the Evansville and Chicago Railroad Co., president and director of the District Telegraph Co., has served as president of several business associations, and in fact is in some way identified with many commercial enterprises of a public character. He is an enthusiastic and an indefatigable practioner, and a fine type of the class to which he belongs. In 1875 the doctor was married to Miss Laura, daughter of G. N. Jerauld, of Princeton, Indiana. Three children have blessed their union, Amelia E., Leartus J. and George N.

Dr. Owen, in connection with Dr. Edwin Walker, established the Evansville Sanitarium which was opened January 18, 1894, he being president and Dr. Walker secretary and treasurer. The sanitarium is one of the most perfectly arranged homes for the sick in the country. Everything in and around it is of the latest and most improved design. Commenting on it the Evening Tribune of August 6, 1896, said: "In January, 1894, there was established in Evansville by some members of the local medical fraternity, a private sanitarium for the treatment and nursing of deep-seated and complicated cases. Also for performing of surgical operations under the highest antiseptic condition. This institution is delightfully situated on Fourth street, opposite the park, and the building is a large and imposing brick structure with white

2

stone trimmings. The halls and rooms are large, well ventilated, lighted by electricity and provided with electric bells. The operating room is a model, it being considered by experts one of the finest in the country. The sanitarium conditions receive the most rigid enforcement. The sanitarium is provided with laboratories, in which the condition of the patient is thoroughly investigated under the light shed by the latest scientific developments. Even the water used in the baths, as well as that used for drinking and cooking, is thoroughly sterilized and made free from all diseased germs. A corps of well trained and experienced nurses are in attendance and everything that medical skill or expert nursing can do to bring about a recovery is at the disposal of the patient."

EDWIN WALKER, M. D., P. H. D.,

A LEADING physician and surgeon of Evansville, was born in Evansville, May 6, 1853, and obtained his elementary training from the public schools, graduating from the high school in 1869. The name of Walker has been closely connected with Vanderburgh county for over a half century. Dr. Walker's paternal grandfather, William Walker, settled here in 1835. He is the son of James T. and Charlotte (Burtis) Walker. Dr. Walker attended the Hanover (Indiana) college, where he for two years pursued a classical course of study, and during that time was a member of the Union literary society and of the Phi Delta Theta fraternity. In 1871 he began the study of medicine, under the preceptorship of Dr. G. B. Walker, of Evansville, attended three courses of lectures in the Evansville medical college, from which he was graduated in 1874. He was afterwards appointed professor of anatomy in that college. He took a course of lectures in New York City in 1877, entered the university again two years subsequently, graduated with honors, was awarded the prize for the greatest proficiency in diseases of the nervous system. He was also a student under Professor Seguin, a most able and scientific instructor. Upon returning to Evansville, Dr. Walker was chosen professor of diseases of women and diseases of the nervous system in the medical college of Evansville. He attended a course of lectures in the New York Polyclinic, also took a course of special study of female diseases and diseases of the throat, under the tutorship of Professor Bosworth. He spent two months attending hospital clinics, went to Europe, where he devoted his time in search of knowledge bearing on the diseases of which he has made a specialty, and was associated with the leading authorities in Berlin, Vienna, London and Edinburgh. He returned to America, and in 1888 devoted himself again to the investigation of medical science in New York. He was county physician of Vanderburgh county in 1876-78, was mainly instrumental in establishing the city hospital. He is a member of the Southern Surgical Society.

JUDGE H. A. MATTISON.

the American Association of Obstetrics and Gynecology, the State of Indiana Medical Society, the Vanderburgh Medical Society, the Mississippi Valley Medical Society and the American Medical society. In 1888 the faculty of Hanover college conferred upon Dr. Walker the degree of P. H. D.

In January, 1893, Dr. Walker, in connection with Dr. A. M. Owen, established, in Evansville, a private sanitarium, which is delightfully situated on Fourth street, facing the park. The establishment in Evansville of such a magnificent and useful institution is a source of great pride to the people of Evansville and the surrounding country. The great good accomplished by an institution of this kind is inestimable. The halls and rooms are large, well ventilated, lighted by electricity and furnished with all modern conveniences. Experts say the model operating room is the finest in the country. The condition of the patient is thoroughly investigated under the latest and most scientific methods, the sanitarium being provided with well arranged laboratories. The sanitary arrangement is perfect, and as a home for the sick, it is complete in every way. The water used for bathing, as well as that used for drinking and cooking, is thoroughly cleansed by filtration and thus rendered perfectly pure. The sanitarium is provided with an efficient corps of well trained nurses.

Dr. Walker was married in 1880, to Miss Capitola Hudspeth, daughter of George and Margaret (Smith) Hudspeth, of Boonville, Indiana.

MAJ. HAMILTON ALLEN MATTISON,

JUDGE of the circuit court of Vanderburgh county, was born in South Berlin, New York, September 23, 1832. His grandfather, Allen Mattison, a Rhode Island Quaker, was in the Revolutionary war in 1775 under General Nathaniel Greene, fought at the battle of Bunker Hill, and removed with his family to South Berlin, New York, where he resided until he died in 1854. Major Mattison's father was Allan J. Mattison and his mother was Miss Lucy Thomas. Hamilton A. Mattison belongs to that large class of men of distinction and public usefulness, who was born to the soil. His early years were spent upon his father's farm in New York, and his first instruction received in the district schools where he attended about three months in the year. When nineteen years old he entered the New York Conference Seminary at Charlottsville and pursued his studies, at the same time earning by his own labor as assistent teacher the necessary means to support him and pay his tuition. He entered Union College, from which institution, under the presidency of the distinguished educator, Dr. Eliphalet Nott, he was graduated in 1860. For two years afterward he was principal of the Bacon Seminary, Woodstown, N. J. In July, 1862, when the war dogs were baying on every side he laid aside his wand, and picking up his musket responded to the call of President Lincoln, enlisted and raised a company of recruits which became members of the Twelfth New Jersey Regiment. He was commissioned second lieutenant and subsequently promoted to first lieutenant, captain and major. He was on the staff of General Alexander Hayes and Nelson a Miles, and was actively engaged in twenty-five battles, wounded three times at Chancellorsville, wounded twice again and had his horse shot from under him in the battle of the Wilderness, and there made prisoner of war. He was introduced to General Lee on the battle field and conversed with him. Now a chapter of hardships in the life of Major Mattison begins, such as only those who have undergone similar sufferings in southern prison pens can appreciate. He was taken to Lynchburg, thence to Macon, Georgia, and there confined "on short rations" from May until July, then taken to Savannah, Georgia. Was one of the fifty federal officers taken from Savanah by the rebel authorities and placed under the fire of the federal guns, while they were shelling the city of Charleston from Folly Island. After several weeks, with others, he was taken to Columbia, South Carolina, and put in a pen exposed to all kinds of weather, without shelter of any kind, and fed only on coarse corn-meal and sorghum. Here through intense suffering he remained until November 28th, when, in company with a fellow prisoner, Rev. John Scamahora, well-known in Evansville, he made his escape. Without money or food and with a scanty supply of clothing, the two took to the woods and started out to meet Sherman's army, which they believed to be on its way to Augusta, Georgia.

They traveled across the state of South Carolina, walking by night and concealing themselves in woods and swamps during the day. Reaching the Savannah river, they took possession of a small boat and ran the gauntlet of rebel guards and steamers until they reached the lines of Sherman's army at Savannah, which place had been captured subsequent to their escape. They had traveled nearly 1,500 miles through a rebel country and were nearly prostrated with fatigue. Gen. Sherman ordered Major Mattison to report to the army of the Potomac as soon as he was able to return to duty. After visiting his home in New York, he rejoined the army of the Potomac about March 1, 1865, and took part in all the battles in which that army was engaged until the surrender of Lee, some six weeks later. He was mustered out of service at the close of the war, and soon after entered the Albany Law School from which he was graduated in 1866, receiving the degree of LL. B. The same year he married the daughter of Hon. Marinus Fairchild, of Salem, New York. He began the practice of law at Salem, in partnership with his father-in-law. In February, 1868, he removed to Evansville and in the following fall took an active part in the political campaign, advocating the election of Gen. Grant for president. In 1870 he was appointed county attorney, but resigned the office in the following year for the purpose of accepting the appointment by the governor to the office of prosecuting attorney of the Vanderburgh county criminal court, to fill a vacancy. In the fall of

1872 he was elected by the people to the same office for a term of two years. In 1876 he was appointed, by United States Chief Justice Waite, register in bankruptcy, and discharged the duties of the office until its abolishment by law. In 1887 he was appointed city attorney for Evansville, and was reappointed to the same office in 1888. Retiring from the office of city attorney he formed a partnership with Messrs. Posey and Clark, and afterwards the firm was changed to Mattison, Posey & Chappell. In the fall of 1896 he was elected judge of the Vanderburgh county circuit court for a term of six years, and it is a notable fact that he is the first republican ever elected as judge of the circuit court in the first judicial circuit of Indiana. He became a member of the Masonic fraternity at Troy, New York, in 1862, and joined Reed Lodge; No. 316, of Evansville, by demit in 1868; became a member of La Valette Commandery of Knights Templar in 1872, and has held many important offices, and is now past master of Reed Lodge, past high priest, past illustrious master of Simpson council and past eminent commander. He joined Trinity Methodist Episcopal church soon after moving to Evansville and ever since has been an active member of both church and Sunday school. His first wife having died in 1873, he was again married February 7, 1878, to Miss Henrietta M. Bennett, of Evansville, formerly of Brooklyn, New York. He had one daughter, the issue of his first marriage, who died in 1892, at the age of twenty. Added to ability and integrity Judge Mattison possesses in an eminent degree those humane impulses which prompts one to temper justice with mercy. It has been his rule to be lenient with youthful offenders brought before him for the first time, his theory being that such cases may be easier and more surely reclaimed to honorable paths by surrounding them with proper influences than by subjecting them to the association of hardened criminals which extreme penalties would necessarily involve. He has not hesitated even at times to set aside the verdict of juries that were plainly excessive, whether from misconceptions of the true import of testimony, from sudden impulse, or from any other cause whatever. Yet where the stern degree of law has seemed to be the only atonement for outraged justice, his decisions have never lacked the firmness and severity which the true minister of the law must know when and how to use.

JOHN H. FOSTER,

EMINENT lawyer and judge of the superior court of Vanderburgh county, was born in Evansville in 1862. He received his early mental training in the common schools of Evansville and entered the State University in 1878 and was graduated in June, 1882. Took a law course in Columbian University, of Washington, D. C., and was admitted to the bar in 1886. He had a successful law practice, which he gave up when called by the people to serve as judge of the superior court, to which office he was unanimously elected in 1894.

Judge Matthews Watson Foster, his grandfather, was born in Gilesfield, county of Durham, England, June 22, 1800. He was apprenticed to a bookseller, which therefore afforded opportunities for literary and legal research. He came to America in 1812 and in 1817 located in Edwards county, Illinois. In 1819 he settled in Pike county, Indiana, and occupied a prominent place in the early history of Pike county, and served several years as associate judge. He was a farmer, miller and merchant in that county until 1846, when he removed to Evansville, where he died April 13, 1863. He married Miss Eleanor Johnson June 18, 1829, who died at the age of thirty-seven years. Their union was blessed with eight fine children. In 1851 he married the second time to Mrs. Mary Kazar, who died in California in 1859. To this union two children were born.

Alexander H. Foster (his father), the fourth child of Matthew W. Foster, was born in Petersburg, Indiana, March 1, 1838, and was educated in the State University of Indiana; was regimental quartermaster of the Twenty-Fifth Indiana Infantry two years, beginning July, 1861; was wholesale grocer in Cincinnati, Ohio, and Memphis, Tennessee. He returned to Evansville in 1866 and engaged in the pork packing business, and was for three years a member of the city council, and in 1888 appointed Metropolitan police commissioner of Evansville, and was also for a number of years engaged in the grain business. He was married April 11, 1861, to Miss Martha, daughter of the late Hon. John S. Hopkins, and to this union four children were born. John H., now judge of the superior court, Frank cashier First National Bank, George and Mary. As a lawyer Judge Foster has always commanded the profound respect of his brethren at the bar. His indomitable energy, his accurate and complete knowledge of the civil code and statute laws, his fair and strictly legitimate manner of conducting his cases, his effort to secure sound and honest legal action, thoroughly equipped in every way for his high calling, courteous and deferential towards his opponent, faithful and persevering in behalf of his client, he commands the respect and confidence of judge and jury and whatever might be the issue he left no doubt in the mind of his client as to the wise and careful management of his case. In the capacity of superior judge, John H. Foster is regarded as one of the best judges on the bench, and has endeared himself to the hearts of the people. His relation to the bar was of the intimate and almost affectionate nature and the practitioners in his court have the highest regard for him. Judge Foster is still in the prime of life and it is the sincere hope of all who know him that he may long be spared to administer justice, as an example of official probity and good citizenship. He served one term in the legislature in the session of 1893. Judge Foster was married December 28, 1887, to Miss Josephine Piper, of Washington,

A. C. ROSENCRANZ.

D. C., and two children bless their union, as follows: Josephine, born November 30, 1888, and John, born October 19, 1896.

MAJOR ALBERT C. ROSENCRANZ,

PROMINENT and worthy citizen of Evansville, president of the Heilman Plow Works, was born in Baerwalde, near the city of Berlin, Prussia, October 26, 1842, and is the son of C. F. Rosencranz, a native of Prussia, who was a watch maker by trade. He married Miss Dorothea Nohse, a native of Prussia, who died in 1884. C. F. Rosencranz was a man of the highest integrity, loved and respected by all who knew him. He took an active interest in the German revolution in 1848. He came to America in 1850 and settled near Evansville, and in 1851 took up his abode in the city, and resumed his business as a watchmaker. In 1867 he returned to Europe, and died there in 1887. The subject of this sketch was the only child, was educated in the private schools and learned the trade of watch maker under his father, while receiving his education. He was engaged in his father's business when the war dogs began to bay, and in 1861 aided in the organization of company A, First regiment Indiana Legion, and when the company was mustered in, he was made orderly sergeant. He recruited compnay F, Fourth Indiana Cavalry, in July, 1862, was commissioned first lieutenant and made captain in 1863. He served as body guard to General Ebenezer Dumont, a Mexican officer of prominence. He engaged in several important battles, notably Chickamauga. In March, 1864, his regiment was ordered to join General Sherman on his famous march to the sea. When near Buzzard's Roost the brigade to which Major Rosencranz was attached, while making a reconnoissance in front of the left flank of Sherman's army, was attacked by the enemy and lost heavily. Here Captain Rosencranz was slightly wounded and captured. He was confined in rebel prisons at Macon, and Savannah, Ga., Charleston and Columbia, S C., and Charlotte, N. C., and while in prison endured a chapter of hardships such as can be appreciated only by men who have undergone similar sufferings in southern prison pens. On March 1, 1865, he was paroled and May 3, following, was exchanged. He rejoined his commandery and was mustered out June 9, 1865. During the winter of 1863-64, he had at times been in command of the regiment, and soon after his release from prison, was commissioned major, his commission being dated May 1, 1865.

After the war Major Rosencranz succeeded his father in business in Evansville, which he operated successfully until 1868, and in that year took charge of the affairs in the office of William Heilman, which kept him very closely confined for five years, at the end of which his health was so impaired as to necessitate a change of climate. He went to Missouri and engaged in stock raising. In 1876 he returned to Evansville, and January 1, 1897, he assumed

active charge of the Heilman-Uric Plow
Co, as manager. Mr Uric retired in
1878, and Mr. Rosencranz has been in
control of the business since. He is a
man of means and affairs, and his mind
is capable of great research. He can
divest difficult subjects of their obscurity and conduct multifarious plans to a
successful issue. Politically, he affiliates
with the republican party, and in March,
1887, served on the committee appointed
by the city council to advise on the city
debt, which at that time was disturbing
the public mind. In April, 1887, he
was elected councilman from the fifth
ward, and was made chairman of the
finance committee when the council was
organized. He served as chairman of
the water works committee. Major
Rosencranz, with all his other duties,
finds time to devote to the following
fraternal organizations, in which he is a
useful and helpful member: Masonic
lodge, Knight Templar and G. A. R.
He was united in marriage May 14,
1868, to Miss Mary Heilman, eldest
daughter of that worthy and honorable
citizen, Mr. William Heilman, and their
union has been blessed with eight children, of whom only three survive, Olive,
Richard and Gertrude.

Major Rosencranz is one of the most
active, energetic and enterprising men
in the community in which he lives. He
is a man of high moral and religious
character, beloved and respected by all,
and stands pre-eminently one of the first
citizens of Evansville. He is a member
of the Trinity Methodist Episcopal
church, has been liberal in his support
of the cause of religion, and has given

to charity with a lavish hand. By these
and kindred actions he has endeared
himself to the people of Evansville and
made a name which will survive him
many years, and his work and exemplary life will be held up as an example
to future generations.

JUDGE PETER MAIER

WAS born August 1, 1834, in the province of Hohenzollern, Prussia, and
is now one of the leading members of the
Vanderburgh county bar. He received
the rudiments of his education in Germany, and in 1848 emigrated to this
country, with his parents, locating in
Cincinnati. He was thrown at once
upon his own resources and worked in
that city until twenty years of age,
when he saved sufficient out of his
earnings to start upon a collegiate course
in the Ohio Wesleyan University at
Delaware, Ohio. He taught school and
attended the university alternately until
1858, when he graduated and commenced the study of law in the office of
Sweetser & Hall in Delaware. While
preparing for the legal profession he
occupied the position of principal of the
public schools in that city. Up to this
point in his career his life had been anything but a bed of roses. It was the
old story of an ambitious but poor
young man, struggling to reach the
first rung on the ladder which leads to
ultimate prosperity. And the natural
result which follows energy, application and indomitable will power came

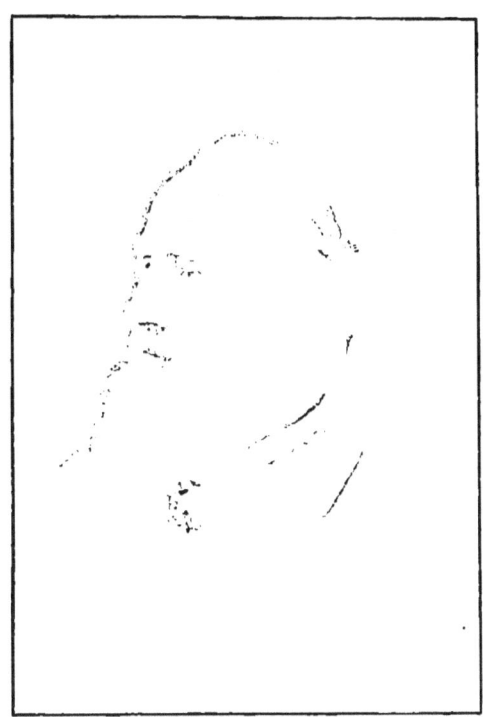

PETER MAIER.

CAPT. J. W. WARTMANN.

to pass. He was admitted to the bar in 1860, at Delaware, Ohio, and upon the advice of a friend came to Evansville, where his star soon commenced to shine in the ascendant In 1864 he began the publication of the Evansville Demokrat, one of the most substantial German newspapers to-day in the country. He sold it to Lauenstein brothers in 1866. In 1865 he was nominated by the democratic party for judge of the court of common pleas, but it was a time when democrat stock was low and he suffered defeat. In 1872, during the famous Greeley campaign, he was nominated for judge of the criminal court, but the entire democratic ticket was snowed under. In 1874 he was appointed city attorney. While attending the Centennial in 1876 he was nominated for state senator. He declined the nomination, but his party insisted and the republican party pitted against him Wm. Heilman, the strongest man in their party, with the result that Mr. Heilman was elected. In 1882, just when he was about to start for Europe, he was appointed without solicitation, city attorney and served one year. He continued the practice of law until 1890, when he was nominated for judge of the superior court, elected and served four years, and in 1894 he went down in the sea of defeat with the wave that swept the democracy at that time. Since he retired from the bench in 1894 he has been engaged in the practice of law. Judge Maier was married in 1864 to Miss Eliza Willey, of Delaware, Ohio, and six children have blessed their union.

3

CAPTAIN J. W. WARTMANN

WAS born is Lewisburg, Green Brier county, Virginia, February 7, 1832, and is the son of Frederick and Elizabeth (Bowlin) Wartmann, natives of Virginia.

Captain J. W. Wartmann spent his boyhood days in Cincinnati, where he attended the famous "Woodward College," from which he graduated in 1847. He was engaged in business at Cincinnati for several years after his graduation, and then removed to Spencer county, Indiana, and began the study of law, under the preceptorship of Hon. L. Q. DeBruler. He practiced first at Rockport. In 1864 he was appointed provost marshal of the first district of Indiana, with headquarters at Evansville, which he resigned, being appointed commissioner of the board of enrollment for the first district. During his service the drafts of 1864 and 1865 occurred, and important and delicate duties devolved upon Captain Wartmann, which he performed to the general satisfaction. After the war was over he returned to Rockport and resumed the practice of his chosen profession in partnership with Hon. Thos. F. DeBruler. He was appointed deputy clerk of the United States Court at Evansville, in July, 1871, and at once entered upon the discharge of his duties, and in September, 1871, he was appointed United States Commissioner, and discharged the duties of that position with dignity and credit. Mr. Wartmann served several years as president of the school board of Rockport, and has always taken an active interest in the common school system. He is a member of Eagle lodge, K. of H., K. & L. of H., and a member of the Methodist church.

Mr. Wartmann affiliates with the republican party and takes an active interest in the welfare thereof. He has excellent practical judgment of men, business and problems, and he has therefore, always had the confidence of the best business men wherever he is known. In all transactions involving money, character and integrity, his reputation is unquestionable and without reproach.

He was united in marriage in January, 1857, to Miss Mary Graham, of Rockport, and they were blessed with five children. Mrs. Wartmann died March 31, 1897.

CAPT. AUGUST LEICH,

PRESENT State Senator from Vanderburgh county, was born in Prussia, in 1842, and came to America with his parents when but six years of age. After receiving such mental training as the common schools afforded, he was thrown on the world to fight life's battles alone. In his boyhood days he achieved an enviable reputation among the news boys of that day, being particularly enterprising and able to sell more newspapers than others. He was cabin-boy and cook on steamboats which plied the Ohio and Mississippi rivers. He served Uncle Sam as postoffice clerk at Evansville and Terre Haute, and also received a good business training, clerking for his brother, Chas. Leich. He learned house and sign painting about 1860; taught a night school of young mechanics and laborers, and it is remembered that those same boys took up the cause of their country and entered the civil war when the call was given. Captain Leich enlisted in company F 24th Indiana Infantry, was appointed fifer of his company and subsequently made principal musician of his regiment. After the war he was employed by Leich & Carlstedt. Later he went to Cincinnati, where he was appointed bookkeeper in the county auditor's office, under General August Willich, and later was employed as bookkeeper in a wholesale liquor house, gaining wide and varied experience in mercantile affairs. He returned to Evansville in 1872, and was employed by Leich & Lemcke for a number of years. He was elected county treasurer in 1886 and re-elected in 1888, and during that period the new court house was built. Mr. Leich handled all the funds and bonds necessary for the construction. He was made assistant cashier in the Bank of Commerce, January 1, 1892, and two years later was appointed cashier of that institution. He was chosen state senator from Vanderburgh county by a large majority in the fall of 1896.

Mr. Leich was married to Miss Matilda Klenk, and two children have blessed their union. He was elected

AUGUST LEICH.

CHAS. H. BUTTERFIELD.

commander of Farragut Post G. A. R. in December, 1895. He is always ready to lend a helping hand in the cause of charity, benevolence and Christianity. His friends are not confined to the orders or the party to which he belongs. He is one of the most universally popular citizens of Evansville.

———

CHARLES H. BUTTERFIELD,

WHOSE distinguished services in war and in peace make a notable figure in the history of the county, was a native of Maine, born in Farmington, May 17, 1833. He remained at home until he was seventeen, assisting his father and attending the winter schools. He then entered the Farmington Academy, and in 1855 completed a preparatory course for college. In the fall of that year he entered Bowdoin college, and was graduated in 1859. His favorite studies were Latin and natural sciences, in which he particularly excelled. In August of the same year, he came to Evansville and became the principal of the high school, in which capacity he acted three years with great credit to himself and satisfaction to the patrons of the school, when the dire necessities of the National government, assailed by rebellion, called upon him irresistibly to drop all civil pursuits and go to the front. In the spring of 1862 he assisted to recruit the Sixty-Fifth

Regiment, expecting ··· it, but was detained by circ ·· beyond his control. He ther ··· Ninety-First, and was appoit r, later promoted to lieuter ·· His command saw acti· ·· ·ortant service. The first ·· ·· ·· y was the chasing of the g·· ·· ·· vicinity of Henderson, and they were then engaged in the expedition after Morgan in the spring of 1863. In the fall and winter of 1863-4 the regiment was a participant in all the battles of the East Tennessee campaign, and in the spring of 1864, it formed a part of the Twenty-Third Army Corps under the general command of General Sherman, and made the march from Chattanooga to Atlanta. This famous campaign ended the regiment returned to Nashville to fight under Thomas, and destroy the hopes of the Confederacy in the crushing defeat of Hood. Then the Ninety-First was transferred to Washington, and took boat for Fort Fisher, North Carolina, landing in time to join Sherman at Goldsboro, and in the final battles and skirmishes that followed, the regiment gallantly did its duty. Colonel Butterfield was in command at Salisbury the first day after the entry of the Union army. In July, 1865, he returned to Evansville and resumed the study of law. He was soon appointed superintendent of schools and he held this position one year, meanwhile improving whatever opportunity offered to keep up his study of law in the office of Hon. Conrad Baker. He was admitted to the bar in December, 1865, and soon after engaged in the practice of his chosen profession. In 1869 he was elected judge of the criminal court, but resigned that position in 1871 to accept the mayoralty, to which he was elected at the death of Hon. William Baker. He served for nearly three years as mayor, and subsequently engaged in the practice of law. He was appointed county attorney by the commissioners, and held that position five years. In April, 1893, he was appointed judge of the police court, which he held with dignity and to the perfect satisfaction of his constituents up to the time of his death, in January, 1897. As a summary of his character we give below the testimonials of the bar of Evansville, which is as follows:

"The members of the bar of Evansville desire to express their appreciation of the life and high character and of the valuable public service of their deceased brother, Charles H. Butterfield; and they wish to put upon the records of this court their sense of the loss the legal profession and this community, have sustained by his death.

"In his long and useful life Judge Butterfield was an accomplished teacher, a fearless soldier, followed, admired and trusted by the men he led in the struggle for the salvation of the Union; a lawyer who took front rank in his profession; an incorruptible mayor of the city and its citizens; an able and upright judge. At an early age he won the entire confidence of this community, and held it throughout all his subsequent life. He has been faithful in every trust."

DR. JOHN BLANCHARD WEEVER,

A LEADING physician of Evansville, was born at Hollowell, Maine, September 25, 1836. He was made president of the Vanderburgh Medical Society the first year he was in Evansville, and read a paper the same year, "Pneumonia." He is a member of the St. Mary's hospital staff and a lecturer on "Obstetrics."

Dr. Charles S. Weever (father) was a native of Maine, and came to Evansville in 1837. He married Miss Mary F. Trafton, and their union was blessed with seven children, the subject of this sketch being the second. Charles S. Weever graduated in medicine at the Jefferson Medical College in 1844, and his son, John B. Weever, took his degree from the same school in 1858, and the grandson of Charles S. Weever, George Slocum Weever, received a diploma from the same college in 1897.

John B. Weever spent his boyhood days in Evansville and his early mental training was received in the schools of this city, and when fourteen years of age his father exchanged places with Prof. Wm. H. Byford, of Mt. Vernon, Indiana, afterwards of Chicago. Dr. Weever received an academic education in the Mt. Vernon Academy, and was graduated from there at the age of eighteen. He then commenced the study of medicine with his father, and later, as before stated, was graduated from the Jefferson Medical College at Philadelphia, after which he began practicing with his father in Mt. Vernon.

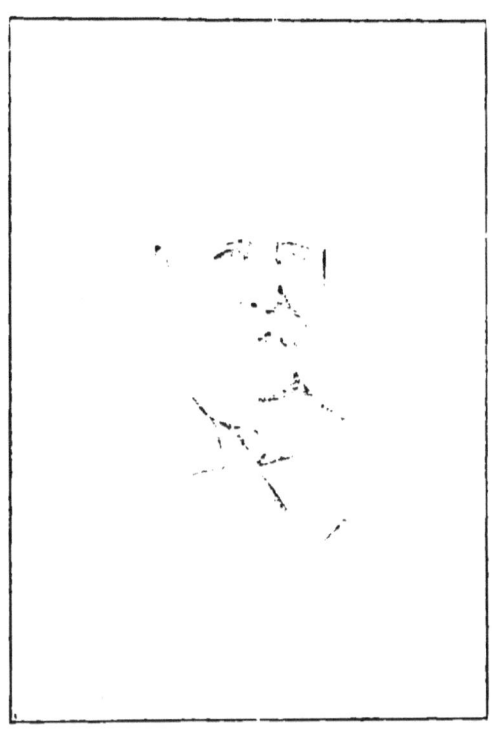

DR. J. B. WEEVER.

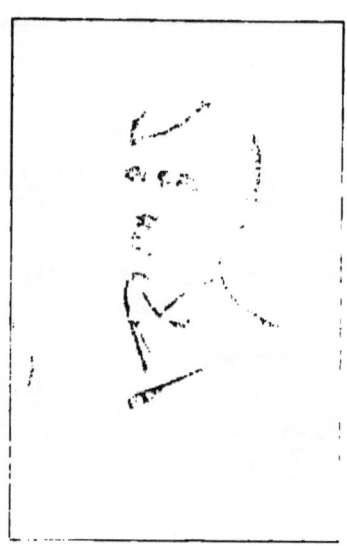

CAPT. LEE HOWELL.

His father died three years later and he continued his practice alone for twenty-eight years. In 1886 he came to Evansville, where he has continually practiced his profession since.

Dr. Weever was united in marriage December 23, 1862, to Miss Emma Slocumb, of Carmi, Illinois, and to them have been born seven children, of whom only three survive, as follows: Walter R., George S. and Paul S.

CAPT. LEE HOWELL,

General freight agent of the Louisville and Nashville railroad, was born in the forties, and is the son of Philip Howell, who, at an early day, located in Lauderdale county, Ala. He was engaged in farming, and married Miss Mary Wesson, a native of Lauderdale county, and their union was blessed with eight children, the subject of this sketch being the youngest son. Capt. Howell was born near Florence, Ala., and belongs to that large class of men of worth and distinction, who was born to the soil. He worked on his father's farm and went to school alternately, and at the age of fifteen became engaged in a large country store as clerk and book-keeper, clerking in the day time and working on the books at night. Here he remained until the war dogs began to bay, when he picked up his musket

in 1862, and entered the cavalry of the confederate army, which he served faithfully until the end of the civil war. After the war he embarked in steamboating on the Ohio and Tennessee rivers, where he served as clerk, and later was promoted to the position of master, having had charge of various steamboats which plied the Tennessee river. While thus occupied he became largely acquainted with the trade and the people, and his worth as a manager of business interests grew rapidly. In 1872 he entered the service of the Louisville and Nashville railroad company as contracting agent, which position he creditably filled until 1880, when he was promoted to the general agency for the company at Evansville. June, 1882, he was appointed division freight agent of the Henderson division, and in the fall of 1882, was appointed to his present position. He was one of the originators of the Evansville, Newburgh and Suburban railroad, and is largely interested in three or four steamboat companies, being president of the Evansville, Ohio and Green River Transportation company which owns and runs two packets —the Evansville and Gayoso, besides several towboats and tugs in Green river. Capt. Howell is an enterprising public spirited citizen, and is a devoted member of the Trinity Methodist church.

He was united in marriage in 1867 to Miss Ottaway, of Tuscumbia, Ala., and four children have issued from their union, two of whom survive, Lee, Jr., born in May, 1872, and Emma, born in August, 1879.

JAMES R. GOODWIN,

PROMINENT business man of Evansville, manager of the Goodwin Clothing Company, was born in Mississippi county, Missouri, June 18, 1853. William M. Goodwin (father) was a native of Daviess county, Indiana, and was engaged in business in Mississippi county, Missouri, and in Hardin county, Illinois. He married Miss Maryetta Wilbur, of Leavenworth, Indiana. They moved in 1859 to Crawford connty, Indiana, where James attended school until he was fourteen years of age.

They moved to Hardin county, Illinois, and he was sent to Louisville. Kentucky, to complete his education. He graduated from the high school there in 1873. Returning to Hardin county, Illinois, he gained a wide and varied business experience by acting as clerk and book-keeper in a general store for four years. At the expiration of that time he moved to Evansville and for one year conducted a branch shoe store for J. S. Morse.

Subsequently he was employed with Miller Bros. Dry Goods Company, and then formed an insurance partnership with Mr. S. W. Cook, which continued successfully until 1888, when he sold out and embarked in the clothing business, and formed the nucleus of the present prosperous business known as the Goodwin Clothing Company. The business was started under the firm name of Pleasants, Goodwin & Co., in a small place on Vine street, the firm being changed to J. R. Goodwin & Co. in 1889, when Mr. Pleasants retired and Mr. S. W. Cook took his place.

J. R. Goodwin is an exceptionally enterprising gentleman of Evansville and a most representative politician, his affiliations being with the democratic party. He has served the city as councilman one term. He is a member of the Knights of Pythias, Elks and Royal Arcanum. He was a delegate to the democratic national convention that nominated William J. Bryan for president of the United States.

Few men have done more for the public good without hope of reward or fear of criticism; and if one were to ask one hundred citizens to write the names of ten of the most worthy and popular citizens of Evansville, the name of J. R. Goodwin would be one of the top, if not the first, in every such list. His career is characterized by great energy, prudence and liberality, controlled by superior judgment, and marked throughout by unquestioned integrity.

W. A. HESTER,

SUPERINTENDENT of the public schools of Evansville, was born in Indianapolis March 17, 1858. Mr. Hester's ancestry is of sturdy pioneer stock, his grandfather, his father and several of his relatives having been members of the Methodist ministry, and being of that noble and self-sacrificing race of itinerant preachers, who, carrying the seeds of religion into what was then a wilderness, were the advance guards of our modern education and civilization.

Rev. F. A. Hester, (father), was born

J. R. GOODWIN.

W. A HESTER.

in 1822, and married Miss R. O. Slack. a native of New Jersey, but residing in Gibson county when married.

W. A. Hester adopted the profession of teaching, and was engaged in the schools of Southeastern Indiana for four years, two years preceding and two years succeeding his graduation from the DePauw University in 1881. In 1882 he became principal of the high school of Owensboro. remaining there until 1890, when he became connected with the schools of Evansville. He was made principal of Campbell street school in that year, and in 1894 was unanimously chosen by the school trustees as superintendent of the public schools. Mr. Hester is thoroughly devoted to the cause of education. The same energy and ability applied to another profession or to mercantile pursuits would undoubtedly bring greater pecuniary results, but he cares not so much for the monetary compensation he receives as for the good he may accomplish in the education and enlightenment of the people of his adopted state.

Prof. Hester has filled the office of school superintendent with ability for three years, raising the standard of the qualification of teachers materially and helping them to attain to that high standard, so necessary to the best school room work. He has been quite successful in all his professional work, as a man must be who loves his vocation. Commenting on his services in the capacity of superintendent, the Evening Tribune of August 6. 1896, said: "The superintendent is a man of marked administrative ability, as has been plainly demonstrated in his successful direction of the school system. This combined with great earnestness of purpose, and a conscientious regard in carrying out whatever may be for the best interests of the schools, distinguishes him as a man eminently fitted for the important position which he occupies at the head of the school system of the city."

He is a member of the Methodist church, a Knight of Pythias, and as such he is an active and helpful worker.

Prof. Hester was married August 18, 1885, to Miss S. H. Ogden, daughter of Mr. L. Ogden. of Owensboro, Kentucky. She was born September, 18, 1879. They have two children, a daughter and son, Wilma Ogden, ten years of age, and Kenneth Owen, two and a half years.

PROFESSOR MILTON Z. TINKER,

OVER whose head has passed three score and three summers, is still an active, energetic, hale and hearty man, and one who bears up well under the weight of years. Born in Kingsville, Ashtabula county, Ohio, June 25, 1834, he belongs to that large class of men of sterling worth, who was born to the soil, and his youth was spent in the ordinary monotony of farm life, where he worked in the summer and attended the common schools in winter. He early manifested a decided taste for music and spent much time in that department of the schools devoted to singing and voice culture. He attended regularly the old fashioned singing schools, as well as the musical institutions and conventions, and gained much useful knowledge and practical training. When but twenty years of age he taught his first school, the compensation being $12.00 per month, which included board, the latter to be obtained only by "boarding 'round" the district, which did by no means guarantee the entire satisfaction of it. But he was young and ambitious and could afford to endure some privations in order to accomplish his purpose. For four years he taught school and at night gave singing lessons in the community where he boarded.

Mr. Tinker went to Chicago, May 1, 1858, and entered the Normal Musical Institute of Messrs. Bradbury & Cady, and there took a five months' course upon practical teaching, which included the subject of harmony and voice training. Leaving there he engaged himself conducting singing classes, musical institutions and conventions, and wherever he went met with very gratifying success. He introduced and superintended the instruction of vocal music in the public schools of Terre Haute, Ind., having been employed for that purpose in the fall of 1863, by the board of education in that city. Four years later he resigned to accept a similar position in the city of Evansville, and, therefore, for thirty years, he has been at the head of the musical department of the schools of Evansville, and there can be produced no better evidence of general satisfaction than his continuity in that capacity. Since 1870, Professor Tinker has also been leader of Walnut Street Presbyterian church choir. During his career in Evansville he has been a leader of the Philharmonic Society, Lyric Society, and Ideal Opera Club, being at all times identified with every movement to advance the musical interests of the people of Evansville.

Professor Tinker was united in marriage in October, 1859, in Sandoval, Ill., to Miss Jennie F. A. Hurd, daughter of Mr. Everett Hurd, a native of Vermont, and four children have blessed their union, one of whom survives. Elbert Moreau Tinker, aged twenty-nine years.

The good accomplished by Professor Tinker in the various capacities of musical director cannot be overestimated. His has been, and is, a most useful life. Old as he is, with a long and busy life behind him, there is no spot, nor smirch, nor stain upon his name. Shame has not known him, nor disgrace abided in his house. It might of him in truth be said:

"Sweet are the thoughts that savor of content,
  The quiet mind is richer than a crown;
Sweet are the nights in careless slumber spent,
  The poor estate scorns Fortune's angry frown.
Such sweet content, such mind, such sleep, such bliss,
Beggars enjoy when princes often miss.

The homely house that harbors quiet rest,
  The cottage that affords no pride nor care,
The man that "grees wi'" country music best,
  The sweet concert of Mirth, and Music's fare.
Obscured life sets down a type of bliss;
A mind content both crown and kingdom is."

PROF. M. Z. TINKER.

PROF. ROBERT SPEAR.

RANE CLAY WILKINSON,

WELL-KNOWN lawyer of Evansville, was born in Gibson county, Indiana, and his boyhood days were spent alternately on the farm and attending the common schools of Gibson county. He was the son of Aaron B. and Lucinda Wilkinson. The subject of this sketch enlisted, in 1862, in the Eightieth Indiana Infantry, and during three years active service was wounded four times. He was first wounded at the battle of Perryville, October 8, 1862, but soon recovered. In the charge on the fortification at the battle of Resaca, Georgia, in 1864, he was shot three times in a space of a few minutes, and was desperately wounded. He was left upon the field of battle for dead, but his magnificent constitution pulled him through. To this day he carries in his right shoulder, as a memento of that terrible charge, a bullet which was never extracted. Mr. Wilkinson served under General Schofield, ex-commander of the United States army. Returning to Evansville he attended a select school for two years, and then was with the Journal Company for five years. Afterwards he read law with Mattison & Gilchrist and formed a partnership with Major Mattison in 1876, which continued until 1883, since which time he has practiced his profession alone. During the late Governor Hovey's administration he was commissioned colonel and chief of staff, and went with that high executive on his trip through Mexico. Colonel Wilkinson is one of our best citizens, respected and esteemed by a large acquaintance.

4

ROBERT SPEAR,

PRINCIPAL of the Evansville high school, was born in Coshocton county, Ohio, February 25, 1851, and is the fourth son of David Spear, who was descended from Irish ancestors of whom the emigrants settled in America in 1796. In the latter part of 1851, the family, then comprising ten children, moved to Indiana and settled in the wilds of Owen county, where the wolves were more numerous than domestic animals, the bridle paths through the forests serving the purpose of highways; where no books were to be procured and newspapers were very rare. It was there the father of Mr. Spear lost his health from exposure, and the hard and ardous work of felling the forest trees and died in 1869. The mother was left with six children at home, three of whom were girls, the oldest being twenty-two years of age. In this wilderness with such surroundings Robert Spear grew to manhood, subject to the privations and the hard work that foster the self-denial and independence. Up to his seventeenth year Mr. Spear had labored hard for the mere acquisition of the simple necessities of life and they were oft-times extremely meagre. In winter he could have attended the log cabin and frame building schools of the day had he been provided with the necessary clothing, which he was unable to purchase. Being ambitious and believing he could accomplished more away from home he set out to find employment which he secured in an adjoining county, where for four years he served as a farm hand. In this capacity the satisfaction of his employer was evidenced by an increase in wages each year. He enjoyed the good fortune of being the son of ambitious parents, ambitious for the advancement and success of their children, and he longed for learning. He secured a spelling book to which he applied himself diligently when not at work; weekly papers were subscribed for and all available books were procured. From this and the stimulus afforded by the association of his employer, a man of considerable learning, a liberal education was obtained while he worked. Later, having accumulated small means he attended the common schools and in 1873 began to teach the three months' winter common schools. He pursued his studies in the summer, and in 1874 attended the Bedford, (Indiana), Male and Female College. He entered the Northern Indiana Normal school in 1875, and at the same time studying medicine under the preceptorship of Dr. Hankinson, of Valparaiso, Indiana. In 1881 Mr. Spear came to Evansville and was appointed teacher of natural science in the Evansville high school. His progressive ideas and thorough knowledge of teaching placed him in prominence and in 1885 he was appointed principal of that institution, which he has filled continually every since. Much of the material growth of the institution, together with the wonderful advancement that has been made in the educational and industrial work of the school are due in a large measure to the indefatigable labor and wise management of its able principal.

Mr. Spear has also for many years been a student of electricity, and when the class of the National School of Electricity was organized in Evansville in 1895, Mr. Spear was selected to deliver a series of forty-five lectures on economic electricity.

Robert Spear is a gentleman of fine personal appearance, a man of large brain, and is one of the men that connect the home-spun clothing and illiterate age with the cultured and learned collegiate system of the present day.

Mr. Spear was united in marriage to Miss Catherine Evans February 25, 1882, that being the anniversary of both his and his wife's birthday, he being just one year her senior. Their union has been blessed with five children: Herbert, Lewis, Walter, Rene and Mary.

PHILIP W. FREY,

ATTORNEY-AT-LAW, prominent member of the Evansville bar, was born in Evansville July 9, 1857, and was educated in the public schools, passing through all the grades, and in 1874 graduated from the high school. His father, Louis Frey, was born in Austria, and married Miss Rosalie Roser, a native of France, and they came to America in 1847, locating in Vanderburgh county in 1856.

Mr. Frey studied law under the preceptorship of Judge Azro Dyer, and in 1877 was admitted to the bar of Vanderburgh county and at once began the practice of his profession. His affiliations are with the democrats and he

PHILIP W. FREY.

DR. W. S. POLLARD.

has always taken an active interest in his party. He was nominated in 1882 for the office of prosecuting attorney for the first judicial district, composed of Posey and Vanderburgh counties, and was elected. In 1884 he was again nominated and elected to the same office. At the expiration of his official career he again turned his entire attention to the practice of his profession. He was united in marriage December 22, 1886, to Miss Hattie Loewenthal, of Leavenworth, Kansas.

WILLIAM S. POLLARD, M. D.,

A LEADING physician and surgeon of Evansville, was born in Carmi, Illinois, November 1, 1838, spent his boyhood days under the parental roof, received an academical education and studied medicine in his father's office.

William Pollard, (father), was a native of Virginia, and was graduated from a medical university of that state. He was prominent in his profession and was very successful. He was a man of means and affairs and owned a large number of slaves, which, on account of his hatred of slavery, he liberated and removed to Kentucky, and from there to Mt. Vernon, Indiana. Later he removed to Cynthiana, Indiana, and died there in 1874. In his practice he exhibited the highest degree of skill and professional attainments. Always upright and honorable, kind and humane, he was much respected and beloved. He married Miss Wilcox, of Carmi, Ill., and their union was blessed with seven

children, of which the subject of this sketch was the fourth.

In 1861 William S. Pollard joined the Federal army as a member of an Illinois infantry regiment, with which he remained however, but a short time. He returned to Indiana and was largely instrumental in the organization of the Twenty-Fourth Indiana Infantry, which was commanded by Colonel Hovey. When the regiment was mustered in Dr. Pollard was commissioned second lieutenant and assigned to Company K. He gradually rose to the rank of lieutenant-colonel, which position was attained by his ability as an officer and his honorable record as a soldier. He saw active service in the battles of Vicksburg, Shiloh, Champion Hills, the siege of Corinth, the battles of Blakely and Mobile, Alabama, and others of less importance. His regiment was mustered out at Indianapolis, Indiana, and Mr. Pollard received an honorable discharge. He was for some time engaged in merchandising, but soon returned to his first love, the medical profession, and in 1869 entered the Miami Medical College, from which he graduated in 1871. He came at once to Evansville and began the practice of medicine in partnership with Dr. James P. DeBruler, with whom he remained until the death of the latter in 1875. He served the county as county physician for three years and was for ten years examining surgeon for the United States Pension Bureau. He is a member of the Vanderburgh Medical Society.

Dr. Pollard is a prominent member of the G. A. R., and in the order of

Masons has filled many important chairs, having at present reached past eminent commander of the Knights Templar

Dr. Pollard was united in marriage in February, 1874, to Miss Mattie A. Sutton, daughter of Gideon Sutton, of Centerburg, Ohio, and their union has been blessed by one child. During Dr. Pollard's residence in Evansville of over a quarter of a century he has thoroughly established himself in public favor as a physician and citizen. Progressive and active, he has kept abreast of the times and has always favored efforts intended to advance the general prosperity of the city.

PROFESSOR WILLIAM McK. BLAKE,

INSTRUCTOR in Latin and civics in the Evansville high school, was born in Delaware county, Indiana, August 21, 1849, and is the son of William Blake a prominent Methodist minister, and a native of Virginia, who came to Indiana and located in Delaware county in 1844. He married Miss Mary Lockhart, a native of Ohio, and four children blessed their union, the subject of this sketch being the first. The father died in 1880 in Green Castle, Indiana, and the mother is still living and resides with her son-in-law, Dr. G. M. Young, in Evansville.

William McK. Blake received his elementary education at home under the preceptorship of his father, and in 1867 entered the preparatory department of Asbury University, now known as De-Pauw University at Greencastle, Indiana, and two years subsequent entered the

college and was graduated in 1873. For three years following Professor Blake was principal of the high school at Rockport, Indiana, and from 1876 to 1879 served as superintendent of schools at New Castle, Indiana. He came to Evansville in the fall of 1879 and taught Latin for two years in the high school. Then for a term of four years was principal of that institution and since 1883 has been engaged as teacher of Latin and civics.

Professor Blake was united in marriage in 1876 to Miss Kate Evans, daughter of Joseph S. Evans, a prominent business man of Rockport, Indiana, and one child, a boy of eight years of age, has issued from their union. Both Mr. and Mrs. Blake are consistent members of the Methodist church. The professor is a musician of considerable note and takes a great interest in vocal music, and the good he has accomplished in that way cannot be readily estimated.

Professor Blake has applied himself assiduously to his work and by economy and good management has succeeded in acquiring a comfortable competence. In his new and beautiful home at the corner of Blackford and Kentucky avenues, he and his family are surrounded by every comfort and many of the luxuries of life. He is a man of great energy and force of character, possessing many of those qualities, without which, few men rise to distinction. Determined and persistent purposes, practical sense and integrity, are the traits which mark the outlines of Professor Blake's chief characteristics.

DR. JOHN E. OWEN.

JUDGE JORDAN G. WINFREY.

JOHN E. OWEN, M. D.,

A PROMINENT physician of Evansville, was born in Madisonville, Kentucky, October 1, 1854, and began the practice of medicine in Evansville in 1880. He is the son of Abraham B. Owen, M. D., a Virginian by birth, and in his day one of the most prominent and successful physicians in Kentucky. Of six children the subject of this sketch was the fifth. He attended the common schools of Evansville and the Kentucky University at Lexington, Kentucky, and in 1875 began the study of medicine in the office of his brother, Dr. A. M. Owen. Later he attended the Evansville Medical College from which he graduated in 1879. In 1880 he attended the College of Physicians and Surgeons, of New York City, from which he graduated. He was a member of the faculty of the Evansville Medical College, of which he was demonstrator of Anatomy. He resigned this position, however, to enter the Hospital Medical College, of Evansville, in which he filled the chair of Professor of Anatomy up to the time that institution was closed. Dr. Owen has served the county as county physician, and is a member of the following medical associations: Vanderburgh County Medical Association, American Medical Association and State Medical Association. Dr. Owen's private practice and the many calls upon him by his professional associates, in many of the surrounding counties sufficiently attest the high estimation in which he is held by the people and medical fraternity. Of very quiet and retiring disposition with no attempt at personal display, his work, not yet finished, has been accomplished quietly and without the use of the ordinary and even legitimate means of advertising, which are so frequently resorted to by ambitious men in the profession. Dr. Owen was united in marriage August 30, 1892, to Miss Maria Louise Linck, daughter of Charles Linck, and to them has been born one child, Mary Linck Owen.

JORDON G. WINFREY,

JUDGE of the police court of Evansville and a prominent member of the Vanderburgh county bar, first saw the light of day in Burksville, Cumberland county, Kentucky, February 24, 1855. His early mental training was received from Columbia and Lexington, Kentucky Colleges. He afterwards entered the law department of the Louisville University from where he graduated at the age of twenty. Then he entered the law office of General James Speed, who was attorney general under Abraham Lincoln. He was admitted to the bar and began the practice of law in 1875, and for two years was associated with his father, also an attorney, at Columbia, Ky.; and while at Columbia he taught school for two years, beginning before he was eighteen years of age. From Columbia Mr. Winfrey went to Owensboro, where he established himself in the practice of his profession and remained one year, doing a lucrative and satisfactory business. In 1878 he removed to Evansville, where he has earnestly and continually followed his profession, to which he is very much devoted. His affiliations have been with the democratic party, in the welfare of which he has taken an active interest. He was appointed judge of the police court of Evansville by Mayor Akin, April 13th, 1897.

Major Winfrey was prosecuting attorney under Judge Brownlee, and served on the staff of Governor Claude Matthews. As a lawyer, he enjoyed an extensive practice, embracing many important cases in the district, state and federal courts. As a judge, Major Winfrey possesses all the qualities necessary to constitute an upright minister of justice.

He was united in marriage September, 1877, to Miss Dora Lee Chambers, of Henderson, Ky. Their union was blessed with three boys, one of whom is dead. He was married the second time to Mrs. Ida N. Carpenter, December 30, 1894, and to them has been born one child, Claude Matthews Winfrey.

STEPHEN BIEDERMANN,

A WORTHY and successful citizen of Evansville, was born in Germany, December 19, 1837, and is the son of Francz Matthias Biedermann, a native of Germany, who came to America in 1853. He married Miss Maria Frances Schwantner, also a native of Germany, and their union was blessed with five children—boys—the subject of this sketch being the second. Francz N.

Biedermann (father) located in Cook county, Ill., where he was engaged in farming for one year, when he removed to Chicago and there engaged in teaming up to the time of his death, which occurred in 1866. Mrs. Maria F. Biedermann (mother) died in Chicago in 1857.

Stephen Biedermann was educated in the common schools of his native land. Until he was twenty years of age he worked in Chicago in the confectionery business and lived with his parents. In 1857 he went to Kansas and located at Leavenworth, where he learned the trade of stone mason. In 1858 he joined the Salt Lake expedition headed by A. Sidney Johnson, and was among the troops of fifteen hundred that crossed the plains and Rocky mountains. He had charge of a wagon and team and drove all the way from Leavenworth to Salt Lake, and, after remaining in the latter place two months, in the meantime suffering many privations, returned to Leavenworth, and from there went to New Orleans, and for some time was engaged in steamboating on the Mississippi and Red rivers. He finally came up the Ohio river and landed at Louisville, Ky., from where he went across to Terre Haute, Ind., and there enlisted in the army, and was mustered in for three years, September 9, 1861, joining Company E, thirty-first Indiana Infantry. He participated in many battles, notably those of Fort Donaldson, Shiloh, Chicamauga, Resaca and Jonesboro, wherein he saw active service and was honorably discharged October 22, 1864. He then went to Chicago to spend a few months

DR. L. D. BROSE.

with his father, and in 1865 came to Evansville, and was at various times, for four years, engaged in mining coal in the mines of and adjacent to Evansville. He would work in the mines in winter, and during the summer, when the weather was suitable, he followed his trade of stone mason. In 1869 Mr. Biedermann went to Washington, Ind., where for ten years he was engaged as mine superintendent, and was one year in the same capacity for a Brazil (Ind.) coal mining company. Leaving there he went to the Patoka Valley Coal Mining Company, and for two and a half years was with that concern in the capacity of superintendent. For two years following he was employed with B. Menden, of Evansville, in the coal mining business, and then began to operate a mine in Pike county, Ind., on his own account, which continued for four years, when Mr. Biedermann returned to Evansville, having previously purchased the coal business formerly run by George Stockfleth, and he has continued it successfully ever since. His office is now at 412 Upper Eighth street, and he handles all kinds of Indiana and Kentucky coal. Mr. Biedermann is an active and energetic member of the G. A. R. During Mr. Biedermann's long residence in Evansville he won the hearty approval and confidence of the people, while his correct and honorable business policy has secured for him a large and increasing patronage He is a man of sterling integrity, and has a high standing, both in business and social circles.

He was united in marriage August 17, 1865, to Miss Katharine Schlotter, of Evansville, and their union has been blessed with eight children.

———

L. D. BROSE, M. D., Ph. D.,

THE eye ear, nose and throat specialist, at St. Mary's hospital, was born in Evansville, April 20, 1859. Daniel Brose (father) was a native of Germany, and he married Miss Christina F. Jenner, of Germany, and ten children blessed their union, the subject of this sketch being the eighth.

Dr. Brose received his elementary education in the public schools of Evansville, and, in 1877, began the study of medicine in the drug store of Dr. John Laval, and in 1877 studied medicine under the preceptorship of Drs. Bray, Wheeler and Austin. He graduated in medicine and philosophy at the university of Pennsylvania in 1881. He then served a year as house surgeon and physician in the German hospital at Philadelphia. He returned to Evansville and continued the practice of his profession until the fall of 1889, when he went to Europe and entered universities in Vienna and Berlin, making a special study of the eye, ear, nose and throat. In 1891 he returned here and was appointed at St. Mary's. His thorough familiarity with the varied branches of the medical science, and the successes achieved in his practice, have gained for him a high rank among the physicians of the city. In 1896 Dr. Brose again went to Vienna, where he spent several months under the leading professors, seeking knowledge of the treatment of the eye, ear, nose and throat.

He was united in marriage in December, 1891, to Miss Matie Munger, of Oshkosh, Wis.

He is a member of the Royal Arcanum, A. O. U. W., Vanderburgh County Medical Society, Indiana State Medical Society, Mississippi Valley Medical Society, the Pan-American Congress and the International Medical Congress.

CHARLES HENRY DAVIES,

A PROMINENT builder and contractor of Evansville, was born in Chester, England, in 1861. His father, Thomas Davies, who descended from a most highly respected English family, was born in Chester, England, and engaged in brick contracting and building. He married Miss Sarah Fellows, also a native of England, and to them fourteen children were born, Charles H. being the sixth. Charles H. Davies came to America in 1883 and located in Evansville in 1885 and followed his occupation of brick layer. Two years subsequent, in connection with Mr. James Scarborough, under the firm name of Davies & Scarborough, he began to do a building and contracting business. There is no more elevating or honorable avocation than that of building and to-day numerous magnificent structures grace the city of

Evansville as the result of the labor of Charles H. Davies.

December 21, 1887, Mr. Davies was united in marriage to Miss Ada Wolf, of Evansville, and two children have issued from their union, as follows: Fannie, born in 1890, and Hugh Gladstone, born in 1892. Miss Ada Wolf was a daughter of Mr. George Wolf, who was a native of Germany.

In speaking of Mr. Davies, one of the leading Evansville daily papers said: "During the years that Mr. Davies has been engaged in the building trades in this city he has built for himself a reputation for workmanship, square dealing and integrity that is equaled by few and surpassed by none. He is popular with all who know him and his acquaintances soon become his warm friends. In the contractor, the man who builds, must repose implicit confidence, and it can be said of Mr. Davies that he has never betrayed a trust, and has always given value received for every dollar expended."

CHARLES F. H. LAVAL,

TREASURER of Vanderburgh county, was born in Evansville, July 27, 1854. John Laval (father) a native of Mainz, Germany, came to America in 1848 and located in Evansville. He was successfully engaged in the drug business up to 1890, when he retired. He married Miss Mary Kron, of Germany, and eleven children blessed their

CHAS. F. H. LAVAL.

FRED. GROTE.

union, the subject of this sketch being the second. Charles F. H. Laval obtained his elementary education from the public schools of Evansville, and in 1872 entered the Cincinnati College of Pharmacy, from which he graduated in 1874. He immediately entered his father's drug store as prescription clerk, remaining there until 1879, at which time he embarked in the drug business for himself, which continued until 1895, when he sold out to his youngest brother, Edward Laval.

His political affiliations are with the republican party, and he has always taken an active and energetic interest in the welfare thereof. In 1892 he became a candidate for county treasurer, but was defeated by only fourteen votes by Mr. James F. Saunders, who was making the race for his second term. Mr. Laval was re-nominated in 1894 and elected by the overwhelming majority of 1,600, the largest majority of any man on the ticket at that time. He is a member of the Masonic body and the Knights of Pythias, in both of which he is an active and helpful worker.

His record as a public officer is clean and honorable, possessing the qualities of true manliness he has attracted many friends and has deserved popularity. Honest purposes and laudable conduct have marked his career.

He was united in marriage December 26, 1877, to Terresa C. Doyle, a daughter of James Doyle, a native of Ireland. Their union has been blessed with two children, as follows: Charles J., born August 23, 1879, and John, born April 23, 1893.

5

FRED. GROTE,

PRESIDENT of the F. Grote Manufacturing Co., was born in Prussia May 4, 1847, and when a boy came to America with his mother and located upon a farm three miles from Evansville.

William Grote, (father), was born in Prussia, and married Miss Laura Konaman, a native of Prussia, and to them five children were born, of which the subject of this sketch was the second. In 1856 his mother moved to a farm on Hickory Ridge, two miles from Henderson. Here F. Grote spent his boyhood days farming and attending school alternately, and at the age of sixteen started out to fight life's battles for himself. He early developed a taste for handling machinery and his first work in that line was in the position of fireman in the Evansville woolen mills. He was subsequently promoted to engineer and remained with that institution seven years, when he entered the employ of Christian Decker, who had the first power wagon manufactory in Evansville. Later Mr. Grote returned to the Woolen mills, where he remained another year. Then with what he earned by hard work and close economy he purchased a threshing machine and followed that business for three years. In 1871 water works were introduced in Evansville and Mr. Grote was employed for six months, putting in machinery for the Holly Co. Afterwards he was engaged by the city as engineer, in which capacity he served five years. His next move was to start a machine shop with William H. Miller and John Mattock as partners under the firm name of Grote & Co. They operated successfully for nearly four years, when they consolidated with Frank Hopkins and established what was known as the Novelty machine works. Three years later Mr. Grote started the F. Grote Manufacturing Co., which he has operated prosperously every since.

Mr. Grote is a democrat in politics and in 1891 he was nominated for water works trustee, and notwithstanding it was a republican year, most of the democratic candidates meeting with defeat Mr. Grote was elected by a majority of 345, and it is a matter of record that he made a most capable and efficient official.

As a member of the Evansville Manufacturers Association Mr. Grote was appointed by the chairman to promote the beet sugar industry in this vicinity. He took up this subject and studied it in all its bearings and soon saw the importance and advantage for Evansville to secure such an industry. He went to work with all the energy he possessed and devoted all his spare time to establish a beet sugar factory there, and at the present time the prospects are that success will crown his efforts. Since he has been connected with the F. Grote Manufacturing Co., he has been granted a number of valuable patents, several of them being on the Grote sectional steam and hot water heater. In fact, his heating system is considered to be one of the most complete in existence, as it works almost automatic in all its details. Mr. Grote

is also the inventor of the Grote perfection elevator, its most specific point being the safety device, which is claimed to be absolutely safe in its action. Another of his noted inventions is the Jarvis tobacco press; also quite a number of inventions for handling leaf tobacco, too numerous to mention.

When Mr. Grote was elected water works trustee he did much to further the interests of that institution. It was he who called the attention of the mayor, common council, manufacturers, business men and citizens to the condition of the water works and the necessity of rebuilding them. He was also author of reconstructing the water mains, so that the pressure would be uniform all over the city for fire and domestic purposes. Mr. Grote was also the promoter of a map, which showed all the underground work of the city water mains, of which there had been no previous record. He was always a strong advocate of filtered water, and is to this day.

When the Southern Hospital for the insane at Evansville, Ind., was completed in 1890, the trustees were in a dilemma as to how to procure water for the institution. They sent for experts from different parts of the country, who came and bored wells on the grounds, and expended a great amount of money, but all without avail. Mr. Grote came to their rescue to solve this vexed question, and he pointed out the spot where the well should be bored, also bored the wells, designed and built the pumping machinery, which is operated by electricity, he being one of the first, if not the first, who applied electric power for

CHAS. S. WOODS.

CHAS. B. HARRIS.

pumping water. He not only furnished the institution with water, but gave them an unlimited supply, which has been used since 1891.

He is a member of the A. O. U. W., Court of Honor and has been a member of the Masonic order, and belongs to the Stationary Engineers' Association, and is a member of the Manufacturers' Association of Evansville, in all of which he is an active and helpful worker.

Mr. Grote was united in marriage June 29, 1875, to Miss Matilda Rahm, and their union has been blessed with five children, as follows: Emil, Ernest, Fred, Laura and Edwin.

———

CHARLES S. WOODS,

CHIEF of the fire department of Evansville, was born December 29, 1860, in Evansville, and is the son of William H. Woods, who is prominently engaged in the decorating and wall paper business on Main street.

After completing his education, which was obtained from the schools of Evansville, Charles S. Woods learned the painting trade, which he followed for eighteen years. Then he engaged from 1889 to 1895 in the wall paper and painting business with his father. He served the city of Evansville as councilman from the Seventh ward in 1894. His affiliations have always been with the republican party, and he is at present chairman of the Republican Central Committee of Vanderburgh county,

which office he has filled since his election, January 2, 1896.

The appointment of Mayor Akin in April, 1897, of Charles S. Woods as chief of the Evansville fire department, was a tribute to his worth, both as a business man and as a leader. Mr. Woods is an ardent republican, and is one of the most prominent young men in local politics, modest and unassumed, yet progressive and aggressive, both in business and politics, and he is steadily preparing the way for a brilliant and useful career.

Mr. Woods is an active member in the A. O. U. W. and the Royal Arcanum. He was united in marriage June 7, 1889, to Miss Laura Heberer, daughter of Peter Heberer, a well-known commission merchant of Evansville, and two children have blessed their union, of whom only one survives.

1588436

———

CHARLES B. HARRIS,

ATTORNEY at law, a member of the Evansville bar, was born in Union county, Kentucky, in 1860, and is the son of Addison J. and Catherine (Bosley) Harris. His father was a native of Kentucky and his mother of Maryland.

Mr. Harris graduated in academics from the Southwestern Presbyterian University in Clarksville, Tennessee, in 1883, and at once entered Washington Lee University, at Lexington, Virginia, where he graduated in the law department, taking the degree of L. L. B. in 1885. He located in Evansville in September, 1885, and was at once admitted to the bar, where he has remained and practiced his profession. He now has a remunerative practice in Vanderburgh and the adjoining counties, and in the appellate and supreme courts, and is occasionally called to the neighboring counties of Kentucky in litigations. He is a gentleman thoroughly prepared to practice his profession, and it is said of him that he has but few superiors in the preparation and trial of cases. He is a prosperous and influential citizen, and a member of one of Kentucky's most distinguished families.

JOSEPH GIBSON,

County Commissioner of Vanderburgh county, a prominent citizen of Howell, Indiana, was born in Scotland, February 10, 1847, and came to America in 1868, locating at Springfield, Illinois, where he remained about one year, moving to Evansville in the fall of 1869. William Gibson (father) was a native of Scotland, where he lived and died. There he was engaged, during his entire life, in mining, and he was united in marriage to Miss Anna Patterson. Nine children issued from their union, of which Joseph was the youngest. Upon reaching Evansville Mr. Gibson at once engaged with the Ingle Coal Company as a miner; has been with that institution continually up to December, 1895, when he was elected county commissioner of Vanderburgh county, from the Third district. He was promoted to higher positions from time to time, until he filled almost every place around the mines, having been made superintendent in 1889. Mr. Gibson is a self-made man in every sense. He has, by careful management and economical disposition of his earnings acquired considerable property, and is identified with almost every movement for the advancement of the community in which he resides.

In 1871 Mr. Gibson was united in marriage to Miss Maggie Russell, whom he had met in Vanderburgh county. She was also a native of Scotland, and a remarkable coincident is, that she came from very near the same part of Scotland that Mr. Gibson did, but they had not known each other previous to their meeting here. Their union has been blessed with seven children, six of whom survive, among them being one grown son and two grown daughters. The son, Mr. Will Gibson, is a young business man of Howell, and, if we may judge the future by the past, we might predict for him a most successful career. He is forging ahead and rapidly placing himself in the front ranks of the leading business men of Vanderburgh county.

In politics Mr. Joseph Gibson affiliates with the republican party, in which he is very much interested, although, by no means a politician in the usual acceptance of that term, but by sheer force of character, has taken a leading position in the republican party, which he is ever ready to serve to the best of his

JOSEPH GIBSON.

J. G PAINE.

ability. He is a prominent member of the A. O. U. W., having passed all chairs in the local lodges, and for the past eight years has been chairman of credentials in the Grand Lodge of Indiana. He is an active and helpful worker in the order, and is justly proud of the record he has made as a member of that order. He was the first past chief of honor of the Degree of Honor, which is an auxiliary order of the A. O. U. W. for Indiana.

———

JOHN G. PAINE,

PROMINENT citizen of Evansville, and commissioner of the First district of Vanderburgh county, was born in England April 22, 1835.

John Paine (father) was born in England, and came to America in 1840. He married Miss Martha Miller, and to them five children were born, John G. being the fourth. The family emigrated to America in 1842, locating in Evansville. John G. Paine received his early mental training in the public schools of Evansville. His father was engaged in the grocery and meat market business, and John was, therefore, afforded an opportunity to qualify himself in a business capacity. He learned to manage a locomotive and for over a quarter of a century was at the throttle of an engine on the E. & T. H. railroad. When elected, in 1892, to the office of commissioner, he resigned his position as engineer. His affiliations have always been with the republican party, and in 1892, he was one of only three republicans who were elected. His satisfactory service was attested in the fall of 1896, when he was re-elected county commissioner. Mr. Paine is an old, honored and respected citizen of Evansville, and one too, who bears up well under the burdens of sixty-two years. He has made a good officer, attending strictly to business. Personally he is temperate in habits, honest in his dealings with his fellow-men, and of genial disposition. He has won a place in the hearts of the people through his modest, unassuming way, and they will surely retain him in office as long as he is willing to serve.

Mr. Paine was married in 1856 to Miss Annie Childs, daughter of Thomas Childs, a pioneer and leader in the livery and feed stable business, of Evansville. Their union has been blessed with five children, three of whom survive.

———

JAMES T. WALKER,

EMINENT, progressive member of the Evansville bar, was born in Evansville October 22, 1850. He is a representative of a distinguished pioneer family. William Walker (grandfather) had much to do with the early history of Vanderburgh county, settled here in 1835, was prominent as a citizen, and was a man of the highest integrity. When war with Mexico was declared, William Walker stepped to the front. He raised a company, among whom were men of high standing, and marched on to the field of battle, and at Buena Vista, while nobly and gallantly leading his command, he fell, pierced to death by a Mexican lancer.

Hon. James T. Walker (father) was born in Salem, New Jersey, in 1806. He married Miss Charlotte Burtis, and died in Evansville May 1, 1877. He was a lawyer by profession, was many years in the office of county auditor, represented the county in the state legislature.

James T. Walker, the subject of this sketch, the second child, received his early education in the common schools of Evansville, spent one year at Wabash college, three years at Hanover, from where he was graduated in 1870. He was admitted to the bar and began to practice law in 1872, and from 1884 to 1887 served the people of Evansville as trustee of the public schools. In his profession he has been associated with Hon. Charles Denby, United States minister to China, and also with the distinguished ex-Judge R. D. Richardson. Mr. Walker's affiliations are with the democratic party, but he seeks no preferment. He is in love with his profession, and follows it assiduously. To be a lawyer in the high sense implies character, love of country, culture, learning and usefulness to the community, has been his hope and settled determination.

Mr. Walker was united in marriage February 28, 1882, to Miss Lucy A. Babcock, a native of Evansville, daughter of Henry O. and Mary E. (Howser) Babcock. Their union has been blessed with three children, Henry B., born

March 10, 1885; James T., Jr., born December 22, 1888, and Mary Howser, born September 24, 1891.

JOHN S. McCORKLE.

AMONG the descendants of the brave and enterprising men who settled in North Carolina, and who afterwards settled in Indiana, were the McCorkles, who were descendants of the Irish emigrants who came over from Ireland in the latter part of the 18th century. Leaving their native state, James S. McCorkle and his wife, whose maiden name was McIntyre, came to the west with pure purposes and dauntless courage and ready and willing to meet any fate. In 1828 they located in Gibson county, Indiana, and in the rude wilderness, he erected a log-cabin, where the subject of this sketch, John S. McCorkle, was born, February 9, 1829. In 1832 the family removed to Evansville, and shortly afterwards Mrs. Dorcas McCorkle expired. James McCorkle was one of the factors in the early growth of Evansville, and saw it rise, Phœnix-like, from the hamlet in swaddling clothes to a beautiful city, the second in Indiana. The advantages afforded John S. McCorkle for mental training when he was a boy were extremely meagre. Notwithstanding, being very studious and diligent, reading books on all subjects, he managed to store his mind with much useful information. He learned the carpenters' trade and worked as a journeyman for twenty years. He

JAMES T. WALKER.

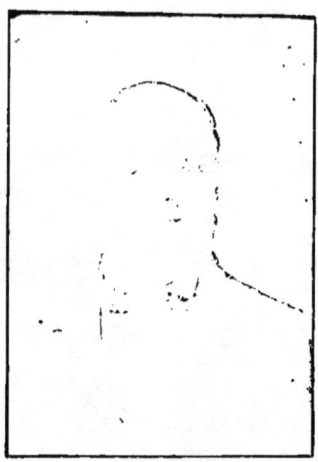

DR. T. E. POWELL.

served the United States government during the civil war, building and repairing hospitals for the sick and wounded who were brought to Evansville for treatment. Having by hard work and close economy accumulated considerable means, in 1866, Mr. McCorkle built a planing mill. This he operated successfully for four years, when it was destroyed by fire. As soon as the flames disappeared and the debris was removed a more complete and larger plant was put in place of the old one, and therefore, the planing mill which stands at the corner of Walnut and Eighth streets has been in existence for over a quarter of a century, and under the control and management of Mr McCorkle. He has been directly or indirectly identified with the prosperity of Evansville, being always ready to assist in any movement that promises to add to its further developments and growth. He has never held any political offices, or had any aspirations in that direction, but his affiliations are with the republican party, and in federal and state elections he always casts his vote in behalf of that party, while in local politics he endorses the men and measures which tend to the improvement and elevation of the public good. He has been prominent as a member of the Business Men's Association, and is a devoted and helpful member of the Methodist Episcopal church.

Mr. McCorkle was united in marriage December 31, 1850, to Miss Mary I. Thorne, a native of Vincennes, Indiana, born in 1836 a daughter of Charles E. and Nancy (Oliver) Thorne. Their

union has been blessed with six children, as follows: John D., born in 1853; William, born in 1855; Charles R., born in 1857; Thomas (deceased); Josie C., born in 1862, and George A., born in 1865.

Both Mr. and Mrs. McCorkle are active workers in the cause of temperance, and by their continuous efforts for many years, have done much to eliminate from the land the vice of strong drink.

THOMAS E. POWELL, M. D.,

ONE of the most successful and popular physicians of Evansville, was born in Union county, Kentucky, March 1, 1848, and his boyhood days were spent on his father's farm in Union county, where he attended the public schools in the winter and worked hard in the summer.

James W. Powell (father) was a native of North Carolina, born about 1810 and died in 1887. He moved into Kentucky at an early day and located in Union county, where he was successfully engaged in farming and was an honored and highly respected citizen in the community in which he resided. Jane (Leach) Powell, mother, was born in Tennessee in 1808, and passed away in 1895, at the ripe old age of eighty-seven.

Thomas E. Powell was the eighth child of nine children born to his parents, and after obtaining his elementary education, as before stated, he entered the Princeton (Kentucky) College, where he completed his literary education, and in 1872 began the study of medicine at Uniontown, Kentucky. In the latter part of 1872 he entered the University of Louisville from where he was graduated in 1874. Then for two years he was engaged in the practice of his profession at Corydon, Henderson county, Kentucky, and moved from there to Uniontown, continuing his practice for two years, when he went to New York to pursue a post-graduate course in a medical college in that city, and obtained his degree in 1885. His next move was an important one, and brought him to Evansville, where he has been continually engaged in the practice of medicine, attaining a high standard among physicians, and he enjoys an extensive practice. He is a member of the American Medical Association, the Indiana State Medical Association, and the Vanderburgh County Association. He was consulting physician for a number of years to St. Mary's hospital, and is lecturing physician to the Nurses' Training School. He is also a popular and influential member of the K. & L. of H. and K. of P., benevolent fraternities.

A man of Dr. Powell's intelligence could not keep out of public life, and he was elected councilman from his ward in 1895, serving in that capacity ably and creditably for one term. He was re-elected in 1897. His election as councilman was a tribute to his worth as a business man and as a true friend to the commercial interests of the city.

Thoroughly equipped for the duties of his profession by study and long experience, he is at once recognized as a skillful surgeon and an excellent physician, and enjoys a large and lucrative practice. He was united in marriage October, 1875, to Miss Mollie E. Dorsey, daughter of William L Dorsey, for many years cashier of the People's National Bank of Princeton, Indiana. Their union has been blessed with three children, only one of whom is living. Mrs. Powell died April 6, 1895. Dr. Powell resides with his son at 1107 Illinois street, where his well appointed office adjoins his home.

WILLIAM HEYNS,

A PROMINENT furniture dealer of Evansville, was born in Germany in 1848, and came to America with his parents in 1865, locating in Evansville. He is the son of Louis and Mary (Page) Heyns. By trade Mr. Heyns is a cabinet maker, and he first worked for the old firm of Bloomer & Hoing, on Water street, and afterwards for the Wetzel furniture factory. He then went with Miller & Karges, now known as the Evansville Furniture Company, with whom he remained a year and a half. He then left the city and went to St. Louis, where he was employed by Aude Brothers for two years, when he returned to Evansville and opened a grocery store at the corner of Michigan street and Third avenue. This he conducted successfully for two years, when he gave it up to travel for Bloomer, Schulte & Reitman, selling furniture in the

G. F. DENBY.

south, and in the three years he was with them, he built up a splendid trade. His next venture was to open a hotel at St. Wendel, which he conducted for five years and then returned to Evansville and started in the furniture business at 226 and 230 West Franklin street. Mr. Heyns has been exceedingly prosperous, which may, in a great measure, be accounted for by the fact that he had a thorough practical knowledge of all matters pertaining to the furniture trade. To-day he owns the largest retail furniture store in Evansville, the building he occupies being fifty feet deep and seventy-five feet front, three stories high, with 25,000 square feet floor room, and which is absolutely packed from top to bottom with furniture of all descriptions. In fact, there are few furniture houses in Indiana that carry as large and varied a stock of all grades of furniture as does Mr. Heyns. He is one of our most enterprising citizens, and is thoroughly up with the times. He manufactures a large part of his furniture, and is building up quite a lucrative wholesale trade with the merchants of the neighboring towns. Mr. Heyns has been a life long democrat, casting his first vote for Seymour. He has served the city four years in the council, and no man who ever entered that body left it with a cleaner record than did Mr. Heyns. The people of Evansville and the surrounding country have the most absolute confidence in him, and he is, in every way, worthy of it. He has erected a new building for his business, which is a model store in every way.

6

He was united in marriage in June, 1875, to Miss Anna Raben, daughter of Anton Raben, and their union has been blessed with five children.

———

GRAHAM FITCH DENBY,

PROMINENT and influential young member of the Evansville bar, was born in Evansville, December 25, 1859. He is the first child of Hon. Charles Denby, a distinguished lawyer and diplomat, and native of Virginia. He was a professor in the Masonic University at Selma, Ala., and came to Evansville in 1853, and edited the Daily Enquirer, the first democratic daily newspaper published in Evansville. In 1885 he was appointed by Grover Cleveland as United States minister to China, which position he has held ever since with dignity and credit. He married in 1858 Miss Martha Fitch, daughter of the distinguished senator, Graham N. Fitch, of Logansport, Indiana. This union was blessed with six children.

Graham F. Denby received his first mental training in the public schools of Evansville. He commenced the study of law in 1881, in his father's office, and the same year was admitted to the bar. He was nominated in 1888 for prosecuting attorney on the democratic ticket, but went down to defeat in the tidal wave that swept the democratic party that year.

From 1889 to 1893 he was in the State of Washington, and since then has been faithfully engaged in the practice of his profession in Evansville. Mr. Denby is a member of the Court of Honor.

LORENZ FRITSCH,

PROMINENT citizen and leading merchant tailor, of Evansville, was born January 7, 1846, in Luxemburg. Frederick Fritsch (father) was born in Barncastle, and he married Catherine Neuman, also a native of France. She died in 1846 and in 1853 he was married again to Tena Von Degan a sister to the mayor of Oberstein, and they moved to St. Wendel, in Prussia, and Frederick Fritsch there engaged in rope making and dealt in cordage, boat supplies, etc. Here Lorenz spent his boyhood days, and learned the tailoring trade. When a boy he left home and worked at Mayence and Frankfort-on-the-Main. He was careful and economic, and, having saved some money, made a trip, during vacation, through old Germany, passing through Hesse Darmstadt, Baden, Wurtenburg, Bavaria and visited Ulm, Oxburg, Munich, Nuremburg, Leipsic and Dresden. He was employed by the court tailor in the latter city, and later accepted a position in the capital of Poland. About the time he arrived there, Poland was having one of her annual revolutions, society was disorganized, and Mr. Fritsch decided to return to Dresden. He went to Prague, Lintz on the Danube, and thence to Vienna. He joined friends and went with Maximillian to Mexico,

sailing from Trieste, the principal seaport of the Adriatic sea, landing at Vera Cruz, Mexico, in the fall of 1861. Here he served as private and was promoted to lieutenant in the Austrian Volunteers under Maximillian. His service in Mexico was so able that when he returned to Vienna, he was made the guest of Maximillian's brother, the present emperor of Austria. He was furnished free transportation and hotel accommodation throughout the empire, and visited all places of interest. Then he went to Switzerland, stopped at Rohrschach on the Boden sea. Here he worked, and during his leisure hours visited all the points of interest in this, the most beautiful part of Switzerland. About this time he was notified by his father that because he had neglected to choose before he arrived at the age of eighteen, the military age, which he would have for his home, Luxemburg or Prussia, as was required by law, he was wanted by the Prussian government for military service. Having no inclination to serve as a private in the German army after having been lieutenant under Maximillian, he decided to travel and give the Prussian government some trouble in finding him.

He went to Lyons, France, where he remained five months, and then to Paris, arriving there in 1867, when the court of Napoleon III. was the most splendid on earth, and France was in holiday attire in honor of the great exposition. He took a course of training under that prince of cutters, De-la-Bye, and acquired the most perfect French art of cutting and draping.

LORENZ FRITSCH.

When the Franco-Prussian war broke out, on account of his Mexican military papers made so as to designate Luxemburg as his birthplace, he was exempt from the general order compelling Germans in war against France to leave Paris. But he was compelled to join the national guard, where he served in company 8, 100th battalion. Mr. Fritsch had become enamored of Paris and intended to make it his future home, and was married on the 5th of February, 1870; but after the war was over and the terrible reign of the Commune was begun, things were in such a complete state of demoralization, and what the morrow would bring forth was so uncertain, that he decided to leave the turmoils and troubles of the old world to be settled by those who could not get away, and he embarked for the land of the free, arriving in New York November 2, 1871. His first engagement was in Boston, where he worked for Rhoden & Townsend, on Washington street, the most fashionable tailors in the city. While in Boston he was offered $2,000 by Henry Schrichte, of Evansville, and he moved to Evansville in 1873. In 1877 Mr. Fritsch began business for himself, and since the first day he threw his doors open to the public, he has been the fashionable tailor of Evansville, making wearing apparel for all of the best people of the city and surrounding country. He has occupied the position of vice president of the "True Blue" and Evansville pump factories, and was for a number of years on the directory and auditor of the Unity Coal and Mining Company, and was a member of the organization committee of the Business Men's Association.

He has been captain of Evansville Division No. 4, K. of P., and is now district deputy Grand Commander of the I. O. K. of P. He is chairman of the committee on military rank I. O. K. of P, with J. L. Bieler and C. J. Many, and is also an A. O. U. W.

LOUIS H. LEGLER,

PRESENT auditor of Vanderburgh county, was born December 21, 1855, in Canada, and came to Evansville with his parents in 1866. Dr. Henry T. Legler, (father), was born in Dresden, Saxony, 1819.

Louis H. Legler received his early mental training in the public schools of Evansville, and at the age of fourteen he was employed as a bundle boy in Coolidge's dry goods store, it being his first attempt to make his own living. In 1886 Mr. Legler was made deputy auditor under James Parvin, and in 1894 he was elected to the office of county auditor, which position he now fills. Efficient, trustworthy and always courteous, he is an acceptable and popular officer. Honest purposes and laudable conduct have marked his career, and the worth of his character have won for him the admiration and respect of all who know him. In all matters appertaining to the city's welfare he will be found in the front rank, ever ready to show the outside world Evansville's advantages.

Mr. Legler's affiliations are with the republican party. He is a member of the Masonic order, Knights of Pythias, Elks and A. O. U. W.

He was united in marriage to Miss Marion Bonnel, a native of Vanderburgh county, in October, 1888, and five children have blessed their union.

WILLIAM G. RALSTON,

WELL-KNOWN physician of Evansville and pioneer citizen, was born in Princeton, Gibson county, Indiana, February, 1819, where he received his elementary education from the then imperfect schools of Gibson county. His paternal grandfather, William Ralston, participated in the siege of Yorktown, when Cornwallis surrendered to Washington, also in the war of 1812. His maternal grandfather, Major Joseph Neely, was major of a regiment in the revolutionary war, and was also in the siege of Yorktown.

Andrew Ralston, (father), was a soldier in the war of 1812, having entered when he was but eighteen years old. He was married in 1818 to Miss Patsy Neely, daughter of Major Joseph Neely, of Kentucky. Their union was blessed with five children, of whom the subject of this sketch was the first.

William G. Ralston spent his early boyhood days working on his father's farm in summer and attending the common schools in winter. This monotonous life continued until 1840, when he realized some better results by teaching

school, which he did for one year. In 1841 he located in Posey county, Indiana, and began the study of medicine under the preceptorship of Dr. Joseph Neely, who was then practicing at Cynthiana. After a four year's course of hard study there he located in Boonville, Indiana, where he practiced medicine until 1863. Then he attended a course of lectures at Cincinnati in the Ohio Medical College and afterwards was graduated from the Medical College of Evansville. From 1845 to 1863 Dr. Ralston followed his profession in Boonville and the adjoining counties of Spencer, Pike and Vanderburgh. In those days when bridle paths served as highways in many portions of the country the physicians who did a riding practice, found it very laborious, and in covering the territory on horseback he endured many hardships that would break down ordinarily the best constitution. No matter how rough the weather, nor how dark the night, Dr. Ralston was ever ready to answer the signal of distress and his indomitable will carried him through and it is a remarkable fact that he was never sick but one week consecutively.

At the beginning of the civil war he was appointed by Governor Morton sergeant of the Eighty-First Regiment Indiana Volunteers. After serving less than one year in the army of the Cumberland and while he was still engaged with his regiment he was appointed sergeant of the board of enrollment of the first congressional district of Indiana. The secretary of war made the appointment without the knowledge of Dr.

DR. W. G. RALSTON.

FRANK TARDY.

Ralston He examined over 10,000 volunteers, substitutes and drafted men, and continued in that position until April 14, 1865, when he returned to the practice of his profession, locating in Evansville. He was appointed United States surgeon of the Marine hospital at Evansville, in which capacity he served four years, and he also served four years as United States pension examiner at Evansville.

He is a member of the I. O. O. F., Crescent lodge No. 122, and for nearly three score years has been a prominent, consistent and helpful member of the Cumberland Presbyterian church. Politically he was originally a whig, but has been a republican since the organization of that party, faithfully exercising at all times the rites of citizenship. By his faithfulness and kindness in the discharge of his duties he has greatly endeared himself to every one throughout this section of the country, and no man has more influence with the people of his community. He is a man of the most remarkable energy, as is evidenced by the fact that while in the active practice of his profession he also finds time to devote to scientific matters and is the patentee of the Ralston bed warmer, which is one of the most useful as well as luxurious inventions of the day. It is a device whereby the comfort and pleasure of a warm bed may be had in a cold room at a nominal expense. It is of incalculable benefit in the sick room and as a sanitary help it is indispensible.

Dr. Ralston was united in marriage in April, 1850, to Miss Isabelle Matthewson, daughter of Dr. R. C. Matthewson. Mrs. Ralston was born September 20, 1830, and died in 1882. Their union was blessed with three children, as follows: William M., Charles N. and Andrew G. The eldest of these died in Texas in 1885.

FRANK TARDY,

PROMINENT business man of Evansville, was born at Vevay, Switzerland county, Indiana, June 24, 1846.

George F. Tardy (father) was a native of France, and married Miss Matilda Martin. Their union was blessed with three children, the subject of this sketch being the first. Frank Tardy's boyhood days were spent in Vevay and he received his education at Hanover college, this state. While quite young he ran away from school and home and took a place as cabin-boy on a steamboat in the Ohio river trade. He continued steamboating from that time until 1880, occupying during that time all the different positions from cabin-boy to captain, including pilot. He came to Evansville in October, 1880, and opened a ship chandler's store, which he has continued up to the present time. He began on a small capital but by industry and economy, has succeeded in accumulating a comfortable competence. Mr. Tardy is a member of the Business Men's Association and the Knights of Honor fraternity, of which he is an active and helpful worker.

He is also a member of the Court of Honor.

Mr. Tardy was united in marriage November 5, 1872, to Miss Annie Yates, a native of New Orleans, and their union has been blessed with three children, as follows: Tillie, Estella and Adah. Adah married Mr. Frank L. Pierce, employed by Bement & Seitz, of Evansville.

MICHAEL CRISLE,

A PROMINENT and successful lumber dealer of Evansville, was born in Hamilton county, Illinois, January 29, 1849. His father, George Crisle, was born in Pennsylvania, and was engaged in farming. He married Miss Delila Stobuck, and six children blessed their union as follows: Michael, William, Henry, Mary, Adaline and Sarah.

Mr. Crisle is in every way a self-made man. He has been dealing in lumber of all kinds and cross ties for a number of years—almost a quarter of a century—and by careful, shrewd and economical means has built an enviable reputation for himself. He is a man of means and affairs and owns large tracts of timbered and farming land in Indiana, Illinois and Missouri.

Mr. Crisle was married in May, 1872, to Miss Caroline Gillman, daughter of Charles Gillman, who was a carpenter and native of Illinois. To them have been born four children, as follows: John, Edith, Eva and Elta. Mr. Crisle is a member of the Masonic order.

GEORGE W. HAYNIE,

A PROMINENT citizen of Evansville, and proprietor of a retail drug house at the corner of Second street and Adams avenue, was born in New burgh, Indiana, February 22, 1857, and is the son of Jefferson and Emma (Hastings) Haynie, both natives of the state of Indiana. His parents died in 1880, the two deaths occurring within one month of each other. George W. Haynie was reared in Evansville, his parents removing to the city in 1868. His mental training was obtained in the public schools. He began to hustle for himself when about eleven years of age, and in 1872 engaged in the drug and prescription business in the store of T. C. Bridwell, ex-mayor of Evansville In 1884 he withdrew from the employ of Mr. Bridwell and opened a drug establishment on Main street, where he remained until October, 1887, when he sold out to Mr. J. M. Compton. He then established himself at his present quarters, where he has one of the best and neatest stores in Indiana. Mr. Haynie has figured prominently in politics, and in 1883 was appointed Metropolitan police commissioner of Evansville, which was quite a compliment to one of his age. He held the position only a short time and then resigned. He is a member of the Orion lodge No. 37, K. of P., and of Leni Leoti lodge No. 43, A. O. U. W.

He was made surveyor of the port of Evansville by President Cleveland in 1892, and no better or popular appointment could possibly have been made.

M. CRISLE.

GEO. W. HAYNIE.

L. J. HERMAN.

H. T. DIXON.

Among his fellows in the drug business he is as generally respected as he is by his life long acquaintances, as is attested by his selection for president of the Indiana Pharmaceutical Association.

LOUIS J. HERMAN,

PROMINENT attorney at law of Evansville, was born in Evansville June 17, 1867. He was graduated from the law department at Notre Dame class of 1890. He began the practice of law with James T. Walker, of Evansville, in June of that year. His grand parents were of the pioneer citizens of Evansville, having located here in 1835. His father, Jacob Herman, an enterprising candy manufacturer, was born in Evansville in 1842. His mother was Miss Mary Marshall, a daughter of Casper Marshall, of Evansville.

Mr. Herman was for two years connected with Judge Peter Maier in the practice of his profession. Their partnership was discontinued in January, 1897, when Mr. Robert M. Cox became the partner of Mr. Herman.

He was married in 1894, to Miss Kate Garvey, one of Evansville's most talented and esteemed young ladies. Louis J. Herman has won distinction as a lawyer of unusual ability, and enjoys a large general practice. He is a man in whom the people have implicit confidence. His reputation is not merely local, for he is one of the best known of the younger attorneys in southern Indiana.

H. T. DIXON,

A PROMINENT and leading physician of Evansville, was born in Henderson county, Kentucky, March 20, 1850, enjoys the distinction of belonging to that large class of self-made men, who are born to the soil.

His father was a native of Henderson county, where he was engaged in farming and died in 1884. He was a man of sterling character, honored, loved and respected by all who knew him. He married Miss Isabella P. Clay, of Henderson county, Kentucky, and to them were born ten children, of which the subject of this sketch was the fourth.

Dr. Dixon spent his boyhood days on the farm where he worked in summer and attended the common schools in the winter. He finished his education by taking a special course of study under the tutorship of Prof. Gibson, an able instructor of Vanderburgh county. In 1868 he began to read medicine under the preceptorship of his brother, Dr. R. S. Dixon, who was then practicing medicine in Posey county, Indiana. He took three courses in the university of Louisville, Kentucky, beginning in 1872 and was graduated in 1878. He immediately began to practice his profession in Posey county with his brother, and subsequently practicing alone in Vanderburgh county. Then for five years he practiced in Henderson county, and in 1884 came to Evansville. In the seventeen years of his active professional life in Evansville, Dr. Dixon has established himself in the confidence of his numerous patrons, who firmly believe in him as a man of honor and a physician of great ability. He attends strictly to his large practice and has no interest in any other kind of business, nor is he carried away with politics or money-making schemes. Of a genial disposition and social nature, he is popular in the society of his friends and in the benevolent orders to which he belongs. He is a master Mason, a member of the I. O. O. F. and Knights of Honor. He is also a member of the following medical associations: Vanderburgh Medical Society, State Medical Society, American Medical Association. He is at present secretary of the board health.

Dr. Dixon was united in marriage October 1, 1878, to Miss Amelia Wilson, of Louisville, Kentucky, and to them were born three children, one of whom Percy Goodwin Dixon, survives.

EDWARD JURGENSMEIER,

A LEADING contractor and highly respected citizen of Evansville, was born in Evansville February 22, 1857.

Joseph Jurgensmeier (father) was a native of Prussia, born October 27, 1823, and came to America in 1845, locating in Evansville and was successfully engaged in the grocery business up to the time of his death, in 1874. He married Miss Wilhelmine Dedank, and to them were born seven children, the subject of this sketch being the fourth. Mrs. Wilhelmine (Dedank) Jurgensmeier is still living, and resides

with her son, Edward, on Columbia street, in Evansville.

Edward Jurgensmeier received his early mental training in the public schools of Evansville, and when he grew to manhood learned the carpenters' trade, and learned it well. This occupation he followed from 1871 to 1880, when he began to do a contracting business on his own account, which he followed successfully until 1888. At that time he discontinued the carpenter contracting business, and began to do slate and tile roofing, which he has followed very successfully ever since. While contracting Mr. Jurgensmeier placed to his credit many handsome structures in and around Evansville, notably, St. Anthony's church, St. Mary's school house, the Vendel-Smith block on Main street and a school building for the Sisters of St. Francis. Since he has been in the roofing business he has covered St. Mary's hospital, St. Anthony's church, St. Mary's school building, the First Presbyterian and the First Baptist churches of Henderson, Kentucky; the German Methodist church in Mt. Vernon, Indiana, Dr. Watson's residence in Mt. Vernon, Illinois, the First Presbyterian and Methodist churches in Carmi, Illinois, William Heilman's residence on Second street and many others which we have not space to mention.

Mr. Jurgensmeier is a member of the Catholic church, St. Anthony's Benevolent Society, C. K. of A., K. of St. J., in all of which he is an active and helpful worker. He served the city as councilman one term, from 1895 to

EDWARD JURGENSMEIR.

THOS. N. BEIDELMAN.

1897, and was re-elected in the spring of 1897 to another term of two years. His affiliations are with the democratic party.

He was united in marriage May 3, 1881, to Miss Anna Lentzenich, and seven children, four of whom survive, have blessed their union. The living children are Frank, born November 4, 1883; Delia, born May 21, 1890; Silvester, born October 6, 1892, and Ida, born November 19, 1895.

THOMAS BEIDELMAN,

PROMINENT citizen and real estate dealer of Evansville, was born in Mt. Carmel, Illinois, July 15, 1850. His elementary education was obtained in the common schools of southern Illinois. George Beidelman (father) was a native of Pennsylvania, but moved to Illinois at an early day, and was engaged as a carpenter and cabinet-maker. He married Miss Jane Ulm, of Mt. Carmel, Illinois.

When sixteen years of age Thomas began to learn the carpenter and cabinet-making trade, in Fairfield, Illinois, which he followed for five years. In 1871 he moved to White Cloud, Kansas, and there for two years was successfully engaged in contracting and building. At the expiration of that time he returned to Carmi, Illinois, working at his trade for three years, and subsequently entered the employ of the Gravett & Johnson Sawmill Company, as bookkeeper, and with that concern

7

he remained two years. Led by the star of ambition, his next move would doubtless have yielded an abundance of fruit, and but for an unforeseen circumstance, he might yet be in the lumber business. He purchased the Moline Plow Company's sawmill plant, which he operated successfully for three years. It was located on the little Wabash river, which was afforded a navigable depth of water by a dam located at New Haven, thirty miles below.

There was an annual overflow of water which was detrimental to the farm land in that vicinity. The state authorities took the matter in hand, the result being the removal of the dam, which, of course, destroyed the facilities for bringing logs to the mill and ruined the usefulness of the plant. Mr. Beidelman entered claim with the Illinois legislature for $17,000, which is still pending.

He removed to Evansville in 1888, and engaged in the real estate business, and in that line has been eminently successful. There was considerable property on Water street belonging to the Conrad Baker heirs which had been idle for twenty years. This Mr. Beidelman opened and sold out in lots, and to-day a number of houses adorn what was once an open field. There was also another piece of ground at the intersection of Second and Emmett streets, belonging to Alvah Johnson, which Mr. Beidelman sub-divided into twenty-seven lots, and it is a remarkable fact that within six days from the time he purchased it, every lot was sold. He purchased several acres of land east of the city and laid out what is known as Clairmont Place. It is now adorned by numerous and handsome cottages.

He was united in marriage December 22, 1869, to Miss Susan B. Fitzgerrell, daughter of Isaac Fitzgerrell, and two children have blessed their union, as follows: Maud, now the wife of E. M. Tinker, and Leonard, employed by the L. & N. R. R. Co. Leonard Beidelman (son) married Miss Ada Bullock, of Evansville, and one child—a boy—has issued from their union.

— · —

JOHN BROWNLEE,

PROMINENT attorney at law of Evansville, was born at Princeton, Indiana, August 23, 1847. His early mental training was received from the public schools of Gibson county. He entered the Albany, New York, law school, from where he was graduated in June, 1866. In 1869 he began the practice of law in Mt. Vernon, Indiana. He was elected, in 1870, prosecuting attorney of the First Judicial District, then composed of the counties of Posey, Gibson, Vanderburgh and Warrick, which office he held for five successive terms. He located in Evansville in June, 1877. Was appointed city attorney in 1889, which position he ably and satisfactorily filled for three years.

Mr. Brownlee has been a successful practitioner, and is prominent as a politician and popular as a man. He is one of the most brilliant attorneys at the bar and possesses the qualifications of a good lawyer, sound judgment, a clear mind, retentive memory, oratorical ability and familiarity with the law. At the age of fourteen Mr. Brownlee enlisted in the Union army, joining Company F, Fifty-eighth Indiana Volunteers, in October, 1861, and served three years with much credit to himself. He is a member of the G. A. R. and Masonic lodge.

Mr. Brownlee was married April 2, 1878, to Miss Mittie Templeton, daughter of Mr. James M. Templeton, of Mt. Vernon, and three children bless their union, as follows: June, Dalmar and Geneva.

Mr. Brownlee's father was John Brownlee, of Princeton, Indiana, who married Miss Jane Harrington, also of Princeton.

——·

WALTER F. FREUDENBERG,

A YOUNG, able attorney and a member of the Evansville bar, was born in Gibson county, Indiana, in 1867. His early mental training he obtained from the common schools of Gibson county. His father, Joshua Freudenberg, was born February 22, 1835. He is successfully engaged in farming in Gibson county, and in 1856 married Miss Elizabeth Fulling, daughter of Clamar Fulling. Their union was blessed with six children, Walter F. being the youngest. In 1889 Walter entered the literary and law department of the State University and graduated with the class of 1892, was at once admitted to the bar and began the practice of law.

W. F. FREUDENBERG.

A. H. SCHROEDER.

Walter F. Freudenberg is rapidly taking his position in the front ranks of the members of the Evansville bar. His intense interest in any case which he undertakes and his deep enthusiasm and great earnestness carry conviction. He is known as a book lawyer, plodding patiently through authorities and works his cases thoroughly. He has not been a creature of advantageous circumstances, but has struggled against adversity, and by dint of persevering industry is achieving rapidly and honorably a brilliant career.

A. H. SCHROEDER,

A WORTHY citizen of Evansville, engaged in electro plating and manufacturing of head lights, was born December 11, 1836, in the Province of Hanover, Germany, and is the son of John Henry and Kratina M. (Heitbrink) Schroeder, both natives of Germany. The father came to America about 1862, and the mother lived and died in her native country. John Henry Schroeder first located in Cincinnati, Ohio, and afterwards moved to Jackson county, Indiana, and later to Ripley county, Indiana. He was a man of sterling integrity, honest, upright and hard working, but having a family of fourteen children to supply the wants of found it impossible to accumulate a very considerable amount of capital. Therefore, A. H. Schroeder was thrown upon his own resources at an early age, and as soon as he had received a meagre education from the common schools of his native land, he started out alone for America, at the age of seventeen. He had not even accumulated sufficient money to defray the absolute expenses of the trip, which were paid by his parents. He landed in the United States, an inexperienced boy, without means and no friends to encourage or to boost him. He located in Cincinnati, and for twelve years was employed in various foundries, and while there met and married Miss Mary E. Wolke, who had come from very near the same place where Mr. Schroeder lived in Germany, although they had not known each other until they met in Cincinnati. In 1866 Mr. Schroeder left Cincinnati to come to Evansville to work for Roelker, Blount & Co., which firm was afterwards changed to John H. Roelker & Co. His work was that of finishing house fronts and fences, and he remained with them ten years or more. He was afterwards employed by J. B. Mesker & Co. and also by Charles Lindenschmidt & Brothers, proprietors of the old Washington foundry, in Evansville.

Having higher aims in view, and believing that the same energy applied in his own behalf would net better results than working for wages, Mr. Schroeder commenced business for himself, in 1884, by starting a nickel plating industry. It required a great deal of courage and self-confidence for a man to embark in an enterprise entirely new to him; but he had determined "to do or to die," believing that "where there's a will there's a way." His was, at that time, the only institution of the kind in southern Indiana. He soon mastered the details of the business, and before many months was doing an extensive and lucrative business in gold, silver, nickel and all kinds of plating. Others watched him with envy, and large manufactories, following his example, added a plating department to their business. This, of course, created great competition, and the supply became greater than the demand. But A. H. Schroeder was not the man to sit idly by and hold his hands. When the plating business became light, he resolved to add another feature to his business, which he did by beginning to manufacture locomotive head lights. He had no knowledge of the business, but took it up and learned it thoroughly, and to-day enjoys an extensive trade reaching to all parts of the United States, and he has even filled orders coming from the Republic of Mexico. In February, 1888, Mr. Schroeder bought the property at 1114 and 1120 Main street, a splendid two-story brick building, and also owns the property at 1047 to 1053 Vine street. There is always a keen sense of delight in chronicling the triumph and success of men who have opened factories, but when a man is found who had courage to start two different enterprises, without any knowledge of either, and succeeds in conducting them both to a successful issue, it baffles one to find words sufficient to sound his praises. The plating done in Mr. Schroeder's establishment is not surpassed, if equalled, by any other concern in the United States.

The general satisfaction of his head lights is amply attested by the ever increasing demand for them. In all his business relations with the public, as well as in the wide circle of personal friends, Mr. Schroeder has enjoyed great popularity, his genial, courteous manner, obliging disposition and natural kindliness toward others winning him a host of friends, while his splendid business qualifications and methods have won the esteem and confidence of the business community.

He is an ardent republican, having cast his first vote for Abraham Lincoln, always liberal in his support of his party, but has never sought, nor would he accept any political office. He and his wife are members of the German Reform church of Evansville, in which they are both useful and helpful workers. Their union has been blessed with eight children, four of whom survive, the other four having died before reaching the age of two years. Of the surviving children two are boys and two are girls, as follows: Charles, A. H., Anna and Lizzie, who married Louis Rieger, a native of Elsas and Lothingen, a province taken from France in the late Franco-German war. She is now a widow, and is employed as saleslady in the millinery department of William Hughes' store, on Main street. Both the boys and also the unmarried daughter assist their father in his business, and they have always worked hard to take care of and foster his interests. The son, A. H., Jr., was married December 16, 1896, to Miss Lizzie Koehnen, of Evansville.

CHAS. H. JOHANN.

CHARLES H. JOHANN,

PRESENT coroner of Vanderburgh county, was born in Evansville July 1, 1857, and is the second child of Albert and Barbara (Spies) Johann. Charles William Johann, (grandfather), a native of Prussia, came to America in 1848, locating at Cannelton, Indiana, where, after a long and busy life he died in July, 1875.

Albert Johann, (father), was born in Prussia July 16, 1831, and was schooled in his native country and he learned to be a carpenter. He has been engaged for over a quarter of a century in the undertaking business in Evansville. He began life a poor man, but by industry and economy has succeeded in accumulating a comfortable competence. He is a member of the I. O. O. F. and K. & L. of H. fraternities. His affiliations are with the republican party and he has served the city as councilman one term. He was united in marriage in July, 1854, to Miss Barbara Spies and eight children have blessed their union.

Charles H. Johann, after receiving his education in the schools of Evansville, was apprenticed to a carpenter, but for the past twelve years has been engaged with his father in the undertaking business, being one of the most efficient embalmers in the state. In the fall of 1896 he was elected by the people as coroner of Vanderburgh county. That he is thoroughly competent all agree, and in his ability the people have unquestionable confidence. He stands at the commencement of his career, and measuring the future by the past, flatter-

ing predictions may be made. He is a member of Leni Leoti lodge, A. O. U. W., Wagner lodge, K. of P., Evansville lodge No. 1, D. of H., and the Evansville Press Club. He is a widower and has a son, Serle, sixteen years of age.

JACOB BIPPUS,

A FOREMOST contractor and builder of Evansville, was born in that city February 9, 1846, and as soon as his elementary education was completed, he started out to do something for himself and decided to be a carpenter, which trade he learned at an early age. He is the son of Gottlieb and Katherine (Loeffler) Bippus, natives of Germany. There are very few contractors in Southern Indiana who are better known or more universally esteemed and respected than is Jacob Bippus. He is known by almost everybody and nearly every town in Southern Indiana is indebted to him for some one or more handsome structures. We might mention a few of the most important buildings which Mr. Bippus has superintended, as follows: Grace Presbyterian church of Princeton, Y. M C. A. of Evansville, Val. M. Schmitz' block, Gilbert Walker's residence, Fowler, Dick & Walker block, Postoffice block of Vincennes, residence of Wm. Decker, president of the German National Bank. He employes a great number of workmen and his treatment to them always gives assurance of his being able to secure all the help needed. His career has been characterized by enterprising activity, able management and unyielding devotion to honorable methods. He has been efficient and trustworthy, and has earned by good work the advancement made.

Mr. Bippus was united in marriage in 1867, to Miss Laura Mathias, and their union has been blessed with ten children.

Mr. Bippus is a member of the Odd Fellows lodge and is also an active Knight of Pythias.

SILVESTER D. MUSGRAVE, M. D.,

ONE of the younger members of the Evansville medical profession, was born in Boonville, Indiana, in 1864 and is the son of Benjamin and Rebecca Ann (Davis) Musgrave. His father was born in Kentucky in 1813 and came to Indiana at an early day and was successfully engaged in farming in Warrick county. He died at the age of eighty-three years. Mrs. Rebecca Ann (Davis) Musgrave, mother, was born in White county, Illinois, in 1829, and died in August, 1896. The subject of this sketch was the tenth of twelve children. He spent his boyhood days on the farm and attended the high school in Boonville, Indiana. After completing his literary education he taught school until 1887, when he entered the Hahneman College, of Chicago, from which he was graduated in 1889, and for four years following practiced his profession in Newburgh, Indiana. He

came to Evansville in 1893 and has succeeded in building up a valuable and gratifying practice. He is a member of the Indiana Homeopathic Medical Society and for four years past has been one of the United States examining surgeons at Boonville. He is also a member of the Evansville Homeopathic Medical Society. He occupies a foremost position among his medical brethren, and is everywhere recognized, not only as an able and successful physician, but as a valuable citizen.

Dr. Musgrave was united in marriage in September, 1888, to Miss Katie B. Werry, daughter of Peter Werry, a native of Warrick county.

HENRY SCHMINKE,

A PROMINENT business man of Evansville, head of the firm of H. Schminke & Co., was born in Germany, April 12, 1854, and is the son of Bernhart Schminke.

Henry Schminke came to America in 1855. Both of his parents expired when he was about ten years of age and he went to live with Mr. Martin Seibert, a farmer of Vanderburgh county. Here he worked for four years and occasionally attended the common schools. He was naturally ambitious and realized that he must make his own way in the world, so in 1865 he went to Grayville, Illinois, and there learned the tinner's trade, which he followed for about eighteen months in Grayville. Then he returned to

DR. S. D. MUSGRAVE.

H. SCHMINKE.

Evansville and engaged his services to Mr. John Scantlin, of Fulton avenue. In 1869 he entered the firm of J. B. Mesker & Co., and when George Mesker succeeded his father, Mr. Schminke remained with the son. He was industrious, careful and economical, and managed to save part of his earnings, and in nine years bought out the business of his employer, which he has conducted most successfully ever since, and which to-day is the leading stove and tinware house in Evansville. Mr. Schminke has not confined himself alone to one enterprise. He was one of the incorporators of the Sunnyside Coal and Mining Company, and for two years served that institution as secretary and treasurer. He has been prominently engaged in teaming, owning a large number of horses and vehicles. He is an efficient business man and a popular citizen. He who starts empty-handed in the race of life and at his prime has gathered about him those things which bespeak successful endeavor, may be said to have made his own way.

The success of Mr. Schminke has been due in a large measure to his untiring zeal, constant watchfulness and unswerving probity. A democrat in politics, faithfully exercising the rights of citizenship, he is never offensive to political opponents in the enunciation of his principles. A man of his intellect and experience could not possibly avoid getting into public life, and he was unanimously elected councilman from the third ward in April, 1895, and in 1897 was re-elected to that position.

and is a useful and helpful member of that body.

H. Schminke was united in marriage in October, 1879, to Miss Julia Bates, and four children have blessed their union.

Mr. Schminke is a member of the A. O. U. W., Improved German K. P. and Macabees.

ALBERT W. FUNKHOUSER.

SOME men achieve distinction early in life, while to others the honors and the plaudits come later. Albert W. Funkhouser, a prominent member of the Evansville bar, belongs to the former class. His success in life is due to his own exertion and energy. He was born in Harrison county, Indiana, October 4, 1863, and is the son of Jacob and Mary L. (Winder) Funkhouser.

The family was founded in America by John Funkhouser, who emigrated from near Zurich, Switzerland, and settled seven miles north of what is now Woodstock, Virginia, in 1682. He was one of that class of emigrants to which Mr. Cooke refers in his "History of Virginia," saying: "To this day the Germans constitute an important element of the population (of the Shenandoah Valley) and in some places the language is spoken It was an excellent class of emigrants. Everywhere was the appearance of reality and thrift; well kept fields, fat cattle and huge red barns." A descendant, Moses Funkhouser, grandfather of the subject of this sketch, settled in Harrison county, Indiana, in the year of 1808. While yet a lad of fourteen he took part in the battle of Tippecanoe as a member of a company organized at Corydon, known as the "Yellow Jackets."

Albert W. Funkhouser was reared on his father's farm in Harrison county. As a boy in school he was quick and bright. After completing the course of study at the public schools he entered DePauw University at Green Castle, Indiana, in September, 1881, as a member of the class of 1885. He took a high rank in college and was recognized as one of the strongest members of his class. In 1884 he represented the Platoneau Society in the Kinnear-Morette contest—the oldest as well as the most honorary forensic contest in that renowned school of learning.

After a thorough course of reading in the office of Messrs. W. N. and R. J. Tracewell at Corydon, he began the practice of law at Leavenworth in 1887, in partnership with Hon. Robert J. Tracewell, afterward a member of the Fifty-third congress from that district. The partnership lasted for nine years and was rewarded with a lucrative business and established a reputation for both members as able, conscientious lawyers.

Mr. Funkhouser was admitted as a member of the bar of the supreme court of Indiana in 1892. He has always been an ardent but a liberal republican politically. In 1894 he was his party's unanimous choice for prosecuting attorney of the third circuit, and was elected by the handsome majority of

498, leading the ticket by 408 votes. As a prosecutor he was fearless, energetic and clean, and was endorsed by the opposition press as having served "with credit to himself and to the district." Though strongly solicited by the people of all parties to make the race for a second term, he declined in order to accept a partnership with his brother, Arthur F. Funkhouser, at Evansville in November, 1896. The firm of A. W. and A. F. Funkhouser enjoys an extensive and growing practice, and is recognized as one of the strongest among the younger class at the bar. Their prospects are second to none.

Mr. Funkhouser was united in marriage January 28, 1891, to Miss Alta Craig and two children - boys—Albert C. and Paul T., have blessed their union. Their home, No. 842 Washington avenue, is one of the most beatiful in the city.

GEORGE W. LOWRANCE,

PROMINENT citizen and proprietor of the popular Sycamore street livery stable, was born in Warrick county April 10, 1852. Jas. W. Lowrance, (father), was born in South Carolina and came to Warrick county with his parents when he was three years old. He grew up to be a farmer and was very prosperous as such and died August 27, 1896, on his farm in Warrick county, where he lived for fifty-five years. He married Miss Fuquay, a native of Warrick county, and their union was

ALBERT W. FUNKHOUSER.

CHAS. SIHLER.

blessed with seven children, the subject of this sketch being the fifth. James W. Lowrance was a most popular and highly respected citizen in the community in which he resided.

George W. Lowrance received his elementary education in the common schools of Warrick county, going to school in the winter and working on his father's farm in the summer, and when nineteen years of age started out on his own account to fight the battles of life. His first move was to engage in the livery business at Newburgh, Indiana, where he formed a partnership with Mr. Albert Alexander. In 1883, having spent twelve years prosperously at Newburgh and having become known all over Southern Indiana as livery men of ability, they began to look out for a larger and better field, selecting Evansville as their future abode, moving there in that year and commenced a livery and feed stable business on Sycamore street, the business continuing successfully and about five years ago Mr. Lowrance, keeping pace with the rapid growth of Evansville, purchased the ground and erected a handsome livery stable on Sycamore street, between Fourth and Fifth, which he at present occupies. It is one of the best in the city, having a capacity for sixty-five head of horses. Mr. Lowrance owns sixteen to twenty head himself, fifteen to twenty vehicles, has thirty to thirty-five boarders and employs regularly five to ten men.

"Duck" Lowrance as he is familiarly called by his friends and acquaintances stands to-day a peer to livery men in
8

Southern Indiana. He is one of the most genial, popular and progressive men in Evansville. He is a man of sterling integrity, loyal and public spirited and numbers his friends by the score.

CHARLES SIHLER,

CLERK of Vanderburgh county, was born in Evansville in 1869, and received his elementary education there in the public schools. Louis Sihler, (father), was born in Wurtemberg, Germany, May 25, 1833, and was a son of L. Sihler, who married Agatha Schleicher, both natives of Germany. Louis Sihler received a good education in Germany, was thrown upon his own resources and developed sterling traits of character, which marked his conduct through life, emigrated to the United States in 1853, locating in Evansville. He was engaged in merchandising for a number of years, when in 1872 he was appointed deputy recorder of Vanderburgh county, and served in that capacity twelve years, when he was elected by a handsome majority to the office of county recorder; was re-elected in 1888. In 1860 he was united in marriage to Miss Charlotte Sixt, a native of Germany, born in 1841, and their union was blessed with five children, as follows: Henrietta, Charles, Lona, Margaret and Clara. Louis Sihler died January 11, 1890.

Charles Sihler served as deputy clerk under Charles Jenkins and also under Mr. Boepple. He served as clerk in the recorder's office under his father, made a race for that office in 1890, but with all other republicans met defeat ; then he served a year in the treasurer's office and then went into the clerk's office. In the fall of '96 he was elected county clerk and in that capacity has demonstrated the wisdom of his con- stituents in placing him there. When but a boy Charles Sihler was serving the people as deputy clerk and so apparent were his abilities and so acceptable his service that it was pre- dicted that he would attain the highest position of trust in Vanderburgh county. He is a man of correct business habits, well qualified, efficient, trust-worthy and popular with the masses. Charles Sihler was united in marriage to Miss Maria Haas in 1895, and one child has blessed their union.

___

HON. H. M. LOGSDON,

EMINENT lawyer, member of the Ev- ansville bar, was born in Spencer county, Indiana, June 28. 1852, and is the son of Samuel Logsdon. The boy- hood days of Mr. Logsdon were spent on his father's farm in Spencer county, Indiana, where he worked in summer and attended the common schools in winter. By diligence he obtained a fair education, and for some time taught school in the neighboring districts, but having higher aims in view, decided to enter the State University, which he did in 1871, and from which he was gradu- ated in 1875. He studied law at the

university and continued his study at Rockport, Indiana, in the law office of Hatfield, DeBruler & Thomas, and in 1877 was admitted to the bar at Rock- port, Indiana. For fourteen years he practiced law in the courts of that thriving little town. He not only won the respect of the courts and the mem- bers of the legal profession, but also obtained a substantial and lucrative practice. Although Mr. Logsdon can- not be said to be an active politician, he has always affiliated with the demo- cratic party, and for two years was chairman of the Democratic Central Committee. In the fall of 1886 he was elected state senator from Spencer and Warrick counties, and it is a remarkable fact that, with him as an exception, the entire democratic ticket that year went down to defeat. No representative in the state had a better reputation as a public officer, or secured more universal and hearty assistance from his associates than did Mr. Logsdon, during the four years of his service as senator. He was appointed a member of the Judiciary Committee, and to Senator Barrett, of Wayne county, and himself, was due the credit for drafting the state election law, which Mr. Logsdon ably and espe- cially championed. He was mainly instrumental in assisting in having passed legislation which had been asked for by Vanderburgh county. He took an active part in the repeal of the Intimidation law.

For two years, from 1891 to 1893, Mr. Logsdon practiced law in Chatta- nooga, Tennessee, but foreseeing, as he believed, that Evansville was destined

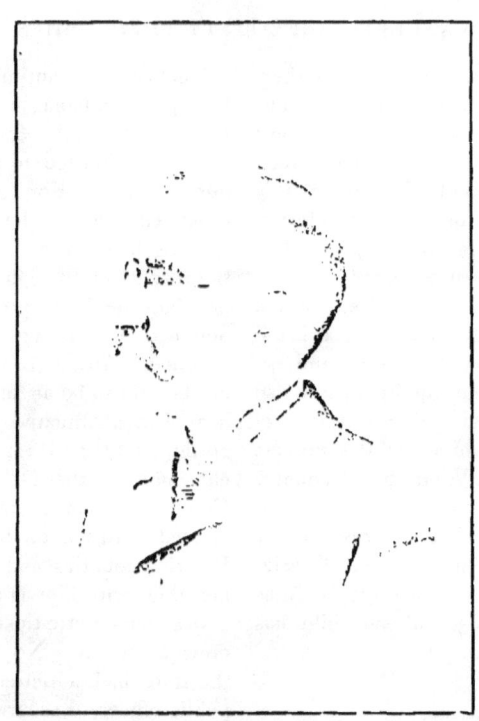

H. M. LOGSDON.

W. S. HURST.

to become the first metropolis of Indiana, he located here in the fall of 1893, and later formed a partnership with Hon. Henry Mason, under the firm name of Logsdon & Mason.

Mr. Logsdon has attained a position at the bar in the very front ranks of the best lawyers in the state of Indiana. He is thoroughly in love with his profession and entertains an exalted idea of the character of a lawyer.

He was united in marriage, May 20, 1891, to Miss Katie Hyland, an accomplished and highly intelligent young woman, daughter of Wilmer Hyland, a prominent business man, of Rockport, Indiana.

Mr. Logsdon is an active and helpful member of the Masonic order, the Elks and Knights of Pythias.

In 1885 he made an extensive trip through Europe, spending four months traveling in that country.

· WESLEY S. HURST,

ATTORNEY at law and member of the Evansville bar, was born November 9, 1846, in Dubois county, Indiana. He started in life with the odds against him, succeeded in obtaining an education which he most desired, studied law and to-day enjoys a gratifying practice.

Ira Hurst (father) was a Virginian, and came to Dubois county at an early date and afterwards moved to Gibson county. He was a prominent farmer and carpenter, a man much loved and highly respected by all who knew him.

He was united in marriage to Miss Phœbe Brinton, a native of Dubois county, who expired in 1847.

Mr. Hurst obtained his early mental training from the common schools of Dubois county, which he attended in winter, working on a farm in summer, and in 1861 he engaged to work in a printing office at Jasper, Indiana. About that time the war dogs began to bay, and Mr. Hurst quit the printing office, picked up his drum and entered the Union army as drummer boy in company E, Fifty-eighth Indiana Infantry. In that capacity he served faithfully one year, when, on account of ill-health, he was honorably discharged and returned home. He at once entered the State University at Bloomington, Indiana, and remained there until 1868, graduating in that year in both literature and law. His great aim was an education, and being of meagre means, and being a firm believer in the gospel of industry and the dignity of labor, he paid his own way through the university by acting as janitor in that institution. To meet his demands while establishing a practice amid all the competition of the day, he readily recognized would be impossible. Therefore, he deferred beginning the practice of law until he could earn sufficient capital to carry him, which he did by teaching school in Pike, Gibson and Warrick counties until 1872. In that year he was admitted to the bar and began to practice law at Vincennes, Indiana, remaining there two years. He removed to Petersburg, Indiana, and in 1883 located in Evansville, where he has continually practiced his profession since, and has been eminently successful, as a man must who is in love with his profession. He is studious, energetic and industrious in his habits.

Mr. Hurst was appointed city attorney December 18, 1895, and served one term.

___

GEORGE F. WEIKEL,

A LEADING builder and contractor of Evansville, was born in Evansville, Indiana, April 23, 1868. At an early age he learned to be a brick mason, and before he was twenty-five years of age, was doing an extensive contracting and building business. His first contract was the building of the Keller printing house, and in 1896 he erected the magnificent structure known as the Delaware street school building. He was also awarded, in December, 1896, the contract for building the new monastery, on Kentucky avenue, in Evansville, a magnificent structure which was completed in June, 1897. In this work Mr. Weikel was his own architect and superintendent, and had entire charge of the work, personally supervising it in every detail, and it is a fact that the building gave entire satisfaction to all concerned.

George Weikel has the reputation of being one of the most "go ahead" men of this section. He stands to-day at the beginning of his career, and, if we shall judge the future by the past, some very flattering predictions might be made.

Frank Weikel (father) was born in Pennsylvania, and was engaged in building and contracting. He moved to Evansville in 1868, and up to the time of his death, in 1887, was a prominent contractor in Evansville, and did a great deal of work in building up the city. He married Miss Frances Rice, a native of Cincinnati, Ohio, and their union was blessed with nine children, the subject of this sketch being the eighth.

George F. Weikel is one of the young men who has achieved prominence early in life. He is always busy, and gives employment to thirty-five or forty men, in various capacities. He is a consistent member of Assumption church. He is a young man of sterling worth, and is highly respected and esteemed by all who know him.

___

ALBERT F. KARGES,

SECRETARY and treasurer of the Karges Furniture Company, a prominent and enterprising citizen of Evansville, was born in German township in November, 1861.

His father, Ferdinand Karges, came to America in 1851, coming direct to Evansville, where he followed his trade, that of cabinet-making. About 1865 he was engaged with Christ Miller in the manufacture of furniture, under the firm name of Miller, Karges & Co., which was dissolved some years later, when Mr Karges assisted in forming the Evansville Furniture Company. Ten years later he withdrew from the latter concern and engaged in farming in White county, Illinois, up to the time of his death, in the summer of 1890.

GEO. F. WEIKEL.

A. F. KARGES.

He married Miss Rosa Dulty, born in Germany in 1836, and she died in Evansville in 1868. Their union was blessed with four children, Albert F, Will T., member of the firm of Karges & Wimberg, and two daughters, one of whom married Mr. J. W. Boehne, of the Indiana Stove Works, and the other is also married and lives in Vanderburgh county. Ferdinand Karges was married (second) to Miss Mary Bohleber.

A. F. Karges received his elementary education in the public schools of Evansville, and took a course in the Rankin & Wright Commercial College. Setting out to fight life's battles alone, he entered the employment of Fred. Brokamp, merchant tailor of Evansville, and remained with him three years. In August, 1879, Mr. Karges engaged as bookkeeper with William Hughes in the dry goods business, where for six years he filled creditably that responsible position. Leaving there, he was for some months in the lumber business, and in the fall of 1885, he became interested with Mr. Henry Stolz in the manufacture of furniture, under the firm name of Stolz & Karges. This partnership continued prosperously until February, 1889, when Mr. Karges, in connection with two others, bought out the interest of Mr. Stolz and organized the Karges Furniture Company, to-day one of the foremost furniture manufacturing establishments in the country, with an ever increasing trade, extending not only all over the United States, but reaching far into other countries, notably South Africa and South America. Mr. Karges was at one time a member of the Business Men's Association and is a prominent member of the Manufacturers' Association of Evansville, having been the second vice president elected to preside over that body, and was strongly solicited to serve as president, which, for good and sufficient reasons, he declined. He is an elder in the Jefferson Avenue Presbyterian church, of which he has for many years been an active and helpful worker. In his contributions to this and kindred organizations for the maintenance and propagation of Christianity, Mr. Karges has been very liberal.

Albert F. Karges is a self-made man, having begun his career without means or influence in his favor, and he has, by hard work and close economy, attained a comfortable competence.

He was united in marriage December 8, 1885, to Miss Lizzie Hauk, of Evansville, and three children, two of whom survive, Albert F., Jr., and Edwin F., have blessed their union.

BENJAMIN HOFFMAN,

CONTRACTOR and builder of Evansville, was born in Dubois county, Indiana, July 15, 1857, and is the son of George Jacob and Stephena Hoffman. He received his education from the common schools of Louisville, Kentucky, and at the age of twenty-three he learned the carpenters' trade, which he followed as journeyman until 1890, when he began to do a contracting business on his own account. Mr. Hoffman has been a valuable factor in the building of Evansville, and a few structures erected by him might be mentioned, viz.: St. Mary's hospital, St. Anthony's church, the residences of Dr. Laval and Frank Pritchett, the Delaware street school and residence of Mr. Louis Legler. His energy and ability have been the chief agents in building up the business which he now enjoys.

Mr. Hoffman was united in marriage May 6, 1884, to Miss Mary Anna Lindenschmidt, and their union has been blessed with four children. He is a member of the Catholic Knights of America, the Knights of Maccabees Supreme Tent and also of the Grand Tent.

————

EMIL WILLIAM SAUPERT,

A SUCCESSFUL business man and enterprising citizen of Evansville, was born in Evansville November 26, 1857, and is the son of Rev. A. Saupert, a native of Bavaria, Germany, who came to America in 1845, was a very earnest and devoted minister of the Gospel and was the founder of Trinity Lutheran church on East Illinois street, where for almost a half century he served as minister, and he continued in the good work up to the time of his death, which occurred in 1893. Rev. A. Saupert was a man of the highest integrity and of sterling worth, honored and respected in the community in which he resided. He was united in marriage to Miss Minnie Schultze, a native of Germany, who came to America with her people

in 1837. She still resides in Evansville. Their union was blessed with twelve children, eight of whom survive.

Emil W. Saupert received his early mental training from the private, parochial and public schools of Evansville, and later entered Fort Wayne Concordia College and afterwards took a course in the Concordia University in St. Louis, from where he was graduated at the age of twenty-four. In 1881 he returned to Evansville and remained for some time, when, on account of ill health, he was compelled to seek a more salubrious clime in the west. He went to Colorado, and for two years taught school and engaged in missionary work for the Lutheran church, and his efforts were crowned with very gratifying success. He returned to Evansville and engaged in the coal business, being elected secretary of the Diamond Coal Mining Company in 1884, and has served that institution faithfully ever since. In 1895 Mr. Saupert became interested in the grocery business, and is now a member of the firm of Koester, Saupert & Korff, proprietors of the "Original" grocery, at the corner of Eighth and Chestnut streets.

Mr. Saupert is still an active and helpful member of the Lutheran church. Politically, he affiliates with the republican party, but has never sought preferment, and has at different times declined the solicitations of his party friends to become a candidate for office, which he could not do without detriment to his business interests. In 1895 Mr. Saupert was married to Miss Lottie Koester, daughter of Mr. Louis Koester,

ISHAM TAYLOR.

F. BOCKSTEGE.

president of the Diamond Coal Mining Company, and partner in the above named grocery firm. Their union has been blessed with three children, two of whom survive—girls—Flora and Edna.

ISHAM TAYLOR,

PROMINENT lawyer of Evansville, was born in Warrick county, Indiana, June 6, 1867. His father, Mr. Hubbard Taylor, was born in Tennessee in 1813. He married (second) Miss Nancy Robinette, and to them three children were born, Isham being the second. He attended the common schools and gleaned therefrom such mental training as they afforded. He first attended the State Normal School of Terre Haute, and subsequently went to DePauw University, where he took a three years' course. He entered the Indiana University in 1892 and was graduated from there in 1893 with the degree of A. B. and in 1895 with the degree of LL. B. He was promptly admitted to the bar and began at once the practice of law, under the firm name of Reister, Taylor & Taylor. That partnership was dissolved in March, 1896, and up to January 18, 1897, Mr. Taylor followed his profession alone, since then he has been in partnership with Mr. William Reister, under the firm name of Reister & Taylor.

Mr. Taylor enjoys a lucrative law practice, to which he is very much devoted. He is a young man of promising future, and has established himself in the confidence of his numerous clients, who firmly believe in him as a man of honor and a lawyer of marked ability.

He was one of the organizers and is the present secretary of the Jualin Mining Company, a company engaged in gold mining in the territory of Alaska. The company is prosperous, and the outlook for the future is most encouraging.

FRED. BOCKSTEGE,

PRESIDENT of the Karges Furniture Company, was born in Germany, April 16, 1861, and before leaving his native land, learned to be a cabinetmaker, having worked in Germany, where he became skilled among the finest workmen. At the age of twenty he came to America, and for several months followed his trade at Akron, Ohio. From there he went to St. Louis, Missouri, where he was engaged for about six months. In 1882 Mr. Bockstege came to Evansville and entered the employ of Joseph F. Reitz, who was engaged in the furniture business, and worked for him as cabinet maker for three years. Then he engaged for some time with Mr. George Mutschler in the planing mill business. Was afterwards, for twelve months, with Schnute, Dubber & Co., who had bought out Mr. Mutschler's mill, and later entered the employ of Stoltz & Karges as cabinet maker. This engagement continued six months, which brings us up to February 1, 1889, when Mr. Bockstege, in connection with Mr. A. F. Karges and John Jourdan, Jr., formed what is known far and wide as the Karges Furniture Company, Mr. Bockstege being chosen president, in which capacity he has served continually ever since. His success has been phenomenal. He started out in life with the odds against him. He came to a new country with no means, no friends and no knowledge of our language, and did not understand the ways of the American people. He was a mere boy, his only possession being the knowledge of his trade, but he had started out to win. He had ample vim and vigor, which are conducive of victory. By hard work and close application, he has succeeded in a decade in raising himself to the presidency of one the most important industries in southern Indiana. He did not have to confine himself alone to his adopted trade, when there was no work in that line, he did something else. Keeping continually at work is the secret of success. Mr. Bockstege is a member of the German Lutheran church of Evansville.

October 30, 1884, he was united in marriage to Miss Alwena Langele, of Evansville. Their union was blessed with one child. Mrs. Bockstege died in 1887, and Mr. Bockstege was again married the same year to Miss Mena Seeger, also of Evansville, and four children have issued from their union.

Fred. Bockstege is a gentleman who is held in the very highest esteem by the citizens of Evansville and is regarded by one and all as a man of sterling integrity and an enterprising business man.

WILLIAM REISTER,

PROMINENT young attorney of Evansville, was born in Gibson county, Indiana, April 3, 1866. He was schooled in the common schools of Gibson county and entered the State University at Bloomington, Indiana, in 1893, where he took a law course and was graduated from there in 1894. He was admitted to the bar in February, 1889, at Mt. Vernon, Indiana, and began the practice of law immediately.

Christian Reister (father) was born in Germany in 1824, came to America in 1848, enlisted in the regular army as soon as he landed in this country and was a captain in the civil war. After the war he was engaged in manufacturing brick and did a contracting business for a number of years. Catherine Reister (mother) was a native of Germany, and was married to Christian Reister in 1848. Their union was blessed with seven children, William being the youngest.

William Reister formed a partnership with Isham Taylor January 1, 1897, as Reister & Taylor. He is a member of the K. of P., I. O. O. F., Royal Arcanum and A. O. U. W. He was a candidate for representative in 1894, but was defeated, like all other democrats at that time. At the age of twenty-four years, he served Smith township, in Posey county, as township trustee.

William Reister was united in marriage May 8, 1889, to Miss Mamie Dunn, and to them four children have been born, three of whom survive. In the short time Mr. Reister has been in

WM. REISTER.

Evansville, he has, by his ability and close application, placed himself in the front rank of the Vanderburgh county bar.

He was one of the organizers and is a stockholder of the Jaulin Mining Company, a company engaged in gold mining in the territory of Alaska. The company is prosperous, and the outlook for the future is most encouraging.

CHARLES P. BACON, M. D.

PROMINENT and leading physician of Evansville, was born in Christian county, Kentucky, September 6, 1836, and received his elementary education in the schools and academies of his native state.

Charles A. Bacon (father) was a native of Virginia, and at an early day located in Kentucky. For a number of years he was engaged in the mercantile business, but the latter part of his life was spent in farming. He possessed a high standard of integrity and both mentally and physically was a man of great natural endowments. He was a man of intelligence, excellent judgment and remarkable industry, and was greatly respected in the community in which he lived. He married Susan Roulette, also a native of Virginia, and a member of one of the best families in that state. Four children issued from their marriage, the subject of this sketch being the third.

Charles P. Bacon began the study of medicine in 1858 under the preceptor-

ship of his brother, Dr. Thomas L. Bacon, an eminent practitioner of Henderson county, Ky., now of Hopkinsville, Ky., and entered the University of Pennsylvania in 1859, was graduated in 1861. For twelve years following he did a successful practice at Cadiz, Ky., and in 1873 he moved to Evansville to make it his permanent abode.

During the existence of the Evansville Medical College Dr. Bacon filled at different times the chairs of anatomy, surgery, gynecology, which he did with dignity and credit both to himself and the institution. He is still a student and a careful reader of medical literature, keeping pace with the rapid progress of medical science, and is a member of the Vanderburgh County Medical Society, Indiana State Medical Society, American Medical Association, and is also consulting surgeon at St. Mary's Hospital and at the Protestant Deaconess Home.

He is a member of the Masonic order in which he takes a deep interest. He is a Past Master, Past High Priest and Past Eminent Commander and is also a thirty-second degree Scottish Rite Mason.

Politically Dr. Bacon affiliates with the democratic party, and although he takes an active interest in the welfare of his party, he is not a politician in the strict sense of the term and never sought political preferment, but a man of his intelligence could hardly keep out of politics, and in 1896 he was induced to accept the position of elector on the national democratic ticket.

Dr. Bacon is a man of means and

9

affairs, and is vice-president of the Citizens National Bank of Evansville.

His literary pursuits have been systematic and thorough and he has grown in the knowledge of men and affairs as he has grown in years; he has contributed his share of work to medical literature and he has taken an active interest in the Methodist church, of which he has been a consistent member for a number of years. Dr. Bacon's practice is not confined alone to Evansville, nor Indiana for that matter, but extends largely into adjoining states.

Dr. Bacon was united in marriage January 23, 1866, to Miss Emma C. Mayes, daughter of Judge Matthew Mayes, one of the leading lawyers of Kentucky. Their union has been blessed with one child, a daughter, Miss Mayes Bacon, who married Mr. Clarence L. Hinkle in November, 1895.

_____

DR. S. B. LEWIS,

SURGEON-DENTIST, was born in Chautauqua county, New York, April 3, 1846. His father, John F. Lewis, and his mother, Mary E. (Brigham) Lewis, were natives of New York, the father born in 1816 and the mother in 1818. When Dr. Lewis was still a boy his parents moved to Clermont county, Ohio, and subsequently settled at Greenville, Ohio. John F. Lewis was a dealer in stock, a prominent and successful man in the community in which he resided.

S. B. Lewis received his education in the common schools of Clermont county. He was only a boy when the war broke out, but when the dogs of war began to bay, he threw down his school books to pick up his musket in the defense of his flag and joined the ranks of the Federal army, enlisting in the 100-day service at Greenville, Ohio, where he joined Company G, One Hundred and Fifty-second regiment O. N. G. He served faithfully from 1864 as regimental musician in the One Hundred and Eighty-seventh regiment Ohio Infantry Volunteers until the close of the war. He studied dentistry after the war under his brother, Dr. Walter F. Lewis. He came to Evansville then and studied under Dr. Isaiah Haas. He returned to Greenville in 1868 and began the practice of his profession. In 1873 he returned to Evansville and has practiced his profession here continually ever since. Dr. Lewis is a member of the G. A. R. and the Royal Arcanum, and in the latter was grand regent one year and represented the grand council at the supreme council two years. He is prominent in the I. O. O. F., having passed various chairs. He is also a useful and helpful member of the Masonic order, having been past master and past high priest, and in 1896 was eminent commander of LaValette Commandery, and has done much to promote the interest of the order.

He was married in 1869 to Miss Emma C. Dorman, of Greenville, Ohio, and two children have blessed their union. The eldest, Ernest Lewis, has been a close literary student for a num-

DR. S. B. LEWIS.

C. L. WEDDING.

ber of years, and recently received the degree of Bachelor of Arts from Harvard University. He is one of the brightest and most promising young men in this community, and, if we are to judge the future by the past, some flattering predictions might be made.

Dr. Lewis has been signally successful as a dentist, being greatly devoted to his profession, and always faithful to the interests of his patrons. He is a man of fine personal bearing, dignified in appearance and genial and cordial in his intercourse with others. He is an exceedingly popular citizen.

— — —

CHARLES L. WEDDING,

ATTORNEY at law, prominent member of the Evansville bar, was born in Ohio county, Kentucky, October 17, 1845, and belongs to that large class of men of sterling worth and usefulness, who was born to the soil. While it is undoubtedly true, according to that great state paper, the Declaration of Independence, that all men are created equal, yet all men do not make equal use of the opportunities afforded them in this country, pre-eminent above all others as the land of opportunities. All lives are full of struggles, and each has its vicissitudes. Some are misdirected and fail of success—others, with no better chances, win the goal. The successful man always has marked characteristics obtained by him in his wrestle with the fates. Either his popularity or his appreciation of his energy has won

the battle, and these leave upon him the characteristics which make his individuality. The subject of this sketch has evinced all these elements--popularity, for his geniality, a place in success as the result of energetic action.

Charles L. Wedding started out in life with the odds against him, courted fortune under adverse circumstances, and has achieved far greater success than falls to the lot of most men. His early boyhood days were spent on his father's farm, where he worked in the summer, attending the common schools in winter. The advantages to be derived from such schools as were then taught in Ohio county were meagre in the extreme. He was not content to remain on a farm and live a monotonous life, but had higher aims, and at the age of sixteen, although equipped with a very limited knowledge of the elementary branches of education, he began to study law. He had an exalted idea of the character of a lawyer. The desire and determination to become a lawyer, in the same sense that implies character, culture, learning and love of country. Although there were difficulties to surmount and many chasms to bridge, he pressed on with determination, eliminating from his vocabulary the word, "can't," and substituting in its place " will." He bought some elementary law books, and it was not an uncommon thing for him to devote sixteen hours a day in gleaning knowledge from their pages. In 1864 he was admitted to the bar, after having passed a successful examination before two eminent and distinguished judges of Kentucky, viz.:

James Stuart, then of Brandenburg, and P. B. Muir, of Louisville and for a while he was engaged in the practice of his profession at Cloverport, Kentucky. At that time Kentucky was very much disturbed and distressed from the effects of the civil war, and Mr. Wedding, therefore, moved to Rockport, Indiana. He arrived at Rockport an inexperienced and penniless boy, with no knowledge of the world nor friends to aid him. At that time the Rockport bar consisted of Judges DeBruler, Laird, Barkwell, Gen. J. C. Veatch, Hon. Thomas S. DeBruler, C. A. DeBruler and others of considerable note. Notwithstanding the weight of this strong competition, Mr. Wedding engaged himself diligently and succeeded in building up for himself a lucrative practice. Before he had reached his majority he had attained considerable reputation as a lawyer and orator. In 1880, seeking a more extended field, Mr. Wedding moved to Evansville, where his career has been marked with continued success. He is in love with and sticks to his profession. He has accumulated a considerable fortune, acquired it all in the practice of law, has built himself a beautiful home on Water street in his adopted city, where he and his family are surrounded with the comforts of life.

In politics Mr. Wedding is and has always been independent, voting as he felt he could best serve his country, but is not a politician in the usual acceptance of that term, yet he has attained some prominence in public affairs as a citizen. He is an able advocate, ener-getic in taking care of his clients, is a sincere and eloquent speaker. He is a man endowed with fine judgment of men, business and business principles, and enjoys the highest confidence of all who know him.

Mr. wedding was united in marriage, December 1, 1866, to Miss Mary C. English, a well known young lady of Rockport, Indiana, and a most worthy and popular woman of this city. They have two children, Webster and Charles Sterling, both now young men.

LOUIS ICHENHAUSER,

A NATIVE of Bavaria, Germany, born at the town of Ichenhausen (which place was named in honor of his grandparents) on September 30, 1832. He came to America in 1850 and located in Hardinsburg, Kentucky, and engaged in merchandising. He removed to Louisville, Kentucky, in 1864, and continued merchandising for one year. Coming to Evansville in 1866, he formed a co-partnership with Charles Lichten, and engaged in the wholesale glass and queensware business, under the firm name of Lichten & Ichenhauser. This firm was dissolved in 1880, by the retirement of Mr. Lichten. Mr. Ichenhauser continued the business, adding thereto the importation of china and queensware in 1883. The business has grown from year to year, until it is one of the leading houses of the kind in the west.

Mr. Ichenhauser is a member of the

LOUIS ICHENHAUSER.

Evansville Business Men's Association. He was for five years treasurer of the Germania Building and Loan Association, and is a member of the Sixth Street Jewish temple, in which he has held various official positions. Mr. Ichenhauser was married in Louisville, Kentucky, in 1859, to Therese Oberdorfer, who was born in Germany, in 1842, and eleven children have blessed their union, nine of whom survive. Three sons, Silas, Nathan and Sidney L., are engaged with their father in his business, the firm being known as L. Ichenhauser & Sons.

CAPT. CHARLES W. MYERHOFF,

WAS born at Cincinnati, Ohio, March 10, 1842, his mother dying, when he was but six years old. He was sent to live with an uncle, residing on a farm in Jackson county, Indiana, with whom, and John J. Cummins, a lawyer of the same county, he remained there until 1855, when he returned to live with his father, who had again married. His father's death occuring two years later. He hired to a gardner near Newport, Kentucky, but soon thereafter followed his only sister to Grandview, Indiana, where he worked on a farm and in a ship yard. He made a trip to Vicksburg, Mississippi, on a flat boat, and in 1858 started out in a sail boat, with three others, to seek adventure and employment. When landing at Evansville a salesman from Robert Barnes' store offered to trade or buy their boat

(Triton). A storm drove them to shore below Hickman, Kentucky, where they took possession of a cabin. For so doing, were set upon by the planter and his hounds. They were thought to be hard characters and roundly abused and ordered out and told to be gone.

As he approached, young Myerhoff stepped out of the door and bowing, said, "good evening." The planter being surprised at his appearance and manner, said, "I beg your pardon, sir, I thought you were river rats." He was profuse in his apologies and offered them all employment in his wood yard. Next day all went to work in the woods and while absent the cabin burned to the ground, by which mishap their clothes and stores were all lost. Two of the men went to the planter for assistance, he told them to go back and send Charley to him. He rendered assistance generously, declining to take their note, considering the young man's verbal promise to pay sufficient.

He was afterwards employed on a store-boat. His refusal to traffic with persons for stolen goods from the planters caused the young man to retrace his steps to Evansville, Indiana, carrying all his possessions in a small bandana. When passing the corner of Main and Second streets, Mr. Krone, the grocer, remarked, "young man, you look as if you have had a hard time."

His brother, John H. Myerhoff, was foreman in the Armstrong furniture factory and here he obtained employment until the tocsin of war was sounded in 1861. He attended the meeting in the old Crescent City Hall when the first two home guard companies were organized. His name was entered on General Blythe's company roll, but when Blythe Hynes moved down the aisle, rapidly vaulted upon the platform, and announced that Dr. Noah S. Thompson had received a commission as captain and orders to organize a volunteer company to start for Washington, D. C. at once to defend the capitol. Young Myerhoff arose from his seat and asked that his name be taken from the roll, then immediately called on Captain Thompson offering to enlist, but was refused, being too young and frail, and that his parents would object. When informed he was an orphan and was determined to go, was examined and accepted as the first enlisted man in the first organized company in Evansville for the war. He was the first man detailed for guard at Klurman's hall. His sternness was long remembered by the boys as being the man that kept them from seeing the first company drill. When Captain Thompson got up his list of non-commissioned officers, he submitted the list to Myerhoff and asked him how he liked the selection. His answer was, "Captain, you have selected the most popular men, but pardon me, when I call your attention to an element in your company you ignore; one half your company are Germans, and not one in the list." The list was changed and Germans recognized. At Terre Haute complaint was made to the captain by the company of unfairness in division of rations. After some parley the men were instructed to elect a member for the duty of dividing rations. Myerhoff was selected, which duty he performed for the company until commissioned first lieutenant. He was captured at Anteitam and performed the same duty for his mess of thirty-two in Libby prison, where he found the prisoners of a certain regiment were favored by an ex-officer of their regiment, then one of the principal officers of the prison. Myerhoff called a meeting in his division: the change following was appreciated by the men.

The regiment was organized at Terre Haute as the Fourteenth. Captain Thompson's company was designated as Company E. Myerhoff was appointed corporal, promoted to sergeant on Cheat Mountain, to orderly-sergeant October 1, 1862, to first lieutenant May 7, 1863, was in command of the company in the famous charge of Carroll's brigade on East Cemetery hill at Gettysburg, had command of Company H in the battles of the Wilderness, Spottsylvania, North Anna and Cold Harbor. Of the twenty-three men that he started with on the fourth of May, three were killed, eighteen wounded, and only two men were left to leave the works when the regiment's term of service expired on the seventh of June, 1864. Captain Myerhoff was seriously wounded thirty feet in front of the breastworks in a lunette he had himself constructed while lying flat behind a log, about five feet long and one foot thick that he had rolled out in front of him to within seventy-five yards of the enemy's breastworks immediately in front of the Fourteenth Indiana. There was an

CAPT. CHAS. H. MYERHOFF.

open space in the enemy's line, and this venture was made to cover that space and to prevent a massing of troops for a charge to break his regiment's line. The breastworks were so close that a cap raised on a bayonet would be immediately fired upon; the log was repeatedly hit. He began his work with a tin cup while lying flat under a hot June sun, afterward he was thrown a spade with which he finished and at dusk the battle began to rage furiously. He still remaining in front and calling to the Fourteenth to hold their fire while he was in front. When dark came some one in the regiment cried "here they come," and in the storm of flying missiles he was wounded; was sent to the officers' hospital in Alexandria, and the fact that he had lived near Gentryville, Spencer county, Indiana, and the threat to communicate with President Lincoln caused a reform in that hospital which was appreciated. His regiment was mustered out long before he was able to leave the hospital. When able to travel he came to Evansville and became interested in a saw-mill in Spencer county, the work being too heavy on account of his wounds he entered the employ of Philip Decker, who was the sutler of the Tenth Tennessee regiment at Nashville, Tennessee. While making efforts to reach Nashville he was arrested four times for not having a pass, and was soon released after each arrest. The regiment moved from Nashville to Knoxville, thence to Greenville. At the latter place he slept on President Johnson's tailoring table for several months.

When the war was over he returned to Evansville. He entered the commercial college of Jeremiah Behm. In 1866 he was employed by Keller & White as bookkeeper, and in the next year went to Boetticher, Kellogg & Co. in the same capacity, where he remained nearly twenty-one years. He was secretary and treasurer of the Evansville Union Stock Yards and is now secretary and treasurer of the Evansville Stove Works.

His civic prominence was principally in connection with drill organizations. He was elected three times successively as captain of the Evansville Light Guards, a prosperous organization. During his captaincy, was elected Sir Knight Commander of Orion Drill Corps, K. of P., and was so thorough in drill that the corps won three prizes, and he was awarded a magnificent gold medal as a prize for best commander at St. Louis, Mo., on August 25, 1880. His drill companies, Red Shirts and Zouaves, in political processions, attracted much favorable notice. He was chief marshal of several large political processions; was on the staff of National Commander-in-Chiefs Kountz, Fairchild and Walker; also on the staff of several department commanders; was member of the national council of administration; district delegate to national encampments; was second commander of Farragut Post.

Capt. Myerhoff was married to Miss Jennie Sharra, daughter of Alexander Sharra, of Evansville. Two children have been born of this union, Carl S. born September 22, 1868, and Zulma

Lois, born October 7, 1887. Two nieces, Miss Emma Wollner and Mrs. Fannie Boicourt, nee Sharra, shared their home with them for years.

ARTHUR F. FUNKHOUSER,

A PROMINENT member of the Evansville bar, was born April 24, 1866, and reared on a farm near New Albany, in Harrison county, Indiana. He entered the Corydon high school at Corydon, and was graduated from there at the age of sixteen, when he entered DePauw university at Green Castle, Indiana, pursuing his studies at Asbury college of liberal arts up till 1886. He was a member of Phi Delta Theta fraternity, and ranked as captain in the military college, and began the study of law in 1886 with Judge W. N. and R. J. Tracewell, at Corydon, Indiana, remaining under their tutorship until August, 1888, the year of the first Harrison campaign. During the remainder of that year and until May, 1890, he edited the Leavenworth (Indiana) News. Although but twenty years of age, he made speeches throughout that campaign in southern Indiana, in the interest of the republican party. In May, 1890, he began the practice of law at Cannelton, Indiana. He succeeded Hon. R. M. Johnson, as prosecuting attorney of the second judicial circuit composed of Spencer, Warrick and Perry counties. December, 1892, Mr. Funkhouser located in Evansville, where he has since continued the practice of his profession.

He is a safe counselor, careful and conservative in his methods, painstaking in the preparation of cases, and always watchful of the interests of his client, and has taken rank among the leaders of the bar. As a member of the bar and as a citizen his probity and high character have won for him the esteem and the kind regard of the community with which he is identified.

Mr. Funkhouser was married to Miss Drude Gray, of Evansville, September 10, 1895

CAPT. JAMES D. PARVIN,

THE newly appointed postmaster of Evansville, was born in Evansville April 8, 1844.

His father, James McMillan Parvin, was born at Winchester, Clark county, Kentucky, May 22, 1818. He came to Evansville in 1840, and for a long time was engaged in the mercantile busines, afterwards moving to Carlisle, Indiana, residing there until his death in 1877. He was a man of prominence in social and business circles, and in politics a staunch republican. He was married September 17, 1839, to Miss Elizabeth Birdsall, a native of New Jersey, and six children were born to them.

When but eighteen years of age James D. Parvin enlisted in the Union army, and was mustered as commissary sergeant in the Sixty-fifth regiment Indiana Infantry, September 1, 1862, and continued as such one year, when, on account of physical disabilities, he was honorably discharged. Regaining

ARTHUR FUNKHOUSER.

J. D. PARVIN.

his health, he again enlisted, May 25, 1864, in Company F, One Hundred and Thirty-seventh Indiana Volunteers, where he served until October, 1864. The following February he was commissioned captain of Company G, One Hundred and Forty-ninth Indiana Infantry, remaining with his command until mustered out at Nashville, Tennessee, in October, 1865. He was engaged in Evansville in mercantile affairs until 1886, when he was elected auditor of Vanderburgh county, and the fact that his majority of 957 votes was more than twice as great as that of any other candidate whose name was on the ticket, demonstrated his great popularity.

Mr. Parvin married Miss Jeannette Ehrman, a native of York, Pennsylvania, October 20, 1868. She was a daughter of Dr. E. J. Ehrman, of Jaxthausen, Wurtemburg, Germany, one of the founders and advocates of the homeopathic schools of medical practice in Pennsylvania. James D. Parvin is a prominent member of the K. of P., I. O. O. F., K. of H., A. O. U. W. and G. A. R. fraternities. He has received from President McKinley his commission as postmaster of Evansville, the duties of which office he will assume when vacated by Mr. John J. Nolan, which will be about September 15.

Mr. Parvin is ever ready and anxious to fight the battles of his party, and he numbers among his friends many who hold opposing political opinions, and not one among them can say he ever sought or accepted an unfair advantage. His friendship is warm, constant and devoted, and it is enough to say that to those who have come within the charming circle that encloses his intimates, he is a friend indeed and in fact.

————

FRANK PRITCHETT,

CHIEF of police of Evansville, was born in Evansville, April 14, 1853. His mental training was obtained in the public schools of Evansville, and at an early age he learned the blacksmith trade, which he followed until 1875, when he was engaged in teaming for three years. He was appointed patrolman of the Evansville police force in 1878, and served one year as deputy city marshal. In April, 1881, he was appointed deputy sheriff, under Sheriff Thomas Kerth, and during that time was made chief of the city police force. This position he filled to the entire satisfaction of his constituents, and when the bill providing for the "metropolitan system" became a law, he was appointed superintendent of the newly organized force, which position he held until 1886. During the session of the state senate of 1887 he served as doorkeeper, having made a successful candidacy against twenty-eight opposing applicants for the position. In 1888 he was elected sheriff by a majority of 634 votes, being the only democrat elected on the ticket. He made a race for a second term and was elected by 2,211 votes. He was city chairman of the Central Committee during the campaign of 1897. True to every trust and in a manly way per-

10

forming every duty as citizen and officer, he has attained a high place in popular esteem. He is a member of the I. O. O. F., K. of H., K. of P. and the B. P. O. E., of which he is an active and helpful member.

Seth Pritchett (father) was born in Evansville in 1819, and for a time was engaged in the blacksmith business, and at one time was engaged in the carriage business. He married Miss Emma Grant, a native of England, and their union was blessed with five children, the subject of this sketch being the second.

Frank Pritchett accepted the position as chief of police April 14, 1897, which he has filled with dignity and credit since.

He was united in marriage October 14, 1878, to Miss Louisa Kerth, and to them have been born six children, as follows: Percy, Frank, Florence, Ralph, Myrtle and Lillie.

HENRY REIS,

CASHIER of the Old National Bank of Evansville, was born in Germany, February 15, 1847, and is the son of Peter and Elizabeth Reis, and came to America with his parents when he was but two years of age. His father located in Posey county, where he engaged in farming. In 1856 the father died, and the family removed to Evansville.

Henry Reis obtained his early education in the schools of Evansville and took a course at Behm's Commercial College. He began his career in the drug business, but later decided to exchange it for banking pursuits, and entered the service of the banking firm of W. J. Lowry & Company, and by close application he made himself so valuable that one promotion followed another until October 5, 1872, when he entered the Evansville National Bank as paying teller and in 1873 was appointed assistant cashier of that bank; was promoted in 1875 to cashier, and, when at the expiration of the corporate franchise of the bank in 1885, the Old National Bank succeeded the Evansville National Bank, Mr. Reis was elected cashier of the latter, and has filled that responsible position with credit and dignity continuously up to the present time. Mr. Reis has been untiring in his efforts in behalf of the Old National Bank, and his zeal and straightforward manner have done much to promote the interests of that institution.

He belongs to the Royal Arcanum and the Court of Honor, having been chosen the first chancellor of the latter, and is an active and helpful member in both. Mr. Reis is a gentleman of fine personal habits, of exceptional ability; greatly devoted to his business, and is one of the ablest and worthy self-made men of this section of the state.

He was united in marriage in 1869 to Miss Caroline Blass, of Erie, Pennsylvania, and he is the head of an interesting family, in which the happiest relations are maintained. His home is characterized by the most liberal as well as elegant hospitality, in which a cult-

FRANK PRITCHETT.

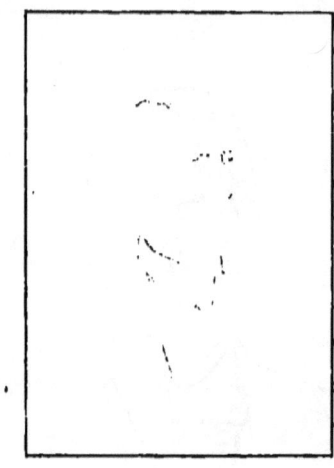

HENRY REIS.

ured wife and daughters, panoplied with the fine graces of womanhood, bear a conspicuous part with charming cordiality.

ANTHONY H. BRYAN, M. D.,

PHYSICIAN and surgeon, inventor, author and a citizen of Evansville, was born in Monticello, county seat of Wayne, Kentucky, August 22, 1832, and obtained his early mental training in the common schools and at an academy in Floydsburg, Oldham county, Kentucky.

His grandfather Bryan was a native of Virginia, and married Miss Hundley, also a native of Virginia. He was engaged in farming and blacksmithing during his life, and moved his family to Kentucky at an early day. Their union was blessed with twelve children, eight of whom were boys. Six of them became physicians, one a lawyer and one a farmer. He and his family were among the best and most highly respected families of Virginia. He was a man of sterling integrity, loved, honored and respected by all who knew him.

Edmund Bryan (father) was born in Virginia, February 19, 1796, and was yet a baby when his parents moved into Kentucky. He was an erudite, and a distinguished physician, and for many years occupied an honorable place in Kentucky both in professional and social circles. He died August 4, 1863. He was a scholarly and skillful physician, and a graduate of the Ohio School of Medicine of Cincinnati, having re-

ceived his diploma in 1836. He married Miss Lettice Pierce, a native of Kentucky, born in one mile of Danville, February 23, 1805, in a stone house which stands there to-day. She was a woman of the highest literary attainments, and one whom any person with aspirations for a higher and better life might wish to imitate. Gentle, kind and conscientious, who performed all the duties of a Christian woman with zeal and pleasure. She was a model wife and mother. She devoted much time to literary research and was a woman of the highest intelligence, and wrote a book entitled "The Kentucky Housewife," which was published in 1841. She afterwards prepared another book of about 400 pages on "Baptism," which, however, was never given to the publishers. She was a pattern of loveliness, kind, delicate and refined, and her deeds of charity made her beloved and honored by every one. She passed to her reward at Bunker Hill, Illinois, Monday, January 29, 1877. Dr. and Mrs. Edmund Bryan were the parents of fifteen children, the subject of this sketch being the sixth.

They moved to Louisville, Kentucky, in 1848, at which time Anthony H. entered the medical department of the University of Louisville, which he attended in winter, working in the summer until 1854, when he entered the class of that year and remained in the university two whole years, graduating February 27, 1857. Dr. Bryan was in the college on that memorable day, the "Bloody 6th" of August, 1855, and helped to care for the unfortunate who were wounded in that desperate riot. Leaving the college, Dr. Bryan began the practice of medicine in Shelby county, Kentucky, March 7, 1857. Afterwards he located in Westport, Kentucky, and in August, 1859, moved to McLean county, Kentucky, where he practiced medicine for seventeen years, and removed to Evansville in 1876, where he has followed his profession continuously, and he has been eminently successful, while his social relations have been of a most gratifying character. He has not sought to obtain a popularity not wholly merited. But performing every duty without ostentation and carrying into his professional work the suggestions of a gentle disposition and a kind heart, he has endeared himself to all with whom he has come in contact. He is still a diligent student of medical science, and readily adopts the new discoveries which promise relief to the suffering, but he is not easily carried away by new and untried doctrines and methods. He is a member of the Vanderburgh County Medical Association, was at one time corresponding secretary of the Green River Medical Society. He was physician to St Mary's hospital charity department in 1876. He was professor of general Pathology in the Evansville Medical College in the fall and winter of 1876-7. He was county physician from March, 1878, to April 23, 1879 and it is a matter of record that the mortality in the almshouse during his administration was less than at any other period in the history of the county, being barely one death per month. He is a master

and also a Royal Arch Mason, having attained the first three degrees at Westport, Kentucky, in 1858, and the chapter degree at Owensboro, Kentucky, in 1865. He has never sought any political preferment, but affiliates with the democratic party, and although, firm, positive and outspoken in his political views, he is highly respected for his fidelity to his convictions and honesty of purposes. He is a strict and consistent member of the Trinity Methodist Episcopal church.

Dr. Bryan is the patentee of the "Automatic Pump and Water Elevator," a device for raising water to any height and distributing it over the house as desired. It is particularly applicable to hotels, where guests may have water at any time, by turning the water cock, thus avoiding much inconvenience and annoyance. It is equally desirable on account of its labor-saving qualities, in ordinary homes, where the spring is far down the hill from the residence.

The machine proper is lined with porcelain and supplied with galvanized pipe, for distribution, so it is impossible for the water to rust or corrode by standing therein. Dr. Bryan's invention is certainly a great stride to the fore and must some day rank with the most useful inventions of the age. Nearly every great invention has had literally to be forced into public acceptance. The Elevator was placed on exhibition at the World's Fair in 1893 and Dr. Bryan was awarded a medal by the executive committee on awards The Inventive Age of February 24,

DR. A. H. BRYAN.

1894, contained the following: The diploma, which is the work of Will H. Low, is pronounced a particularly fine piece of art. In the upper portion is an arch, through which is given a view of the Court of Honor and surrounding buildings, as if taken out in Lake Michigan, looking down over the Peristyle. To the left of this arch is Columbia in a reclining position, resting on a buffalo's head stretching forth her hand to three young Americans, located just to the left of the base of the archway birdseye view of the White City. These three young Americans represent the white, the colored and the Indian children of the land. The keystone of the arch is formed of the American coat of arms, with the eagle quite pronounced. Resting on a console in the upper right hand corner of the diploma form is art, with the mechanical industries similarly represented on the opposite side. Below the arch giving the view of the Exposition grounds is the blank space for the language of the award, about eight inches square. The base line supporting Columbia and the young Americans is sustained by massive columns on either side, on which appear the names of the countries, which by exhibition and otherwise assisted in making the Columbia Exposition a grand success. Just to the left of the space for the inscription of the award is the figure of Fame standing, tiptoed, upon the stern of a barge and handing to Columbia a laurel wreath. In the stern of the barge stands Columbus, with face and line of vision raised toward Columbia. His left hand rests

upon the rudder of the bark, and in his right he holds a globe, mounted with a cross. On the side of the barge is shown the coat of arms of the countries most prominently represented at the Fair, while the four figures which propel the craft are typical of Europe, Asia, Africa and South America. The blank space for the language of the award is intended to hold three hundred words of printed matter, the fac simile autograph of the individual judge, the attest of the international committee of judges by its presiding officer, and the autograph signatures of the proper exposition officials.

DESCRIPTION OF MEDAL.

One side of the medal is historical and the other emblematical. The historical side represents Columbus stepping from his boat. This view of the medal is not in the least perspective in design, that effect or quality having been cut off by the broad folds of the flag of Spain, which is borne by the sailor who stands directly behind the figure of Columbus, whose head is raised on high, giving thanks to the Almighty. The reverse or emblematical side is supposed to typify America. It represents a splendid specimen of lusty young manhood. This figure, entirely undraped, leans easily against a ponderous oak tree, and holds in his right hand three wreaths. In the distance stand the pillars of Hercules, bearing in scroll the legend of "Plus Ultra." The oak is intended to typify great strength, and the boundary posts of the ancient world, with their legend, suggest how much the new world surpasses that known to the inhabitants of classic lands. The original plates have been so arranged that the name of the recipient will be placed on each medal and the whole will appear as complete as if each single medal was the only one struck off.

Aside from his professional and other duties, Dr. Bryan finds considerable time to devote to scientific research, and is now preparing a work of science in which he proposes to elucidate many important and heretofore unsolved questions. He will give a complete explanation of sun spots and also of the incandescent state of the earth's interior. He will tell what a comet is and how and why its nebulosity is effected and affected, and why it describes a circuit different from the orbit of the planet and how and why the tail of the planet is formed. He will also make plain many other questions which are puzzling the scientists of the day. The work which was sent to Washington, D. C., some time ago for copyright comprises a system of philosophy entitled "Philosophic Consideration of Universal Cosmogony and Electro-Planetory Phenomena." His thoughts are original and his mind is capable of great research. He can divest difficult subjects of their obscurity and readily see through the mazes of mystifying and intricate problems.

On May 25, 1897, there was an entertainment at the Peoples Theatre in Evansville commemorating the 53d anniversary of the first telegraph message, and the manager, Mr. N. M. Booth, advertised that at the close of the program a gold medal would be awarded for the best answer to the first message "What hath God Wrought?" Dr. Bryan's reply was among a great many others and the committee, after examining each and every one, quickly decided that Dr. Bryan had answered the question most completely and comprehensively of all and he was duly awarded the medal. His answer was, "The annihilation of distance." There could not be a more perfect answer to that question and a notable thing is that the answer contained the same number of words as are in the question. The telegraph has practically annihilated distance. There was a time when regions and places on the surface of the earth were in all respects separated from each other by measurable distance. The time required for communication from point to point was governed by the speed of such methods, horse or ship, or foot, as might convey a man, a messenger. Very nearly in a related correspondence was there a wideness of separation in feeling among communities and nations. Sympathies were narrowed, neighborly feeling could not grow, and in times of trial the hands which might have helped were too late in coming. Numberless were the instances of resulting evils, greater or lesser, for even battles were fought after the nominal return of peace, but before it could be announced in the opposing camps. The world before the telegraph and the world since its coming are hardly the same, in many great features, but the transition from the old to the new is already an almost forgotten story. We are so accustomed to the news of all the earth that we receive it like the air, and think and talk as if our ancestors had done as we do. Dr. Bryan received many congratulations upon the reply given, among them being those of the editor of the Telegraph Age

Dr. Bryan was united in marriage April 21, 1857, to Miss Irene Josephine Thomas, a native of Kentucky, who died May 25, 1880. Their union was blessed with eight children, five of whom survive. He married (second) October 5, 1881, Mrs. Anna Eliza Neale, a native of Kentucky, who died July 19, 1894. He again married (third) Mrs. Naomi Turnock, a native of Evansville, and in their comfortable home at 209 Chestnut street, they are surrounded by every comfort and many of the luxuries of life.

THOMAS KERTH,

Ex-senator. A crowning glory of the United States is that the paths to wealth and to fame and to social distinction are open to all—to the adopted as well as the native-born citizen; and there are few whose histories better illustrate what can be accomplished by energy and integrity, under republican institutions, than the subject of this sketch. Mr. Kerth was born in Bavaria, Germany, in 1829, and came with his parents to this country in 1840, where they went to farming eight miles north of Evansville. His early years were divided between attending school in the winter and working upon the farm during the summer. In 1846 he went into the grocery business with his brother, Jacob Kerth, on Water street, near the corner of Vine street. His brother had preceded the family to America, was one of the oldest settlers in the county and died in 1850. In 1848 the subject of this sketch went to Cincinnati and engaged in the butcher business for ten years. While in Cincinnati he married Miss Louisa Renner, and in the fall of 1858 returned to Evansville and entered into partnership with his brother-in-law in the leather and hide business, on Main street. The following year he erected the store at 219 Main street, and for twenty-four years successfully conducted that business. His political career is most interesting. In 1870 he was elected councilman from the old eighth ward (now the fifth) and during his term was appointed one of the water works trustees when the water works were being built. In 1880 he ran on the democratic ticket against J. August Lemcke, a political opponent of elephantine strength for sheriff and astonished his party by beating him 597 votes. He was renominated in 1882, and pitted against Chas. Schaum, whom he defeated by 919 votes. In 1888 he was nominated and elected state senator, and made a most enviable record in the Upper House. All the bills that Evansville asked for were passed. He repealed the Intimidation act, passed the state school book law, obtained appropriations for the insane asylum and the right to issue bonds for the completion of the court house; in short, his career as state senator will bear the highest eulogy. After leaving the senate, Mr. Kerth established with his son, William G. Kerth, an insurance office at 207½ Upper Fourth street.

WILLIAM MORRISON DUNHAM,

THE leading bicycle dealer of Evansville, was born in Uniontown, Kentucky, July 13, 1861, and received his early mental training from the common schools of Union county. His father, William Dunham, M. D., was a native of Virginia, having left his native state when about eighteen years of age and located in Kentucky. He was one of the foremost men in the medical profession in Western Kentucky, and at Uniontown, where he practiced for years, enjoyed an extensive and lucrative practice. He was a man of the highest integrity and was loved, honored and respected by all who knew him. He married Miss Susan Hardin, whose ancestors were one of the first and best families of the state of Kentucky, and their union was blessed with twelve children of whom William M. was the first boy. The mother died in 1872 and the father in 1874, thus leaving William to fight life's battles alone. For a number of years William Dunham was engaged in the practice of medicine in Evansville in partnership with Dr. Casselberry, but removed to Uniontown when the partnership was dissolved.

William Dunham, the subject of this sketch, at the age of eighteen years, returned to Evansville, and for a number of years was employed as clerk, first in the store of Parsons & Scoville and afterwards with Viele, Stockwell & Co. In 1885 when Evansville was undergoing something of a panic and many persons were seeking the west believing they could better their condition Mr. Dunham went to Kansas City, Missouri, and for several years was there engaged in the hardware business, and later was manager of the Monehan Coal and Iron Company in that city. It was a very responsible position for so young a man as Mr. Dunham to hold, but he did it with dignity and credit to both himself and his employers. In 1890 he decided that Evansville was best for him and he returned and engaged in the bicycle business, which he has followed continually and successfully ever since.

William Dunham is a young man holding an enviable position in the business and social circles of Evansville, and if we are to judge the future by the past, some flattering predictions might be made. He is a member of the Court of Honor, the Y. M. C. A., and the Bicycle Club, and takes an active and energetic part in all of them.

He was united in marriage April 11, 1882, to Miss Nettie Reavis daughter of William Reavis, a prominent citizen of Evansville, and two children—girls —Pansy and Mazelle, bless their union.

To William Dunham much credit is due for the great interest that is to-day taken in cycling in Southern Indiana. He

HON. J. J. NOLAN.

was the pioneer in the business in Evansville, having in connection with Mr. Will Paine opened the first bicycle store in Evansville. Mr. Dunham was mainly instrumental in organizing the Cycle Club of Evansville, and has done much to keep that institution alive.

in Evansville is more popular nor more respected.

Mr. Breger was united in marriage to Miss Lizzie Steinhauser, of Jasper, Indiana, in 1887, and their union has been blessed with two children—boys, one nine and the other seven years of age.

MICHAEL W. BREGER,

COUNCILMAN-AT-LARGE of Evansville, was born in 1861, at No. 19 East Delaware street, and has ever resided in the place wherein he was born. He is the son of John and Rosa Breger, and his education was obtained from the schools of Evansville. He is a self-made man in all that the term implies. He has by hard work and perseverance raised himself from the ranks of a laborer to the presidency of one of the most important industries in Evansville. And he is still a worker, giving all his time to his business and to the interests of the people of his native city. He served as councilman two terms, and hir career in that capacity in 1889-91 is remembered by all, and especially by the taxpayers. He was a prominent and useful member of many important committees, and his counsel was sought by his colleagues. He voted against granting a forty years' franchise to the street railway company some years ago. He was in attendance at the midnight meeting of the council when the ordinance was rescinded. He is fearless and expresses his views on any subject with emphasis and decision. No man

11

MICHAEL SCHMITT,

A PROSPEROUS farmer of Center township in Vanderburgh county, was born February 18, 1819, in Germany, and came to America in 1842. He was educated in Germany, and located first in Ohio, where he was engaged working in a foundry. Mr. Schmitt came to Evansville in 1857, and thus for four decades has been identified among the successful farmers of Vanderburgh county.

He married Miss Christina Schmitt, a native of Germany, but not related to him prior to their marriage. The wife died about eight years ago. Their union was blessed with seven children, six of whom survive. His sons, Michael, Jr., and Jacob, aged about thirty-five and thirty-two respectively, reside on the farm and operate it.

Mr. Schmitt affiliates with the republican party, but has never sought nor accepted public office. He is a member of the German Presbyterian church.

Michael Schmitt's life has been a useful one and now, when nearly three score summers have passed over his head, he can look back over the past with a keen satisfaction of having done his duty. He is an honored and respected citizen in his community.

HON. JOHN J. NOLAN,

PRESENT postmaster of Evansville, was born in Evansville September 1, 1859, and is the son of William J. and Anne (Roche) Nolan. His elementary education was obtained in the public schools of Evansville, and at an early age he entered the service of the Western Union Telegraph Company as messenger boy, picked up telegraphing while filling that position, and fourteen years of his life were spent in the service, and in course of time he became receiver of the Associated Press dispatches. In 1886 he was nominated by the democratic party as representative to the legislature. It was a republican year, however, and while he ran 700 votes ahead of his ticket, he was defeated, and in 1888 he was again nominated and elected to that office. He introduced a bill for the repeal of the Intimidation law, which was passed after a hard fight.

In 1890 he was renominated for the legislature by acclamation and elected. During his second term he succeeded in getting through what is now famous in local history, under the title of the "Nolan Bill." The bill prevented the street car company from getting an extension of their old franchise, limited the franchises of all corporations in Indiana to twenty-five years, and pro-

vided that the city receive no less than two per cent of the gross receipts of all corporations receiving franchises. In addition to the above, he had passed numerous other bills, among them the metropolitan police and fire department bill.

He returned to Evansville at the expiration of his term, and for some time occupied his old position with the Western Union, and later was appointed general manager of the People's Electric Light and Power Company. May 23, 1893, President Cleveland commissioned him postmaster of Evansville.

He was united in marriage October 18, 1887, to Miss Vallie Fitzwilliams, of St. Louis, and two children—boys—have blessed their union.

DAVID A. COX, M. D.,

A SCHOLARLY and able physician of Howell, Ind., was born October 1, 1865, in Vanderburgh county. A true and impartial history of Vanderburgh county could not be written without mention being made of the Cox family, who have been prominently identified with the county since its infancy. The subject of this sketch is the son of Major Joseph B. Cox, a prominent farmer and distinguished soldier, and who was at one time surveyor of United States customs for the Evansville district and at various times served the county as public officer. He raised a company for service in the civil war, was soon promoted to Major and saw active and

DR. D. A. COX.

valuable service until ill-health caused him to tender his resignation. .

James Cox (grandfather) was a native of Pennsylvania, born in 1800 and died in Vanderburgh county in 1834. He came with his brother Joseph, to Vanderburgh county in 1818, and was one of the pioneer farmers. They lodged in a log cabin in a dense forest about where the site of Evansville now is which at that early day was a wilderness.

David A. Cox received his early mental training from the public schools of Evansville and in the fall of 1884 entered the Indiana University from which he was graduated in 1888. He attended the Ohio Medical College of Cincinnati, graduating March 6, 1890. He at once located in Howell, Indiana, and began the practice of his profession, where he has since been successfully engaged. Dr. Cox occupies the important post of consulting physician of St. Mary's Hospital and delivers lectures on chemistry to the school of nurses and is the medical examiner at Howell for the leading life insurance companies. He is a member of the Masonic order, Reed Lodge, No. 316, F. & A. M., also of LaValette Commandery No. 15, Knights Templar.

Dr. Cox belongs to that class of men who achieve success early in life, and if we are to judge the future by the past some flattering predictions might be made.

He was united in marriage September 26, 1894, to Miss Gertrude Alma Walsh, daughter of Thomas Walsh, a prominent and representative citizen of Howell, Indiana.

Dr. Cox is a member of the Howell Land Company, which laid off and started the building of houses in Howell. He has always taken an active interest in the welfare of its citizens, and was the first one to urge the people to incorporate Howell as a town.

COL. CHARLES C. SCHREEDER,

A PROMINENT, enterprising citizen of Evansville, was born in Berlin, Germany, January 19, 1847, and is the son of Frederick Schreeder, a native of Germany.

In 1852 the subject of this sketch came to America with his widowed mother, who located at Huntingburg, Ind., being induced to locate there by relatives. In the spring of 1853 the mother was united in marriage to the Rev. Frederick Weithaup, minister of the German Evangelical association, who was stationed in Evansville, where he had charge of a congregation. This caused the removal of the family to Evansville. The mother died on December 26, 1890. During the pastorship of Rev. Weithaup the church, which now stands at the corner of Eighth and Division streets, was erected.

Col. Schreeder's father was one of the German Revolutionists in 1848, and died of cholera in 1849. The early mental training of Col. Schreeder was obtained in the common schools. He was but thirteen years of age when the war dogs began to bay, and at the age of fifteen he enlisted in Company D,

Second Ohio Volunteers, and for nearly three years saw active service. In September, 1864, he was discharged on account of disabilities and came to Evansville to recuperate his health. When he was again able he re-enlisted, January, 1865, in Company E, One Hundred and Forty-third Regiment Indiana Volunteers, and was mustered out October 23, 1865. Then he returned again to Evansville to live. He early manifested an active interest in politics and was chosen city assessor when but twenty-one years of age. Subsequently he was elected township assessor and afterwards chosen to fill the important office of city clerk, and it is a notable fact that he was the youngest man that had ever been elected to that office. He removed to Huntingburg, Ind., in 1876, where he was soon afterwards appointed postmaster, holding the office under Presidents Hayes, Garfield, Arthur and Harrison. He was commissioned lieutenant-colonel of artillery, Indiana Legion, in 1892, by Governor Chase. Shortly afterwards he was promoted to chief of ordinance, with the full rank of colonel, on the Governor's staff. April 27, 1897, he was recommissioned by Governor Mount as colonel of engineers on the Governor's staff. He served five terms as commander of Shively Post, G. A. R., at Huntingburg, which he organized in 1881. He represented the Second Congressional district at the National encampment at St. Louis in 1887, and at Indianapolis in 1893. He served as aide de camp of the staff of the late Commander-in-Chief Fairchild, ex-Commanders-in-Chief Rhea, Palmer,

Adams and Walker, and is now serving as aide de camp on the staff of Commander-in-Chief Clarkson. His record in this capacity is a brilliant one, and we doubt if any other man has served as long and with as much credit and dignity.

Col. Schreeder's affiliations are with the republican party, and for sixteen years he was recognized as the leader of that party in the Second Congressional district of Indiana. For twelve years he was chairman of the republican central committee of Dubois county, himself organizing the first republican central committee in that county. He also represented the Second district on the republican state and was a delegate to national conventions in 1880 and 1884. He was elected in 1887 chief doorkeeper of the Indiana house of representatives, this being the first session that met in the new building, and also one made famous by the terrific scenes caused by the robbing of Lieut. Robinson of his place as presiding officer of the senate by the democratic majority.

In 1880 Col. Schreeder, appreciating a long-felt want of the republicans of Dubois county, established the Huntingburg Argus, a weekly paper which strongly championed the cause of republicanism, and which he edited and was the proprietor of during the time he remained there.

Col. Schreeder is one of the most enterprising men of Evansville, and stands in the front ranks of those who are instrumental in making the Crescent City. He is a man of means and affairs, a large property owner in Evans-

COL. C. C. SCHREEDER.

MRS. C. C. SCHREEDER.

ville and elsewhere. He is identified with the best interests of Evansville and is known as one of her most public-spirited citizens. He is a man of fine personal appearance and pleasing address, of kind disposition and sympathetic nature. He is a careful and diligent reader, keeping pace with the advancement of the times. He is a member of Farragut Post, G. A. R., in Evansville, and also one of its trustees. He is a member of the Business Men's association, the Press club, and the Vanderburgh club. Col. Schreeder was united in marriage in 1868 to Miss Louisa C. Behrens, of Huntingburg, with whom he lived happily until her death in 1892. Their union was blessed with two children: Emma M. and Walter D. He was married (second) March 27, 1894, to Mrs. Rebecca Keller, of Evansville, and at their beautiful home at 710 Locust street they are surrounded by every comfort and many luxuries. Success is like a pyramid, broad at the base as the thronging millions that crowd it, towering upward its point narrows; scattered along its sides are the men who have achieved something more than usual prominence in the world's affairs. At the top are the few who have grandly succeeded, their forms lit up by the sunshine of merited fame. Among those who have achieved a place in the history of Southern Indiana is the subject of this sketch, Col. C. C. Schreeder. He is still in the prime of life, and it is the hope of all who know him that he may long be spared as an example of good citizenship. He is kept very busy in looking after his and his wife's property interests, which are largely centered in Evansville.

Col. Schreeder is second vice-president and a director of the North American Benefit Association of Evansville

---

REBECCA SCHREEDER,

WIFE of Col. C. C. Schreeder, of Evansville, was born at Portsmouth, Ohio, May 31, 1845, and is the daughter of Rev. John and Margreta Hoppen.

Rev. John Hoppen was one of the pioneer ministers of the German Methodist church, and died at Indianapolis, Indiana, where he was pastor, September 10, 1861. The mother died in Evansville February 10, 1859.

Rebecca Hoppen lived with her parents, and her father's calling varied their residence, which at different times was in the following cities: Evansville, Madison, Indiana; Evert street, Cincinnati, Dayton, Pittsburgh, Wheeling, Race street, Cincinnati; Clay street, Louisville, where Rev. Hoppen had a charge as pastor, and he was presiding elder in the Evansville district.

After the death of Rev. Hoppen, the subject of this sketch returned to Evansville, where she has resided continuously since. She was united in marriage August 13, 1879, to the late Mr. Charles Keller, in his day a prominent and influential citizen of Evansville. Their union was blessed with two children, Carl P. and Oscar H. At his death, February 10, 1892, Mr. Keller left his family a handsome estate.

Mrs. Rebecca Keller was married (second) March 27, 1894, to Col. C. C. Schreeder, whose biography appears in this volume. Mr. and Mrs. Schreeder are the head of a delightful home, where the happiest relations are maintained, and where their four bright and cheerful children play a conspicuous part with charming cordiality.

Mrs. Schreeder is a consistent and helpful member of the German Methodist Episcopal church, with which she has been continuously related since her youth, having joined at about the age of ten years. She is also an active and energetic member of Farragut Corps No 18, of the Woman's Relief Corps, an auxiliary to the G. A. R.

the city of Evansville as attorney from 1892 to 1897.

Mr. Cunningham was united in marriage November, 1881, to Miss Susan S. Garvin, daughter of Hon. Thomas E. Garvin, of Evansville, and three children have blessed their union.

He is a man of much application and greatly devoted to the interests of those who entrust their business to him. He is distinctively a lawyer, and stands in the front rank of the members of the Evansville bar. His practice has been very large and general, and his knowledge of the law is not confined to any one branch, but extends through all. He has always been a close student and a hard worker. His achievements are proof of his ability.

GEORGE A. CUNNINGHAM,

PROMINENT attorney at law, member of the Evansville bar, was born in Gibson county, Indiana, April 4, 1855, and is the son of Joseph and Mary J. Cunningham. His father was a prosperous Gibson county farmer, born in 1807, and George spent his boyhood days there, where he worked on the farm and attended the common schools of Gibson county alternately. In 1874 he entered the old Asbury College, now DePauw University, and remained one year, and there fitted himself for teaching, which he followed for a number of years in Gibson county. In 1877 he came to Evansville, and was admitted to the bar in 1878. His affiliations are with the republican party, and he served

THOMAS EDGAR GARVIN.

AN EMINENT lawyer of Evansville, was born in Gettysburg, Pennsylvania, September 15, 1826. His father, John Garvin, was descended from the Scotch and married Mrs. Providence Summers, February 21, 1821. Their union was blessed with five children, as follows: Laura, Louisa, Thomas Edgar, Jane and John Reuben.

Thomas E. Garvin graduated from Mount St. Mary's College at Emmettsburg, Maryland, after a number of years' hard study. He came to Evansville in the fall of 1844, and has watched the city grow from an isolated acorn to a staunch and hearty oak. He wanted to be a lawyer and soon after coming

Geo. A Cunningham

Yours truly

Thos. E. Garvin

to Evansville began to read law in the office of Hon. Conrad Baker, Governor of Indiana, and a leading and forcible lawyer of his day, and who afterwards became a relative of Mr. Garvin. He taught school and thereby earned sufficient means to meet his obligations and prosecute his studies. He managed by close application and frugal living to finish his law course and was duly admitted to the bar March 27, 1846, and he at once formed a partnership with Hon. Conrad Baker, under the firm name of Baker & Garvin. For eleven years this partnership continued successfully. In 1876 his Alma Mater Mount St. Mary's College conferred upon him the degree of L. L. D., a distinction rarely granted. In 1862 he was elected representative of Vanderburgh county to the State legislature. He is not only a lawyer of ability, but a man of affairs and means. He was one of the first stockholders of the First National Bank of Evansville, a director therein for a long period. He has been for many years actively engaged in real estate. He is an able and profound scholar, deeply interested in literature and natural history. Was one of the first trustees of Willard Library and one of the board to whom the property was deeded, and for many years has been president of that institution. Mr. Garvin was state commissioner at the Centennial Exposition at Philadelphia in 1876 and National Commissioner at the World's Fair at Chicago in 1893.

He was married November 11, 1849, at Penn Yan, New York, to Miss Cornelia M. Morris, a descendant of the Morris family of Morristown, New York, a family of revolutionary fame. This union has been blessed with eight children, five of whom are living, as follows: Thomas Edgar, Ford Morris, Susan Shaw, Cornelia Imogen and Isaac Casselberry.

JOHN A. REITZ.

IT was the fortune of John A. Reitz to realize the fruits of a successful career whose course had been guided by honor and integrity. His ability was recognized by all while he was living, and in his death there were left behind him none but the most pleasant recollections and the tenderest sorrow. His generosity as a citizen, affability as a gentleman, and kindly treatment of all with whom he came in contact, were alone sufficient traits to have drawn to him warm friends, while his energy and perseverence left an indelible stamp upon the business and social community of this section.

John A. Reitz was born December 17, 1815, at Dorlar, Prussia, where his father, Francis Joseph Reitz, owned large estates. His childhood received careful training at home. When only twelve years of age he was sent to Osloh, one of the important education centers of Prussia, where he pursued his studies four years under a capable tutor. The five years next succeeding were spent in work at home. On attaining his majority, inspired by a spirit of adventure and a desire to enjoy the blessings and opportunities afforded by a free popular government, he turned his face toward and set sail for the United States. He was the first immigrant to leave his native village for America, and it required courage to break home ties and start alone on a voyage of nearly four thousand miles. The sturdy German races have long been noted for courage and determination, and he possessed the characteristics of his race. His ancestors were long lived. It is related that his grandmother lived to the age of one hundred and sixteen years, and, on the death of her husband, at the age of eighty-one, managed successfully for nearly thirty years, the business of manufacturing salt, inaugurated by him.

After a long voyage the young man landed in Baltimore, but in a short time crossed the Alleghenies and located in Louisville. Soon afterwards he was induced by a practical potter to establish a pottery in Evansville, where clays adapted to that industry had been discovered. The business proved unprofitable, for want of demand for the ware, and was abandoned after a few kilns had been burned.

After spending a year in Louisville, he settled permanently at Evansville, in 1838, taking employment in a saw and planing mill owned by Judge Stephens, which was soon afterwards destroyed by fire. For several years after that he was in a saw mill, and then with his half-brother built a mill in that city. At the end of ten years his brother retired and the mill burned. It was rebuilt immediately, and in 1873 was again rebuilt and enlarged until it became one of the substantial and profitable manufactories of Evansville. Subsequently his sons were taken into partnership and the firm became John A. Reitz & Sons. The firm is probably the largest manufacturer of hardwood lumber in the country. In 1857 he formed a partnership with John A. Haney, to operate a foundry, which was continued with great success for a period of twenty-four years, and then sold to other parties. He assisted in organizing the Crescent City bank in 1856, and became one of its directors, subsequently filling the offices of vice-president and president. This institution was one of the solid banking organizations of the state and continued to transact business until the national bank law was enacted. It was then succeeded by the Merchants' National bank, of which Mr. Reitz was a director. Later on he transferred his interest to the German National bank, in which he held the position of director for several years, then was elected vice-president and afterwards president, holding the presidency at the time of his death, May 12, 1891. He was not only a successful manufacturer and banker, but was associated with other enterprises and organizations that promised remuneration to their founders and benefit to the city. Realizing the value of transportation as a factor in the building up of a commercial center, he became an active promoter of railroads, was one of the incorporators of the Evansville, Carmi and Paducah road and president of the company. It is now known as the St. Louis division of the Louisville and

Nashville system. He was for years also a director of the Nashville division of the same system, from Evansville to Nashville, Tenn. Mr. Reitz was charitable as well as public-spirited. He was liberal in the expenditure of his means to benefit the poor and the unfortunate. As a memorial to his daughter, Louise, who died some years ago in California, he built a commodious home for the aged poor on a site selected for its beauty and pleasant surroundings. This home he presented to the Little Sisters of the Poor, in order to insure the proper care of the inmates. The number cared for is about one hundred. He was a devout Roman Catholic in his religion and a member of the Church of the Holy Trinity. No member was more generous in contributing to the erection of its building and the maintenance of its worship. He built at his own expense the church of the Sacred Heart, and presented it to the bishop as a place of worship for Irish Catholics. His liberality was characterized by a catholicity not confined to the church of his own belief. Protestant churches received liberal contributions from his abundance. Every public enterprise that tended to advance the interests of Evansville or better the condition of mankind found in him an active supporter. His charity was as broad as humanity. There is no sectarianism in the home which he founded. The deserving poor, whose weight of years incapacitates them from earning a livelihood in the ordinary pursuits, are welcomed to its privileges, without regard to their creed or nationality. He con-

tributed liberally to build and maintain Evans Hall, dedicated solely to the cause of temperance.

Whatever he undertook was prosperous, not through luck, but on account of prudence and foresight, which determined the character of his undertakings. His real estate investments were immensely profitable. His sympathy for the unfortunate prompted the greatest liberality in their behalf, and sometimes prevented that careful investigation of the merits of an appeal which he would have given to a business proposition; hence, he was frequently imposed upon by unscrupulous and designing men, who took advantage of his generosity.

When the town of Lamasco was incorporated, in 1846, he became its chief executive officer, and managed its affairs with ability until it was consolidated with Evansville. He was largely instrumental while president of the board of trustees in advancing the interests of the Evansville, Indianapolis and Cleveland railroad. He embarked in some very large real estate enterprises with the late Willard Carpenter, which proved to be very profitable. In 1862 Mr. Reitz was elected to the state legislature, as a joint representative from the counties of Vanderburg and Posey, and served during the memorable session of 1863. He was also a member of the city council. He was very active in all public enterprises that had for their object the advancement of his city. While he always acted with the democratic party, he did not allow his devotion to party politics to so control his actions that he could not support all

12

measures which were for the general good of the community. He was not a partisan in any sense of the word. He never acted hastily in anything he undertook, but when he had reached a decision could not be swerved from his course. The relations between himself and his employes have always been cordial and sympathetic. Though a large number of men have been employed, the business, extending over a period of nearly fifty years, has never been interrupted by a strike. Mutual confidence between employer and employe is firmly established. This condition has always existed, not only when John A. Reitz conducted the business, but under the present management as well. The result of this humane treatment is that the men who have grown old in his service (and there are some who have been employed forty-one years) are not discharged by reason of their advancing years; but their names hold the same place on the pay roll at the same wages they received in their strength and vigor. Such a policy is creditable to the conscience and the sagacity of the successful man who inaugurates it. It makes friends of employes, and the increased interest which they take in their employer's business no doubt insures better returns than if he exacted hard conditions. It is evidence of a high type of humanity and tends to mitigate the antagonism between capital and labor.

Mr. Reitz was married in 1839 to Miss Gertrude Frisse, who came from a locality in Prussia not far from the place of his nativity. Ten children were born to them, all of whom are living but two —the daughter, who died in California in 1886, and a son, who was drowned in Colorado in 1892.

The subject of this sketch was a man of strong convictions and character. He was deliberate in forming his judgment and unyielding in his firmness when it was formed. He was ready to stand alone if necessary in defense of what he conceived to be right. He was a man of such wide experience in business and such excellent judgment that he was consulted freely regarding the management of large financial institutions and important enterprises He was conservative and honest. It was the policy of his business life to owe no man. He kept free from debt and was able to devote all his thought and energy to the prosecution of his work without annoyance or embarrassment incident to debt. He never entered into a contract to pay without having the cash to meet the payment at once. The freedom from obligations due in the future contributed much to his success and infinitely more to his happiness. He was a man of fine physique, fond of outdoor exercise and manual labor.

His family life made his best traits conspicuous. He was devoted to his wife and children, with affection that sought to provide for their comfort and happiness. Business affairs were not permitted to enter the precincts of home. His supremest enjoyment was around the hearthstone, as the central figure in the circle cemented by love and confidence. In that home circle, where the happiness of each was the desire of all,

ALBERT JOHANN.

he found rest and recreation. His wife was helpful by her sympathy and advice. She was a charitable woman, contributing her full share to the support of the church and worthy benevolent objects in the community. She supplemented and made complete the home life of a happy family.

(A portion of this biography is copied from Biography of Indiana, 1895, by G. I. Reed.)

ALBERT JOHANN,

THE leading undertaker of Evansville, was born in Prussia July 16, 1831. His father, Charles William Johann, harness-maker, came to America in 1848, and after living a few years in Evansville, removed to Cannelton, Indiana, where after a long and busy life, he died in July, 1875, at the age of seventy-four years. He married Miss Elizabeth Worth, who died in Cannelton in 1895, at the age of eighty-six years.

Albert Johann received his early mental training in his native country, and when a young man learned the trade of a moulder. His frailty did not permit him to work at his trade, and he learned that of a house carpenter, at which he worked occasionally, in connection with other business until 1880. In 1865 he began to do an undertaking business.

He began life a poor man. When he began business he bought a small house, but was able to make a cash payment of only $25.00. By industry and economy he has accumulated a comfortable property. He is a member

of the I. O. O. F. and the K. and L. of H. fraternities. He is a republican in politics, and his popularity is evidenced by the fact that for four years he represented his ward in the city council.

He was married in July, 1854, to Miss Barbara Spies, a native of Germany, and daughter of Henry Spies. Eight children have blessed their union: Amelia K., Charles H., Lydia, (who died at the age of twenty-one years in 1880), Emma L., Albert H., Edward W., Mary A. and Eva A.

He is a consistent member of the German Methodist church. He has been connected with the Deaconess' Home, and as one of the trustees, purchased the original property where that institution stands.

PROFESSOR WILLIAM MUSHLITZ,

PRINCIPAL of the Fulton Avenue school, of Evansville, was born in the eastern part of Pennsylvania on March 6, 1851, and is the son of Monroe Mushlitz, a native of Pennsylvania.

William Mushlitz received his early education in the public schools of Pennsylvania and attended Beaversville Academy and the Lehigh University. He was engaged in the public schools of Pennsylvania for seven years, and came west in 1877, locating in Clinton county, Indiana, where he was made superintendent of teachers, in which capacity he served one year, and from 1879 to 1885 he occupied the position of superintendent of the schools of Clinton county. In 1885 he removed to Evansville, and since that time has been principal of the Fulton Avenue school.

He is a member of the Masonic order and is a Knight Templar and is also a member of the Royal Arcanum, council No. 491. He is a consistent member of Trinity Methodist Episcopal church, and is a most highly respected citizen.

He was united in marriage in 1878 to Miss Ida Holliday, of Frankfort, Indiana, and to them have been born two boys, DeEarl and Curtis T. The elder, DeEarl, served for some time as reporter for the Evansville Journal and also for the Courier.

Professor Mushlitz is a man of great ability as a teacher, and much of the prosperity of Fulton Avenue school is the result of his untiring efforts. Always courteous, and his pleasing manners have made him exceedingly popular in educational and social circles.

GEORGE L. LOUDEN,

MANAGER of the Southern Planing Mill company, of Evansville, was born in Keokuk, Iowa, September 17, 1856.

George Louden (father) was a native of Germany and came to America at an early day, locating at Mt. Vernon, Indiana, where he remained for two years, when he removed to Keokuk, Iowa, and was there successfully engaged in the brewery business. He

married Miss Elizabeth Pfeifer, a native of Germany, who came to America in 1836. They met in Posey county, where they were united in marriage, and their union was blessed with three children, the subject of this sketch being the youngest. The father died in 1857 and the mother is still living and resides with her son, a brother of George Louden's, in Evansville.

George Louden received his education in the common schools of Keokuk, Iowa, and when he left school went into a planing mill, where he learned to be a machine hand. He came to Evansville February 4, 1879, and engaged to work for Swanson Brothers and was afterwards employed in the McCorkle planing mill as machine hand. In 1881 he, in connection with J. M. Overell, Gus Schellhase and Henry J. Ashley, organized the Ohio Valley Planing Mill company. Six months afterwards Mr. Schellhase went out of the business and Mr. Overell sold his interest to Messrs. Louden and Ashley. The plant was destroyed by fire November, 1886, but no sooner was the debris cleared away than they began to rebuild and by February, 1887, a new planing mill was in operation at the corner of Main and Iowa streets, the same being known at present as the Mechanics' planing mill. Mr. Louden continued with the concern until 1893, when he sold out and for some time afterwards he was engaged in the real estate business. In 1896 he organized the Franklin street planing mill company and later the business was merged into the Southern planing mill company and the plant

G. L. LOUDEN.

JOSEPH C. SAUM.

moved to the corner of Water and Goodsell streets.

Mr. Louden was united in marriage August 5, 1880, to Miss Carrie M. Roesner, of Evansville, and five children, four of whom survive, have blessed their union. The living children are Harry, Willie, Mamie and Arthur.

Mr. Louden is a member of the Odd Fellows and of the Chosen Friends. His career as a business man and progressive citizen is beyond reproach and he performs every duty in the manner suggested by his conscience and judgment. His excellent business qualifications have made him an influential factor in working out the success which he has achieved.

LEE M. CASSIDY,

PROMINENT business man of Evansville, was born in 1857, in Gettysburg, Pennsylvania, and is the son of William and Mary Cassidy. The father was born in Pennsylvania and the mother in Kentucky.

The boyhood days of Lee M. Cassidy were spent in Pike and Davies counties and he was graduated from St. Meinrad's seminary at Washington, D. C., in 1879. He lived in Washington for a number of years and afterwards spent a number of years in the west and came to Evansville in 1883. He was engaged in the railroad business for a few years and for the last eight years has been contractor and builder. In April, 1897, he was elected councilman from the

seventh ward, and it is a notable fact that he was the first democratic councilman elected from that ward, and he received the largest majority of any councilman ever elected.

He was united in marriage in May, 1885, to Miss Mattie L. Mortore, of Davis county.

By honest and industrious effort, by wise and skillful management Mr. Cassidy has achieved a large measure of success. He enjoys the confidence of the business community and a high social position.

The sketch of Mr. Cassidy would not be complete without mentioning that he is a man of unblemished moral character, and for a number of years he has been a consistent member of the Assumption church, and a liberal benefactor to all the religious and philanthropic enterprises of the day. Both as a business man and citizen, Mr. Cassidy carries with him the esteem of the community. Surely, his life career has been a success.

JOSEPH C. SAUM.

COUNCILMAN of Evansville, a native of Vanderburgh county, was born June 12, 1860, and is the son of James and Elizabeth Saum. The father was born in Ohio in 1837, came to Evansville in 1854 and was successfully engaged in farming.

Joseph Saum, the subject of this sketch, spent his early days upon his father's farm and attended the country schools. At the age of eighteen he began as an apprentice in a blacksmith shop, where he served for seven years, at the end of which time he purchased the shop where he had learned and for two years following operated it with gratifying success. In 1888 he sold his blacksmith interests and embarked in the grocery business at the corner of Fountain avenue and Park street, in connection with Mr. Dickmeier, under the firm name of Dickmeier & Co. Two years subsequent he erected the house which he now occupies at the corner of Park and Maryland streets, where he has done a prosperous business ever since.

He is a member of the K. and L. of H. and also of the Knights of St. John. He was elected councilman from the fourth ward by the democrats in the spring of 1897, and the manner in which he has conducted himself in the capacity of councilman amply attests the wisdom of those who placed him there.

Mr. Saum was united in marriage October, 1887, to Miss Carrie Dickmeier, of Evansville, and three children —two boys and a girl, have blessed their union.

VERY REV. EUGENE F. McBARRON,

DEAN, member of the bishop's council and immovable pastor of the Church of the Assumption, was born in Floyd county, Indiana, near New Albany, June 18, 1844, and is the son of John McBarron, who was born in 1807 in the northern part of the Emerald Isle.

John McBarron married Miss Mary Ann O'Daly, who was born in Madison, Jefferson county, Indiana, in 1822. The father came to America in 1837, locating in New York. He remained in New York and Boston for a few months and in 1838 removed to Floyd county, and was engaged in farming and contracting. The boyhood days of E. F. McBarron were spent on his father's farm, and his early education was obtained from the public and catholic schools of Floyd county. He took a classical course under the preceptorship of Father Louis Neyron, of New Albany, and in 1863 entered Notre Dame university, and in 1864 attended the St. Thomas seminary at Bardstown, Kentucky, remaining there one year. He then spent a year and a half at St. Meinrad, Spencer county, Indiana. His theological course was finished at St. Sulpicien seminary of Montreal, Canada, and he was ordained to preach at Vincennes, Indiana, June 8, 1871, by the Right Reverend Bishop de St. Palias. He was appointed pastor of St. Mary's of the Woods in Vigo county, Indiana, and in 1879 was appointed pastor of the Assumption church of Evansville, and on June 8, 1896, celebrated his Silver Jubilee as pastor.

Rev. McBarron is a man of large mental attainments and ranks among the best pulpit orators in Southern Indiana. He is a profound thinker, a good reasoner, logical and eloquent in the presentation of his sermons. For over eighteen years he has occupied this field of labor, and all who know him love him and delight to do him honor.

HENRY MASON.

HENRY MASON,

ATTORNEY at law, prominent member of the Evansville bar, was born on a farm in Hancock county, Kentucky, May 4, 1859. He attended the common schools and his boyhood days were spent in the monotonous routine of farm life. He entered Asbury University, where he attended in 1879-80, and then went home to teach school, which he did for two years. He then entered his brother's law office at Hawesville, Kentucky, studied law and was admitted to the bar at Hawesville, where he practiced until 1891. He served the people of Hancock county as legislator in 1889-90, and a notable feature of his election was that the county went largely republican, he being the only democrat elected. His affiliations have always been with the democratic party, and he has at all times manifested an active interest in the welfare thereof. Mr. Mason removed to Evansville in 1891, and in 1893 became engaged with Mr. H. M. Logsdon, under the firm name of Logsdon & Mason, and their efforts in the practice of their profession have met with gratifying success.

James Mason (father) was a prominent farmer of Hancock county, and married Miss Nancy Blincoe, a native of the same county. To them twelve children were born, Henry being the ninth.

Henry Mason was united in marriage June 24, 1896, to Miss Mattie Robb, daughter of James C. Robb, a successful farmer of Hancock county, and a most highly respected citizen.

GEORGE J. VENEMANN,

A LEADING and representative grocer of Evansville, was born January 13, 1852, and is the son of Joseph and Eliza Ellen (Aiken) Venemann. The father was born in Germany and the mother was a native of Vanderburgh county.

The early education of George J. Venemann was obtained from the common schools of Evansville, and he was graduated from the Third Street Catholic academy. He entered his father's store as clerk, and remained there for seven years and gained a wide and practical experience in business affairs. Leaving his father's employ he became engaged with the dry goods establishment of Frank Hopkins & Company as clerk, in which capacity he remained for fifteen years. He then embarked in the grocery business with his brother, Theodore J. Venemann, which continued with marked success up to four years ago, when George J. began to do a grocery business on his own account. Actual merit and continued fair dealing have been the main factors in the achievement of his success, and the reputation he has established and maintained is second to none for honesty and genuine business acumen.

Mr. Venemann is a member of the K. of P. and takes an active interest in the welfare thereof. Public-spirited, energetic and liberal, he is a highly respected citizen in all the various walks of life, and his able and judicious management has made his grocery one of the most enterprising and complete establishments of the kind in the city of Evansville.

Mr. Venemann was united in marriage in 1879, to Miss Helen Cook, daughter of Charles Cook, of Evansville, and four children have blessed their union, as follows: Maud, Eloise, Helen and Carl.

JACOB ULRICH SCHNEIDER,

PASTOR of Zion Evangelical church, Evansville, was born in Ohio August 5, 1859, and is the son of George S. and Margaret (Traxell) Schneider. The father was born in Wittenburg, Germany, in 1827, and came to America at the age of eighteen, locating at Winesburg, Ohio. For a number of years he was engaged in blacksmithing and is still living and resides at Sabetha, Kan. The mother, a native of Switzerland, was united in marriage to Mr. Schneider in Ohio, and their union was blessed with six children, of whom the subject of this sketch was the second. The early education of J. U. Schneider was obtained from the common schools of Ohio and he took his first collegiate course at St. Joseph, Mo., attended Bryan's business college and was graduated in 1879. He then entered the Protestant seminary of the Evangelical synod at Elmhurst, Ill., where he remained four years, graduating in 1883. The three years succeeding he attended the Eden Theological seminary of the Evangelical synod of St. Louis, Mo. Was graduated from there and on June

21, 1886, was ordained for the ministry. He at once entered upon the service and took charge of a congregation at Castle Shannon, Pennsylvania, remaining there until the fall of 1888. From there he went to Jefferson City, Missouri, where he took charge of the Centennial Evangelical church, which continued until the summer of 1893. He was principal of the Wabash, Mo., high school for two years, and in 1895 assumed the duties of pastor of Zion church, Evansville, on Fifth between Ingle and Bond streets. In connection with the church is a school house, which has been renovated under Rev. Schneider's administration. His church has a large membership and the school building is used for various meetings, the Deaconess and other societies holding their meetings there. September, 1886, Rev. Schneider was united in marriage to Miss Rosa Langtim, of St. Joe, Missouri, and three children, two boys and a girl, have blessed their union.

Rev. Schneider is secretary of the board of directors of the Protestant Deaconess Home and is a member of the board of home missions of the Indiana district of the Evangelical synod.

Besides his many duties as a minister and in other relations, Rev. Schneider contributes frequently to the theological periodical, "Theologische Zeitschrift," published at St. Louis, Missouri, and at present he is engaged in revising the Evangelical catechism.

During his ministry, and very largely under the inspiration of his faithful and enterprising labors, many additions to the church membership have been made

G. J. VENEMANN.

ISAAC CASSELBERRY.

and many improvements accomplished. Rev. Schneider is a learned gentleman and greatly beloved by his congregation, and his efforts are meeting with deserved success.

ISAAC CASSELBERRY, M. D.,

DECEASED, was born on his father's farm in Posey county, Indiana, November 26, 1821. The impartial historian who writes a complete record of southern Indiana cannot fail to accord proper place to the Casselberry family, who were important factors in the history, and took a conspicuous part in the affairs of Posey and Vanderburgh counties.

Paul Casselberry, grandfather of the subject of this sketch, was of German descent, and in 1806 removed from Norristown, Pennsylvania, to Posey county, Indiana, and his family was among the prominent pioneers of that county.

Thomas Evans Casselberry, his father, was a gentleman of the highest honor and integrity, and was one of the commissioners who located the county seat of Vanderburgh county at Evansville. He married Miss Rachel J. Carson, daughter of Charles Carson, of Posey county. Their son, Isaac, was five years of age when the father died, and, therefore, the training of the boy devolved upon the mother. She was a woman of unusually strong character, and reared a family of children who

13

were noted for their honor and true citizenship.

Hamilton S. Casselberry, twin brother of Dr. Isaac Casselberry, represented Posey county in the state legislature in the session of 1848 and 1849.

Isaac Casselberry, after receiving an academic education from the Rev. Lamon, rector of St. Paul's Episcopal church, began the study of medicine, in 1841, in the office of Dr. M. J. Bray, of Evansville. In 1843 he went to Cincinnati, where he continued his medical studies under the preceptorship of Dr. R. D. Mussey, and was graduated with honor from the Medical College of Ohio in 1845. Returning to Evansville, he entered upon the practice of his profession in partnership with his former preceptor, Dr. Bray. His efforts were crowned with gratifying success, and he obtained a large and lucrative practice in Vanderburgh and adjoining counties.

He was a strong Union man, and when the war broke out, volunteered his services. He was appointed surgeon of the First Indiana Cavalry, Twenty-eighth regiment, and in that capacity served until the close of the war. He received high commendations from his superior officers for his faithful and efficient service. While he was acting as surgeon general of the corps in which his regiment was incorporated he was taken prisoner at the battle of Mark's Mills, Arkansas, April, 1864. After his return to Evansville he was appointed by President Johnson as collector of customs for the port of Evansville, which position he sustained with dignity and credit until a change of administration took place.

Dr. Casselberry filled the office of secretary of the board of health from the time Evansville was placed under sanitary regulations up to the time of his death. He was one of the founders of the Evansville Medical College, being one of its first trustees, and occupied the chair of Clinical Medicine and Physical Diagnosis in that institution until he died. He was also one of the trustees of the Orphan Asylum. He was a member of the council in 1866 and was one of the school trustees in the same year.

Dr. Casselberry was a man of fine personal appearance and pleasing address, of kind disposition and sympathetic nature; a constant and diligent student, keeping pace with the advancement in medical science; was a member of the Indiana State Medical Society almost from the date of its organization, having united in 1852, and he was elected president of that body in May, 1873, at the annual meeting. He was a permanent member of the American Medical Association, and, aside from his many professional duties, found time to contribute largely to medical literature, and was extensively known both in and out of the state as a strong and forcible writer.

A few of the important papers prepared by him were, "An Inquiry Into the Physiology of the Organic Nervous System"— American Medical Journal, 1852; "Causes of Fever"—Ibid, 1856; "Ancient Marriage of Consanguinity" —Nashville Journal of Medicine and

Surgery, 1859; "Use of Iron"—American Medical Journal, 1858; "Use of Water in the Treatment of Fever"— American Medical Journal, 1857; a series of articles on "Historical Views of the Causes of Epidemics"—Nashville Medical and Surgical Journal, 1857 to 1858. In 1857 Dr. Wright, of the Memphis Medical Recorder, made an able review of some of Dr. Casselberry's articles, in which he remarked "that much credit was due him for the boldness and industry with which he strove to throw life on pathological subjects.

In his professional career he at all times manifested those exalted virtues that assure success to the profession and honor to his calling. Endowed by nature with a keen perception and a logical mind which long experience had polished and a profound study had stored, to these he super-added the virtues of diligence, accuracy, patience, integrity and trustworthiness.

Dr. Casselberry was united in marriage at Gettysburg, Pennsylvania, in 1847, to Miss Louisa Garvin, daughter of John and Providence Garvin, and sister of Thomas E. Garvin. Their union was blessed with two children, one of whom survives, Mrs. Laura Dunkerson, wife of R. K. Dunkerson, a prominent citizen of Evansville.

Dr. Casselberry died July 9, 1873, and another link was broken which bound the history of that time to the early history of southern Indiana, and in his death the community lost one to which many clung with loving remembrance. For over a quarter of a century he practiced medicine in Evansville, a calling that required him to move along the private pathways of life that led within the home circle, and is associated with family affliction. There are no memories so tender as those which cling around the name of one who brings comfort to us at such a time.

The announcement of the death of Dr. Casselberry moved across the community like a shadow, and tears came even in eyes that were unused to the melting mood.

He was a modest, unassuming man. In all his surroundings, whether as citizen, physician, friend or father, he might have been taken as a model, and humanity would have been elevated by the pattern. Upon his monument it could be carved,

"The earth has lost a man
Whom Heaven has claimed."

REV. SAMUEL A. JOHN,

PASTOR of St. Lucas Evangelical church on East Virginia street, Evansville, was born and reared in St. Louis, Missouri. He is the son of Rev. Dr. R. A. John, a native of Prussia, who came to America in 1842.

Rev. R. A. John was educated in his native land and was graduated from the university at Breslau and also from the university at Berlin. He completed his theological education and served as pastor before coming to America. He married Christina Koph, a native of Stuttgart, in Wurtemburg, and their union was blessed with five children, the subject of this sketch being the second. An older son, brother of Rev. S. A. John, is pastor of St. Paul's Evangelical church in Chicago, while a younger brother is pastor of the First Evangelical church at New Albany, Indiana.

Rev. R. A. John located at Washington, Missouri, but removed from there to St. Louis, where for many years he had charge of a large parish. He is is now located in the country, near Trenton, Illinois, where, although eighty years of age, he still has charge of a congregation. He is a senior in the church, and is the oldest active pastor in the service. He is also editor of the church organ, an influential paper, "Friedensbote," published in St. Louis Missouri.

Rev. Samuel A. John attended the Parochial schools in St. Louis until he was twelve years of age and spent three years in the public schools of that city. He then entered the Smith Academy in St. Louis, and afterwards for two years, 1873-5, attended the Washington University in St. Louis. He went to Chicago and took a preparatory course, attending the Elmhurst Seminary, from where he was graduated in 1884, when he returned to St. Louis and entered Eden Theological Seminary of the Evangelical church, graduating at the end of a three years' course. He at once entered upon the service as minister and his first appointment was in Cincinnati, where he organized the St. Matthews church at Elmwood place, under the auspices of the Evangelical Mission Board. He remained there three years when he returned to St. Louis to take charge of the Ebenezer Evangelical church, which he served as pastor for four years. He then came to Evansville and assumed the duties of his present charge, St. Lucas Evangelical church, which has a membership of 180 families. Aside from his many duties as pastor Rev. John finds time to devote to literature and frequently contributes to the religious journals, and he publishes a local church paper called the St. Lucas Herald. Rev. S. A. John was united in marriage May 28, 1889, to Miss Emma Tuxhorn, a native of Edwardsville, Illinois, and their union has been blessed with three children. As a man and citizen Rev. John stands in high esteem, respected by all denominations for his religious tolerance, and loved by all his parishioners. He is a man of large mental attainments and ranks among the best pulpit orators in Southern Indiana.

GOTTLEIB WILLIAM BAUMANN,

ENTERPRISING citizen of Center township, in Vanderburgh county, was born May 18, 1849, in Switzerland, and came to America when four years of age, with his parents, who located at Evansville. His father, Rudolph Baumann, was a carpenter, and died about twelve years ago.

The subject of this sketch was the second youngest child born to his parents, and his education was obtained in the public schools of Evansville. His mother having died when he was five years of age, he was bound out to another family to remain until he reached his majority, but at the age of nineteen left his adopted home and went to Posey county, Indiana, and there learned the trade of blacksmithing. For four years he lived in Kentucky, and then returned to Evansville and for eleven years was engaged with the Blount Plow Company. In March, 1883, he purchased ten acres of land where he now resides in Center township, and also bought the blacksmith shop there, which he runs at the present time. Mr. Baumann's home and small farm is a model and is one of the most attractive places on the Stringtown road.

Mr. Baumann is a member of the A. O. U. W., Center Lodge No. 42, and in politics he affiliates with the republican party, and has always taken an active interest in the welfare thereof. He is one of the school directors of Hooker school house, which position he had filled eight years before. Honest, hard working and conscientious, he has achieved a position of high standing in his community, and by close economy succeeded in acquiring a comfortable competence.

Mr. Baumann was united in marriage to Miss Amelia Reichelt, of Evansville, and five children, four of whom survive, have blessed their union. The living children are: Willie, age twenty-three; Virginia, age seventeen; Allen, age twelve, and Oliver, age nine.

O. M. ADAE.

CHARLES T. SHERMAN,

THE leading house decorator of Evansville, was born in Oliver, New York, in 1858, and is the son of William J. and Charlotte (Morris) Sherman. The father, born in 1829, was prosperously engaged in farming and also in the hotel business, and both parents are still living.

Charles Sherman's education was received in the eastern schools, and his boyhood days were spent in different parts of New York and in the oil regions of Pennsylvania. In 1879 he became connected with the oil wells in Pennsylvania which continued for a term of three years. He then went to New York city, and afterwards spent two years in Batavia, and for five years lived in Rochester, New York. He came to Evansville in 1890, and was engaged by William E. French as manager and decorator, and by close application and strict economy succeeded in accumulating considerable means, which afterwards led to his embarking in business on his own account. The decorating and wall paper business of Mr. Sherman, which is carried on at 513 Main street, has grown and prospered under his guiding hand until it has taken the lead in that line of trade. He decorated the Borman residence and business house, Muschler's residence on Third avenue, Court Place, Wilhemeyer's residence on First avenue, Poor Clare Monastery, and made improvements in the Vanderburgh court house.

Mr. Sherman was united in marriage September, 1882, to Miss Katie Andrews, of Alexandria, New York, and their union has been blessed with three children, Harry, age fourteen; Carl, age ten, and Howard, age six.

Early thrown upon his own resources, the strength of his character was developed in the rough experience common to all men who make their own way in life. He began to maintain himself when he was not yet of age. His candor and congenial manners have made him popular, while sagacity and qualification have gained him prominence as a valuable citizen.

He is a member of the Masonic order and is a Knight Templar.

───────

OTTO M. ADAE,

SECRETARY and manager of the Evansville Ice and Storage Company, was born in Wurtemburg, Germany, and came to America when sixteen years of age. His ancestors were a patrician family from the free city of Ulm. His father was a physician and for many years member of the Reichstag. Mr. Adae's first engagement was with his uncle, C. F. Adae, engaged in banking in Cincinnati, and also consul for all German states. He remained there until his twenty-fifth year, when he went to Chicago and was with the Union National bank of that city for some time. Later he was engaged in the manufacturing business, operating a bent wood factory in East Tennessee. He was afterwards connected with the Cincinnati Ice Machine Company, and in

1888 came to Evansville and was the prime mover in establishing the Evansville Ice and Storage Company. At the time of its organization it was the largest plant of the kind in the world and it was an attestation of the confidence of Mr. Adac in the future of Evansville. The business has grown and prospered under his guiding hand and its success is largely due his energy and untiring zeal.

_____

JOE V. WALZ,

PRESIDENT of the Walz Seed Company of Evansville, was born in Evansville January 20, 1860, and is the son of Vital and Fredericka Walz. His father was a native of Germany and was one of the pioneers of Evansville, and a man loved, honored and respected by all.

Joe V. Walz was educated in the Catholic schools of Evansville, and as he grew to manhood formed the purpose of carving out his own career. He took up the study of telegraphy and in 1876 took a position as telegraph orperator on the St. Louis and Southeastern Railroad, worked for many years in that capacity and in 1884 entered the employ of the E. & T. H. R. R. as ticket agent at Evansville, which position he filled ably and with satisfaction up to July, 1897, when it became necessary for him to resign and to give his entire attention to seed and and agriculturial implement business, which was established in 1895 and which

has grown prosperous even beyond his most sanguine expectations. The business is located at 418 and 419 Fourth street, where all kinds of field and garden seeds and everything in the way of agricultural implements, phaetons, etc., are handled.

Mr. Walz is a consistent member of St. Mary's church. He married Miss Minnie Folz, daughter of Jacob Folz, Sr., and four children, three girls and one boy have blessed their union. Honorable and upright in all life's relations Joe Walz commands universal respect, and not a small element in the causes of his success is his power of making and holding friends. From his youth he has made his own way in life and has been eminently successful. His life has been one of industry and constant effort, and the success which has come to him has been well deserved.

_____

HON. FRANK B. POSEY

WAS born at Petersburg, Pike county, Indiana. April 28, 1848. He received his earlier education in the public schools and academy of his native county. At the age of sixteen he became a student of DePauw University and Indiana University law school.

Mr. Posey entered the legal profession in 1869 and enjoyed a lucrative practice from that time, escaping the "starvation period" usually experienced by young lawyers. In 1872 he was appointed district attorney for the counties of Knox, Pike, Davies and Martin, in

J. V. WALZ.

Your Obt. Servt

J. B. Posey

which position he acquired an enviable reputation as a criminal lawyer. From his first appearance in public he has been acknowledged an orator of more than ordinary ability. In his chosen profession as a trial lawyer and advocate he occupies a position sought by many but achieved by few.

"Frank Posey," as he is familiarly known in Southern Indiana, has from boyhood been an enthusiastic republican; he was elector in 1880; delegate to the National convention in 1884, and soon after chosen chairman of the republican executive committee of the First Congressional District. At all times, in all cases and under all circumstances, he proved himself a careful, earnest, intelligent representative of the people. In 1888 Mr. Posey was nominated for congressman of the First Congressional District, which for forty years, had been considered democratic. After a hotly contested campaign the usual majority of 2,000 was reduced to 21 in a total vote of 40,000. Two months after the regular election, a vacancy having occurred by the resignation of Gen. Hovey, Mr. Posey was elected for the unexpired term by a majority of 1,100 over his former opponent. Having served with distinction for the unexpired term he returned to his home and to the practice of his profession.

In 1893 he removed to Evansville and has since been a member of the law firm of Posey & Chappel. In 1896 he was a prominent and popular candidate before the republican state convention for Governor of Indiana and

14

was only prevented from receiving the nomination for that office by reason of the location of candidates for offices, notwithstanding he immediately entered into the campaign and labored unceasingly for his party's cause until his work helped to achieve a great State and National victory for his party. During this campaign Mr. Posey spoke in all the principal cities of his state, and in many places in other states. There was no more eloquent and earnest orator in this campaign than Mr. Posey. His services as an advocate, orator and lecturer are in constant demand, not only in Indiana, but adjoining states. As a citizen, lawyer and statesman, Mr. Posey has a made a reputation which is a credit to himself and an honor to the state.

REV. JULIUS BLASS,

PASTOR of the German Evangelical Protestant, St. John's church, of Evansville, was born in Erie, Pennsylvania, May 1, 1861, and is the son of Rev. Jacob Blass, a native of Germany, who came to America in 1859, and who had studied for the ministry at Heidelberg, Germany, and Utrecht, Holland. He married Catherine Barthel, a native of Rhenish Bavaria, and the subject of this sketch was the first of eight children born to them. The father died in 1890, in Erie, Pennsylvania. The mother is still living and resides with her son in Evansville.

Rev. Julius Blass received his early education in the public schools of Penn-

sylvania, and in 1877 entered the Theological school at Meadville,Pennsylvania.
from where he was graduated in 1882.
Having taken a post-graduate course of
one year in the same school, he was
ordained for the ministry at Meadville,
1883, and began in the service immediately. He located at Jackson, Michigan, and there had charge of the First
Unitarian church. After remaining
there two years he removed to Mill-
bury, Massachusetts, and for four years
was pastor of the First Unitarian church
there.

He came to Evansville in 1889, and
for one year was assistant to Rev.
Runck, who had charge of the German
Evangelical Protestant St.John's church.
When Rev. Runck was called to his
reward in 1890, Rev. Blass was elected
as his successor. This church has the
largest membership of any church in
Evansville, comprising about 630 families. Rev. Blass is admirably fitted for
his responsible position. He adds to
his knowledge a spirit of retirement,
and to his zeal an excellent judgment.
His ability as a scholar and his worth
as a man have given him a strong hold
upon the affections of the people.

DeWITT Q. CHAPPELL,

ATTORNEY at law, was born in Pike,
county, Indiana, January 22, 1861.
His early life was spent on the paternal
farm near Petersburgh, Indiana, where
he also attended the common schools of
the county. As he grew older he went
to the State Normal School at Terre
Haute, which course was supplemented
by additional training at the State University at Bloomington, Indiana. His
father dying about this time Mr. Chappell was obliged to quit school and
manage the family estate. This inter-
ruption in his studies, however, did not
cripple the young man's spirit, and
though much of his time was taken up
by the management of the farm, he
pushed onward bravely, devoting all
his spare hours to study, and thereby
acquiring those habits of close application, which form the basis of his subsequent success in life.

After leaving college he was appointed
principal of the schools of Stendal, a
town of his native county, which position he filled with distinction.

In 1885 he removed to Evansville,
where he read law in the office of J. S.
and C. Buchanan. Returning to Petersburg in 1887, he was admitted to the
bar of the Pike Circuit Court. It was
but a short time until the fellow-citizens
of Mr. Chappell recognized his abilities,
and hence entrusted to him a fair quota
of their legal business. The skill and
assiduity the young attorney evinced in
the management of these affairs showed
that their confidence in him was rightly
placed. His practice began rapidly to
increase, and his reputation as a "safe"
counselor and skillful advocate soon became firmly established.

In 1889 Mr. Chappell was united in
marriage to Miss Anna F. Summerville,
of Vincennes. Indiana.

In the following year he formed a
partnership with Hon. Francis B. Posey,
which partnership still exists. In 1894

DEWITT Q. CHAPPELL.

C. A BREHMER.

Mr. Chappell was urged to make the race for the lower branch of the legislature on the democratic ticket. The times, however, were not favorable to that party's success, and he, like so many others of his political complexion, was defeated. In the same year he became a member of the law firm of Mattison, Posey & Chappell, in Evansville, still, however, remaining in charge of the Petersburg office.

Two years later he removed with his family to Evansville, the occasion of this change being the election of the Hon. Hamilton A. Mattison, the senior member of the firm, as Judge of the Vanderburgh Circuit Court. Since 1896 Mr. Chappell has been a member of the firm of Posey & Chappell.

Though the residence of Mr. Chappell in our midst has been a short one, he has already achieved an enviable reputation as a profound lawyer and an intrepid debater. He is painstaking, conscientious and thoroughly devoted to the interests of his clients. As a man he is "of the tribe of God Almighty's gentlemen," a genial companion and a steadfast friend.

CHARLES A. BREHMER,

ARCHITECT, of Evansville, was born September 23, 1860, at Glencoe, Cook county, Illinois, and is the son of Charles A. and Mary A. (Uthe) Brehmer. The father was born in Elsas, Germany, in 1833, was general speculator, and came to America when quite young, locating at Tonawanda, New York. From there he removed to Michigan where he operated lumber camps for a New York syndicate. He died in Lansing, Michigan, in 1890. The subject of this sketch spent his boyhood days in Bay City, Michigan, and was educated in the common schools there. At the age of sixteen he entered the Notre Dame University at South Bend, Indiana, and was graduated from there at the age of twenty-one, having first attended the industrial school, and later took a finishing course. After completing his education he settled in Bay City, Michigan, and was there engaged as contractor and architect for two years when he returned to South Bend, Indiana, and remained until he came to Evansville in May, 1893. In September, 1893, Mr. Brehmer entered into partnership with Mr. C. C. Shopbell, under the firm name of Brehmer & Shopbell engaged in the architect business, and the partnership continued with gratifying success until the 15th of June, 1897, since when Mr. Brehmer has prosecuted the work alone. He is an active and helpful member of the Knights of Maccabees, Knights of St. John, and Y. M. I. He has furnished plans for some important buildings in Evansville, among them being J. G Lannert & Son's carriage factory, Bernard Reitman's residence, L. C. Bomm's residence, William Seiffert's residence, Joseph Schaefer's business block, Poor Clare Monastery, Edwin Taylor's residence, Robert Davidson's residence, J. H. Borgman's business house and residence, Court Place, P.

W. Frey's residence, H. Wilkemeyer's residence, Vanderburg county court room improvements and O. S. Week's residence.

He was united in marriage in 1883 to Miss Mary A. Reilly, of South Bend, Indiana, and nine children have blessed their union, as follows: Charles Edward, Mary Gertrude, Olivia,. Louis, Mary, Bernard, Genevieve, Lillian and Margaret. In business Mr. Brehmer is active and sagacious. His enterprises are remarkably successful: not only in business is he active, but also in those enterprises which make men beloved by their fellow-citizens, in those things which work for the general good and in his attitude toward benevolent movements of society. Industry, integrity and wise management have been the chief factors in building his prosperity.

DANIEL AIKEN.

THE history of no county in America contains the record of a more honorable and successful career than that of Daniel Aiken, deceased, in his day one of the foremost farmers of Vanderburgh county. One little expects to find startling events in the life of a farmer, but he does not understand the forces which contribute to the advancement of the moral, social and political interests of our people if he leaves the careful and conservative farmer out of his calculations. Daniel Aiken was born in what is now Vanderburgh county, in 1813, and was the son of David and Elizabeth (Noble) Aiken.

David Aiken was born in Genesee county, New York, in 1788, and emigrated to the Indiana Territory in 1808, passing down the Allegheny and Ohio rivers on a raft. He located at Rising Sun and there erected the first log-cabin in that vicinity. From there he went to Darlington, then the county seat of Warrick county. He participated in the battle of Tippecanoe and also the battle of New Orleans. He erected the first jails in Boonville, Indiana, and Henderson, Kentucky. The mother, Elizabeth Noble Aiken, was a native of Virginia, and was a woman of the highest character.

The early life of Daniel Aiken was spent in the wilderness, assisting his father in felling the forest and participating in the monotonous routine of clearing land and raising crops. Education was little thought of, no books were to be procured and newspapers were rare, indeed. In a wild, primitive country Daniel Aiken grew to manhood, subject to the privations and the hard work that foster self-denial and independence. He was favored by being the son of ambitious and intelligent parents—ambitious for the success of their children, intelligent in providing the means of educational improvements to the best of their ability.

Late in life Daniel learned the alphabet from his father, and he became ambitious for knowledge. Weekly papers were subscribed for and all available books were procured. Many a night he was found poring over the pages of some old book by the dim light of a log fire, and in that way he obtained suffi-

DANIEL AIKEN.

cient knowledge for ordinary business transactions. In addition to this he had a head full of good common sense, which was, not only then, but is now more valuable than "book learning." From 1836 to 1848 Daniel Aiken was engaged in flat-boating to New Orleans and by hard work and close economy, succeeded in accumulating considerable means, which in 1839 led to the purchase of 320 acres of land which is to-day a part of the present homestead. Among the pioneers of Indiana there were few, if any, better men than Daniel Aiken. He was deservedly popular and widely respected for his qualities of genuine manliness. He was a plain man, practical and unostentatious.

In his social relations he was universally respected and by his more intimate friends who knew him best, he was sincerely loved. When released from the cares of business he cared more for the domestic circle and comforts of home than the demands of society. Prudently careful of his own interests he was economical without being miserly, and yet charitable without being injudiciously or excessively indulgent. Remembering his own struggles, his hand was ever ready to help the needy who were objects of charity. He was always ready to interest himself in the welfare of the deserving and his practical wisdom enabled him to be advisor and helper of a number of young men, who owe their prospects in life to his judicious counsel and aid. Amid all of the pressing engagements of his active life he never failed in the conscientious, punctual performance of

his religious duties. On December 15, 1884, Daniel Aiken was called to his reward, and he died as he had lived in the clear hope of immortality through Jesus Christ.

His excellent wife, Mrs. Elizabeth Aiken, who for many years was his efficient help-mate, who shared with him the toils and enjoyed with him the prosperity of a long and useful life, still survives him and resides at the old homestead on the farm, about five miles above Evansville. They were married in 1848. She was the daughter of Conrad Stacer, who was a native of France. He was associate judge of Vanderburgh county for fourteen years and for the greater part of his life was connected with some public office in the service of the people. He was a man of sterling integrity, public spirited and enterprising and took an active part in all interests for the betterment of his fellowmen. Mr. F. Stacer, brother of Mrs. Aiken, was a soldier in the Mexican war, having run away from home at the age of eighteen to enter the service. Two other brothers served faithfully in the Union army and were honorably discharged at the close of the rebellion.

Mrs. Aiken's magnificent farm consists of 720 acres of as fine river bottom land as will be found in the Ohio Valley. It requires the services of thirty men to attend the farm and they are now under the supervision of Mr. Joseph Angel, who has served as Mrs. Aiken's foreman since the death of her husband. She has large numbers of mules and horses and her farm is run on a metropolitan plan. For thirty-five years Mrs. Aiken has been a consistent and helpful member of the Union Christian church. She was instrumental in establishing the church in Vanderburgh county. The church was presided over by Rev. J. T. Philips for over a quarter of a century. He was called to another field some few years ago but is now coming back to his old church Although she has passed many mile stones of life's journey, she is still apparently hale and hearty and takes an active part in the management of her farm. She is a true christian, exemplifying in her life the ideals of perfect womanliness.

REV. JOSEPH DICKMAN,

PASTOR of St. Mary's church, was born in Oldenburg, Franklin county, Indiana, December 26, 1849. His father, Frederick Dickman, was born in Hanover, Germany, in 1809, and came to America in 1836, settling in Oldenburg, Indiana, where he was engaged in farming up to the time of his death, September 2, 1881. He was a man of sterling integrity, and in his death society lost a good citizen and his family a counselor whose worth was beyond estimate. He married Elizabeth Fischer, a native of Germany, born October 20, 1820. The elementary education of Father Joseph Dickman was obtained in Oldenburg, where he went to school and worked on his father's farm alternately. In 1863 he attended St. Meinrad Indiana school

and later attended at Bardstown, Kentucky, his classical and theological education being obtained in those institutions. He was ordained at St. Meinrad's September 21, 1872, by Right Rev. De St. Palias and for nineteen years succeeding he was pastor at Joseph's Hill, Indiana. February 1, 1892, he came to Evansville, having been appointed pastor of St. Mary's church, in which capacity he has served continually since. He is admirably fitted for the responsible position which he holds. To his knowledge he adds the spirit of retirement, and an excellent judgment he unites with his zeal. In the pulpit he is of great force. He is known as an eloquent and earnest preacher. He is possessed of an excellent education and many charming qualities of mind and heart.

SAMUEL ORR.

THREE score and two years ago a young man from Ireland, rich in energy, integrity and moral character, became a resident of Indiana, after having spent two years in the eastern part of the United States. He had resided in Pittsburg, Pennsylvania, where he was employed in a grocery store. In 1835, he was induced by friends to come to Evansville. The man was twenty-five and the town less than twenty years old. For nearly five decades thereafter the two were scarcely separated. He and the town grew and prospered together, mutually de-

SAMUEL ORR.

pendent and mutually helpful. This man was Samuel Orr, of Scotch-Irish descent. He was born in Newtownards, County Down, Ireland. The necessity of gaining for himself a livelihood allowed little time or opportunity for acquiring higher education. So he left his native land in the strength of young manhood, with scant knowledge of science and the classics, but with broad views of life and its obligations. He had inherited large mental capacity, and a splendid constitution; a tendency to business pursuits and the exercise of benevolence. A careful home training and the necessities of his early environments had fixed in him habits of industry and thrift. He established for others in Evansville a pork packing and wholesale grocery and an iron business which prospered under his management. But a man of his ability and independence could not be contented to manage the business of other men and in a short time he became a partner and afterwards owner of the business which he had inaugurated. All of his business undertakings prospered and his accumulations were wisely invested. It naturally followed that he grew rich, twenty years afterwards becoming sole proprietor of the business in which he was engaged. His interests were divided into two branches, his son, James L. Orr, and Matthew Dalzell, being admitted as partners in the grocery department, wherein they continued until the beginning of the rebellion. After the close of the war James L. Orr (his son), and James Davidson, were taken in as partners in the iron trade and the

firm name changed to Samuel Orr & Co. The business grew and prospered under the guiding hand of Samuel Orr until the operations of the concerns become the largest and best known in the west. In all of his plans Samuel Orr considered the future. Temporary expedients found no favor in his sight. Great in his conceptions, broad minded, large hearted, whether in the conduct of personal business or in the management of a public enterprise; whether in his permanent investments for an income or the endowment of an institution for public benefit he considered the decades and the centuries hidden in the womb of futurity.

He stood for the public spirit of the community, and favored whatever would insure to the permanent prosperity and welfare. Mr. Orr was elected a director of the branch at Evansville of the State Bank of Indiana, November 2, 1846. On May 10, 1855, was elected president of the branch bank, and remained in that capacity until the expiration of the franchise and until the final dividend from the assets in December, 1858. Upon the organization of the branch at Evansville of the Bank of the State of Indiana as the successor of the State Bank of Indiana, Mr. Orr was elected a director and served in that capacity until 1865, when by an act of congress national banking was ushered in and the ten per cent tax imposed on the circulation of state banks, which forced the Bank of the State of Indiana into liquidation Mr. Orr immediately, in connection with others, organized the Evansville National Bank, was one of the directors and members of the executive committee and took an active part in the management of the bank up to the time of his death in 1882. In 1873 the German National Bank of Evansville was incorporated and Mr. Orr was elected president, in which capacity he served until his death. He was one of the incorporators of the Evansville and Illinois railroad, now known as the Evansville and Terre Haute Railroad Company.

The objects of his private bounty were almost infinite and always deserving; he gave with a definite purpose in view and his gifts were helpful. The world can never know of the myriads whom he assisted. His most intimate friends were not informed to the extent and variety of his good deeds. He sought to avoid publicity and the only complete record of his benefactions is in the courts of Heaven. He was a consistent member of the Walnut Street Presbyterian church, of which for a quarter of a century he was an elder. The church was deeply in debt, and it was largely through the aid of Mr. Orr that the debt was cancelled. He was for many years trustee of Wabash College, of which he left a bequest in aid of its library. Dr. Tuttle, the venerable president of the college, officiated at Mr. Orr's funeral on the 10th of February, 1882.

A few sentences from his sermon are in place here: "He was a husband. And one who has leaned on him these many years finds her strong staff broken. He was a father. These children suddenly find the fatherly heart has ceased to beat, and the fatherly hand closed. He was a friend. Hundreds outside his home called him their friend. They loved him. His presence was as sunlight to them. How much it meant when they said: 'He is our friend.' He was a philanthropist. Such were his varied relations to the suffering that he might have said: 'When the ear heard me then it blessed me, and when the eye saw me it gave witness to me, because I delivered the poor and the fatherless, and him that had none to help him.' The honored and beloved wife of Mr. Orr, who had been a loved and loving companion for a half century, followed him to the tomb in a few months. She was reared with sterling purposes under the drippings of the Old Scotch Presbyterian Sanctuary. Her active interest in all good work as well as her example were a great benefit to humanity. Of the children of Mr. and Mrs. Samuel Orr, two, a daughter and a son survive—Mrs. Bayard, wife of a prominent citizen of Evansville, whose biography appears in this volume, and Mr. James L. Orr, who succeeded to his father's business. To commemorate the life and work of Samuel Orr and his good wife, their children erected a beautiful parsonage adjoining the Walnut street Presbyterian church, where their parents worshipped and labored for so many years.

Mr. Samuel Orr at his death left to his family ample means to secure to each of them the comforts of life. They also inherited from him a legacy of higher value, an example of a whole life of honorable and indefatigable industry, with no spot or smirch resting upon his character. Such a character built up, as it was, by strict fidelity to every trust, is more precious than riches, or station, or rank, or the fulfillment of every desire which ambition incites in the minds of her votaries.

CHARLES RUSSEL BEMENT,

Deceased, in his day one of the foremost business men of Indiana, was born at Stockbridge, Berkshire county, Massachusetts, March 4, 1829, and received his early mental training in the schools of Stockbridge. With a somewhat limited education he found himself when he had grown to manhood confronted with the problem of life. Bright, energetic and determined he bravely faced the difficulties of his position and decided to carve out a career for himself. He was descended from fine old Scotch-English ancestry and had a grand, good mother who reared a family of children everywhere noted for their honor, culture and true citizenship. In strength of character, resolute and inflexible devotion to principal, her devotion to family, church and her section was evidenced by tireless ministrations to the afflicted. Under the influence of such a mother he acquired naturally honor, charity and love of liberty and a spirit of independence.

Russel Bement came west about the age of twenty-five and reached Evansville a poor boy as far as this world's goods go, but rich in energy and true

15

manliness. When he arrived in Evansville he had the princely sum of a quarter of a dollar and at his death his estate was worth near a quarter of a million dollars. He attributed his success to the fact that he attended to his affairs himself, and never asked others to do for him what he could do himself. His first engagement was in the capacity of clerk in the grocery store of his brother, Asa Bement. He soon developed superior business ability and tact, possessing many qualities without which few men rise to distinction. So when his brother married and went to Connecticut Russel Bement assumed full charge of the business. He met with success and had the courage to manage a wholesale business during the civil war and maintained a splendid trade with southern merchants, although Mr. Bement's affiliations were with the Union. He finally became the head of the concern which he had served as a clerk, and under his guiding hand the business grew and prospered until its operations became second to none of the kind in Indiana. He was for twenty years president of the Merchant's National bank and gained wide reputation as a financier by familiarity with the principles of banking. The bank thrived and prospered under his direction until it went into voluntary liquidation. He was a man of means and affairs and had extensive real estate interests in and around Evansville.

While a reticent man, he was not taciturn, and people who were thrown with him through business relations or by personal contact, bear testimony of his genial manner and warm hearted friendship and generous hospitality.

He never sought prominence as a politician, but he was well informed in all matters pertaining to local, state or national government, and could have wielded a strong influence, but he simply voted the republican ticket and was satisfied with having done his duty.

His counsel was sought and his judgment relied upon by his fellow-citizens. He was one of nature's noblemen, and had a strong hold upon the affections of the people. Suave and courteous in manner, warm hearted and kind to his friends, but in business dignified and firm, and his decisions were strong and always just. As a citizen he shirked no duty or responsibility, and while rarely concerned in the conduct of public affairs, he took a live interest in all that affected the common welfare. He was a friend alike of his people and his country, equally attached to the rights of one and the glory of the other.

As a man, he was of strong will, industrious, honest, brave, magnanimous and true, faithful and confiding with his friends, unswerving in his attachments, fixed in his principles, a pleasing companion, and devoted and affectionate to those bound to him by natural ties. Simple in tastes, frugal in habits, dignified and decorous in manners, gracious in address and at all times and in all companies by his bearing and appearance showing that "His tribe was God Almighty's gentlemen."

In his family circle Mr. Bement was kind, affectionate and unselfish to a fault. Wherever his name was known it was strongly fettered with honor and fidelity on the one hand and modesty, purity and benevolence on the other. Chaste and delicate in his tastes, he could not brook that which savored of coarseness and unrefinement. He was the proudest of men and yet the humblest, and so rare was the blending, so admirable the balancing that he was the esteemed friend of the prosperous, and the ready counselor and help of the poor. He gave alms lavishly, although he guarded his charitable work as a secret, and the only true record of his deeds of kindness is in the court of Heaven.

Russell Bement married Mary Charlotte Ruby, of Ohio. Mr. Bement left his family a large fortune, and also something more precious than riches— a fair name. His death was an irreparable loss to the community and to his friends.

WILLIAM HEILMAN.

THE faithful and impartial historian of Indiana, who prepares a roster of her greatest men, will not fail to accord the proper place to Hon. William Heilman, senator, congressman and business man, who was born at Albig in Rhenish Hesse, October 11th, 1824, and was the son of Valentine Heilman, who died when William was eighteen months of age. His mother was united in marriage (second) to Mr. Peter Weintz, a native of Germany, and the family came to America in 1843, landing at New Orleans. From there they removed to

WM. HEILMAN.

St. Louis and shortly afterwards took up their abode in Posey county, Indiana. The conditions of William Heilman's childhood were not more favorable than those common to the frontier boys of the epoch. He had almost no advantages in school during childhood and his early life was spent in the monotonous routine of farm life. In 1847 in connection with Christian Kratz, his brother-in-law, an experienced hand in the foundry business, he started a small foundry and machine shop in Evansville, occupying a rude frame building on Pine street. They manufactured dog irons, stoves, plows, etc., and employed a half dozen men. In 1850 they added a blacksmith shop and supplemented their horse power with a steam engine and boiler, and in 1854 manufactured the first "portable steam engine," and five years later made their first threshing machine, patterned after the "Pitts machine." Their business progressed marvelously. During the war Mr. Heilman took an active interest in the cause of the Union, but notwithstanding that, southern merchants, who had always liberally patronized him, continued to do so without intermission. In 1864 Mr. Kratz withdrew from the business and received $100,000 for his interest.

In 1852 Mr. Heilman was elected councilman of Evansville and served in that capacity several terms. Subsequently, in 1870, his party friends elected him representative to the State Legislature. He was nominated in 1872 as the congressional candidate. The district had always given a demo-cratic majority of 2,500, but he reduced it to 112. In 1874, a year fraught with disastrous defeat for the republican party, he again had the satisfaction of reducing the majority, and in 1876 was elected State Senator. Some time afterwards he visited Europe but was not permitted to remain in private life, as the qualities of leadership which he possessed were demanded by his party, and in 1878 he was called home to serve the people as congressman from the first Indiana district, being elected by nearly one thousand votes, and he was the first republican who had ever carried the district. No representative from Indiana ever established a better reputation as a public officer or secured a more universal or hearty esteem from his associates than did Mr. Heilman. In evidence of this fact a portion of the speech delivered by him in the House in 1879 on the "Warner Coinage Bill" is quoted below. He insisted that "honesty is the best policy" in Governmental matters as well as in anything else, and thus expressed himself:

"I am strongly in favor of well considered, practical legislation to benefit the agricultural and manufacturing interests, to increase our commerce and wealth, but by all means let us have some stability in our financial legislation. The condition of the country is at least, although perhaps slowly, getting better, and what commerce and finance need just now more than anything else is to be let alone."

Mr. Heilman rose, phœnix-like from an unsophisticated German boy, who had never entered a school house after he was thirteen years of age, to the position of statesman and successful business man. He organized the Cotton Mill company of Evansville. Was a large stockholder in the Evansville Gas Works, director in the Evansville National Bank, director in the Evansville and Terre Haute and other Railroads. His fortune was not acquired by objectionable methods, but by persistent exercise, for forty-four years of industry, economy and sound judgment. His individuality was strong. In intercourse, he showed little consciousness of self but in all circumstances a strict regard for dignity. He had extraordinary pertinacity and self-reliance. His intelligent gaze went straight to the heart of the most complicated questions. No fallacy, no scheme, no contrivance could ever evade his glance. His judgment was as profound as his penetration was acute. He had the ability to make conclusions clear, the honesty to make them right and the generosity to make them beneficial. He was pre-eminently a man of reason. His intelligent sagacity, not less than his moral integrity kept him ever away from the illusions, the ambiguities and the torments of the world of chance. Mr. Heilman's greatest endowment was strong practical common sense. He calculated shrewdly the cost of an enterprise before embarking in it. He went to work with tireless industry and firm determination to win success.

He was united in marriage in 1848 to Miss Mary Jenner, and their union was blessed with nine children. His death occured September 22, 1888. Although he had rounded out more than the allotted age of man, to those who had known him, his span of life seemed far too short; but his memory lingers with them like a benediction and in his fame and fair name his descendents have a precious heritage.

JOSEPH ANGEL,

FOREMAN of the Aiken farm, was born in Vanderburg county, Indiana, December 17, 1849, and is the son of Matthias and Elizabeth (Murphy) Angel. The father was born in Ohio in 1819 and the mother was a native of Vanderburg county. Mr. Angel came west in 1821 with his parents, who were among the first settlers of this section. He was for a number of years engaged as a pilot on flat-boats and steamboats. He was a man of high integrity and his efforts were crowned with gratifying success. He was honored and respected by all who knew him. Joseph Angel received his education in the common schools of Newburg, Indiana, and his first business engagement was in the capacity of clerk in that town. For twenty five years he has been engaged as farm overseer, and for the past fourteen years has been acting in that capacity for Mrs. Elizabeth Aiken, whose biography appears in this volume. Mr. Angel is an overseer of ability as is demonstrated by the manner in which he handles Mrs. Aiken's large farm He is a member of the

Masonic order and of the Knights of Honor, belonging to Silver Cloud Lodge of Evansville. In 1870 he was united in marriage to Miss Anna Roberts, who died one year afterwards. In 1872 he was again married to Miss Mollie Bullett. She died in 1880 and Mr. Angel was again married to Miss Lollie Butts, of Evansville. Mr. Angel is the father of five children, all living. One the issue of his first marriage, two of the second and two of the last.

Mr. Angel is recognized as an enterprising and progressive business man, and by fair and honorable conduct he has placed himself in the good-will of the people.

ASA IGLEHART,

Iఄ his day the leading legal light of Evansville and one of the most foremost lawyers of this county, was born in Ohio county, Kentucky, December 8, 1816. His grandfather was John Igleheart, of Prince George county, Maryland, and his father was Levi Igleheart, the fifth son of John Igleheart. Levi Igleheart married Annie Taylor and in 1815 left Maryland for the west and settled in Ohio county, Kentucky. Asa Igleheart was seven years of age when his parents removed from Kentucky into the wilds of Warrick county, Indiana, and the name of Igleheart is one of the oldest and most highly respected in the county. They trace their ancestors back to Germany and it is recorded that over two hundred years

ago the first people of that name landed on American soil in Maryland.

In a wilderness in the midst of wild animals Asa Igleheart grew to manhood, and the privations and hard work that foster self-denial and independence, were his. There he underwent the monotonous routine of clearing the forest and farming, and little opportunity was afforded for procuring an education. He never attended college but his massive head was filled with that superior knowledge, common sense. It was not until he had formed a matrimonial alliance that he decided to take up the law as a profession. He commenced the study of law on the farm and pursued it with eagerness a little short of romance. He was admitted to the bar of the State of Indiana in 1848 and that event marked an era in his career. He devoted himself with zeal to the study and practice of his profession from then up to the time his health failed several years before his death, which occurred February 5, 1887.

He removed to Evansville in 1849 and at once became a member of the law firm of Ingle, Wheeler & Iglehart, where he remained until he was appointed common pleas judge to fill a vacancy in 1854, and afterwards he was elected without opposition to the same position. In 1858 he resumed his practice after thorough elementary training and four years experience on the bench and his success came rapidly and surely. He served in the administration of the law as judge and wrote a valuable treatise on practice and made other numerous digests and expositions.

His personal acquaintance with the leading lawyers of the state was great. He was active in organizing the first State Bar Association and was its first president. He was an original promoter and member of the Bar Association of the United States and for many years contributed editorially to the Central Law Journal. He took up and revised "McDonald's Treastise," and that work subsequently became known as "Iglehart's Treatise," and also prepared an original work on "Pleading and Practice" in Indiana. He performed these and many other minor literary labors while actively engaged in his profession.

He practiced successfully for many years in the supreme court of Indiana, and his opinions were always respected by that court. His mind was naturally capable of great research, and he could see readily through the mazes of intricate problems and divest difficult subjects of their obscurity. He practiced regularly in the federal courts of Indianapolis before it was established in Evansville, and was often associated with such men as Hendricks and McDonald, and a number of other important cases were conducted by him through the supreme court of the United States. His reach and grasp of thought was clear and incisive and at the same time it was broad and comprehensive. No scheme, no fallacy, no contrivance, no fraud could ever evade his glance. He had the ability to make conclusions clear, the honesty to make them right and the generosity to make them beneficial. His judgment was as profound as his penetration was acute. Sophistry was not employed by him, nor did he seek by rhetorical outbursts to darken counsel.

He was a trustee and steward of Trinity church for many years, and in a broader sense a steward of the Lord's vineyard; dispensing charity as a trustee among the worthy poor, helping such as were in distress, inspiring more hopeful views of life and aiding in the attainment of better conditions. He took a prominent part in the proper education of the young and his good work in that way could not be calculated. He was a member of the Evansville board of education, and for twenty years a trustee of Asbury and DePauw University.

In speaking of Judge Iglehart, one of his contemporary and fellow-townsmen said: "He was a lawyer, pure and proper—imbued with respect for his profession, abiding by its etiquette and illustrating its high intellectuality. His appropriate place was the court room, and his greatest pleasure the argument of an abstruse question of law. My mind often reverts to law and to lawyers. Among them there was no stronger or clearer mind, no greater equity pleader, no professor of more profound legal learning."

He was a man of means and affairs and successful in accumulating property. His home was noted for its hospitality, which was dispensed with a lavish hand. The surviving children of this notable man are as follows: Rev. Ferd. G. Iglehart, now pastor of Simpson Methodist Episcopal church, Brooklyn, New York, well and favorably known as a writer, lecturer and orator; J. E. Iglehart, prominently engaged in the general practice of law, a competent and well qualified corporation lawyer and solicitor for several railroad companies. The daughter is Mrs. Annie Taylor, wife of lawyer Edwin Taylor, of Evansville.

PROFESSOR KARL KNORTZ,

SUPERINTENDENT of the German department of the Evansville City and High Schools, was born in Garbenhiem, Rhenish, Prussia, August 28 1841, and attended the Royal Prussian Gymnasium at Wetzlar, and studied philology and philosophy at Heidelburg University. He came to this country in 1863, when he engaged in teaching at Detroit which continued until 1868. He taught at Oshkosh, Wisconsin, 1868-71, and at Cincinnati 1871-74. For a number of years he edited a German newspaper at Indianapolis, and in 1882 removed to New York City where he devoted himself to literature. He came to Evansville five years ago and took charge of the German department of our school. Professor Knortz is to-day the most prolific German writer in America. Speaking of his achievements Appleton's Biographical Encyclopodia of America, says: "Mr. Knortz has done much to make American literature known and appreciated in his native country." He has published besides translation of American poetry, "Marchen und Sagen der nordamerikanischen Indianer," (Jena 1871);

"Amerikanische Skizzen," (Halle 1876): "American Shakespeare Bibliography," (Boston 1876); "Humoristische Gedichte," (Baltimore 1877); "Longfellow: Eine literarhistorische Studie," (Hamburg 1897); "Aus dem Wigwam," (Leipsic 1880); "Kapital und Arbeit in Amerika," (Zurich 1881); "Aus der transatlantischen Gesellschaft," (Leipsic 1882; "Staat und Kische in Amerika," (Gotha 1882); "Shakespeare in America," (Berlin 1882); "Amerikanische Lebensbilder," (Zurich 1884); "Eines deutchen Matrosen nordpalfahrten, (1885); "Representative German Poems," with translations,)New York 1885); "Goethe und die Wertherzeit," (Zurich 1885); "Brook Farm und Maragreth Fuller," (New York 1886); "Gustav Seyffarth," (1886).

Of his recent productions may be mentioned "History of American Literature," in two volumes, a critical study of Longfellow, whose writings he translated into German. He wrote a book on Shakespeare, and one on Walt Whitman, translating the latter's principal work, "Leaves of Grass," into the German language. Professor Knortz has written a history of three of the most important German Communistic Colonies in the United States. The first was the "Colony of the Harmonies;" second the "Colony of the Inspirationists" at Amina, Iowa, and third the "Colony of the Separatists" at Zoar, Ohio. He also wrote "Rome in America," and published a book on "Folklore" and one entitled "Individuality in Education," which was his latest effort.

Professor Knortz was united in marriage in 1878 to Miss Anna Singer, a native of Leipsic, Saxony, but at the time a resident of Pennsylvania. Their union has been blessed with one child, a daughter, seventeen years of age.

WILLIAM BOWER,

PROMINENT farmer and stock raiser of Scott township in Vanderburgh county, was born February 5, 1836 or 1837, in Scott township and is the son of Thomas and Lucinda (Lee) Bower. The father was a native of England and came to America in the early twenties. The mother was a native of Ireland and came to this country when a young girl.

Thomas Bower was engaged as a horse trainer and married Lucinda Lee in New York city. They came west and located in Scott township about 1836. Their union was blessed with four children, the subject of this sketch being the oldest. Thomas Bower was a successful man and farmed and raised stock on a large scale. He was a democrat in politics and served the people as public officer at various times and in various capacities. True to every trust he was a man honored and esteemed by his fellow-men. He took a prominent part in the civil war and rendered valuable service as a recruiting officer.

William Bower received his education in the schools of Vanderburgh county and worked on his father's farm in the summer. He now owns a fine farm of 300 acres in Scott township and gives a great deal of attention to the raising of stock, especially to sheep and wool growing. On his farm seven to ten men are given employment. Mr. Bower's affiliations are with the democratic party and he served the people of Vanderburgh county as commissioner during the time the new court house was being erected. He has been county assessor and has filled various minor offices in the township, and it can of truth be said that he discharged every duty with grace and dignity, both to himself and to his constituents.

Mr. Bower has accumulated a considerable fortune and is a large taxpayer. He is a man of means and affairs, owns considerable property in the city of Evansville, which calls him there about once every week to look after it.

Wm. Bower was united in marrige in 1860 to Miss Martha J. Stacer, of Vanderburgh county, and three children, two of whom survive, issued from their union. Martha J. Bower died in 1865, and Mr. Bower married (second) 1866, Miss Charlina Morrison, of Warrick county. Three children, only one of whom survive, were born to them, and the mother died in 1881. Mr. Bower was again married in 1883 to Miss Anna Denison, of Scott township, and five children have blessed their union.

As a public spirited, loyal and enterprising citizen Wm. Bower has no superior. He is a man of great energy and force of character, possessing many of those qualities without which few men rise to distinction.

WILLIAM BOWER.

LOUIS PUSTER.

THE life of Captain Louis Puster, of Evansville, may be profitably considered in three distinct relations, all of them important. First, in the relationship of private citizen, occupied with every day work of securing a livelihood, the performance of social, domestic and religious duties, and gaining position in the commercial world; second, in the relation of a soldier, defending the flag and fighting for the restoration of national unity; third, as an eminently successful business man, the head of one of the most important manufacturing concerns in Indiana.

Louis Puster was born July 25, 1832, in Germany, and is the son of Jacob and Katrina (Kerth) Puster. He received his early education in the schools of his native land and in 1850 came to America seeking his fortune. He was for five years in St. Louis, where he learned the trade of wood-turner. Later he was engaged in Keokuk, Iowa, Quincy, Illinois, and Cincinnati, Ohio.

Of his war record we have no more illustrious example of bravery and efficient service. When the war dogs began to bay, Mr. Puster returned to Missouri, and on June 15, 1861, enlisted in Company K, Twenty-first Missouri Volunteer Infantry as a private. He soon became first sergeant and was promoted to captain March 6, 1863. The following is a complete record of the service actually performed by Mr. Puster, compiled by Mr. F. H. Dyer, compiler of war records at Washington, D. C. He served altogether four years

16

and nine months, having enlisted July 1, 1861, and was discharged April 19, 1866, and we venture to say that not another man from Evansville served so long and faithfully.

"SERVICE.—Battle of Shiloh, Tenn., April 6-7, 1862. Advance on a siege of Corinth, Miss., April 17, May 30. Occupation of Corinth and pursuit to Boonville, May 31, June 12. Duty at Corinth until September 19-20. Battle of Corinth. October 3-4. Grant's central Mississippi campaign, November and December. On post and garrison duty at Columbus, Ky., Union City, Tenn., Clinton, Ky., and Memphis, Tenn., until January, 1864. Ordered to Vicksburg, Miss. Action at Islands Nos. 70 and 71, Mississippi to the river while en route, January 29. Meridian campaign from February 3 to March 5. Action near Black river, February 5. Slightly wounded in leg by cannon ball but remained on duty. Meridian, February 14-15; at Columbus, Ky., April, 1865. Smith's expedition to Tupelo, Miss., July 5-23.—Near Ripley, July 7; Pontotoc, July 11-12. Camargo cross roads, July 15; Harrisburg, near Tupelo, July 14-15; Old Town Creek, July 15. Smith's expedition to Oxford, August 5-26.—Tallahatchie river, August 7-9; Abbeville and Oxford, August 12; Hurricane creek, 13-14; College Hill, August 21-22; Abbeville, August 23. Moved to Duvall's Bluff, Ark., September 1. Marched through Arkansas and Missouri in pursuit of Price, September 7 to November 16, marching over 700 miles. Moved to Nashville, November 25 to December 1. Occupation of Nashville until Hood's investment, December 1-14. Battles of Nashville, December 15-16. Pursuit of Hood to the Tennessee river, December 17-28. Moved to Clifton, Tenn., thence to Eastport, Miss., January 2-7, 1865, and duty there until February 9. Moved to Vicksburg. Miss., thence to New Orleans, La., February 9-21. Mobile campaign, March and April. Siege of Spanish Fort and Ft. Blakely, March 26, April 8. Ft. Blakely, April 9. Marched to Montgomery, Ala., April 13-25, and duty there until June. Moved to Mobile, June 1. In command of U. S. arsenal at Mt. Vernon, Ala., June 15 to August 16, 1865. Provost Marshal at Pollard, Ala., to March, 1868. In command of battery Gladden, near Mobile, until April. Mustered out April 19, 1866, and honorably discharged from service."

"This is to certify that the above has been compiled and arranged from official records and sources only, and was not furnished in particular by Captain Puster, whose military record it presents.   (Signed) F. H. Byer."

Soon after the war Mr. Puster located in Evansville and embarked in the furniture business, at first being connected with the Union Furniture Company and afterwards with the well-known Armstrong Company, with whom he remained until the organization of L. Puster & Co., in 1881. The business of this concern has grown and prospered under the guiding hand of L. Puster until it has become one of the largest and best known manufactories in the west.

Mr. Puster is a progressive citizen, has been a member of the Business Men's Association, and is also an active and helpful member of Farragut Post, G. A. R. and Loyal Legion. He has always been a friend and patron of education, an earnest supporter of the church, being a member of St. Lucas Evangelical church, and all instrumentalities for the promotion of religious principles and moral reforms. His long life has been filled with usefulness and crowned with honor. He has been successful in accumulating the means essential to personal comfort, without neglecting any of the higher duties of life, which contribute to the intelligent, spiritual and moral growth.

Mr. Puster is the head of a delightful family, in which the happiest relations are maintained. His home is characterized by the most liberal as well as elegant hospitality, in which a cultured wife, panoplied with the refined graces of womanhood bears a conspicuous part with charming cordialty.

ALFRED BERNARDIN,

PRESIDENT of the Bernardin Bottle Cap company, was born in France, 1845. He came to America in 1856, locating in Ohio, and in 1873 removed to Evansville, and since that time his success as one of the foremost business men of Evansville has been gratifying.

The Bernardin Bottle Cap company was organized to manufacture the celebrated Bernardin patent bottle cap in

LOUIS PUSTER.

1885. The incorporators were C. R. Bement, F. W. Cook and A. L. Bernardin. In 1893, the two sold their entire interest to Jacob Haas and A. Bernardin, who are now the sole owners of this mammoth plant, which is located at the corner of First Avenue and Ingle street. The products of this concern are shipped to every state in the union and to the following foreign countries: England, Australia, South America, Mexico and Canada. Mr. A. L. Bernardin is president of the company and Mr. Jacob Haas, secretary and treasurer.

CHANDLER H. PEIRCE,

INSTRUCTOR of penmanship, was born June 13, 1850. in Clarke county, Ohio, and is the son of Jacob and Marian (Chandler) Peirce. The father was born March, 1821, in Chester county, Pennsylvania, where he lived until he was fourteen years of age, when he removed to Ohio and was there successfully engaged in farming. He was a man of highest integrity, loved, honored and respected by all who knew him. His mother died in 1892.

The early education of Chandler Peirce was received in the common schools of Clarke county, Ohio, and he attended the National Normal at Lebanon, Ohio, and was graduated in 1870. He entered Eastman's Business College at Poughkepsie, New York, in 1870, where he took a course which prepared him for teaching. This led to his removing west and he located at Keokuk, Iowa, where for twenty-three years he was engaged as supervisor of writing, and for fifteen years he was principal of the business college in that city.

January 1, 1895, Mr. Peirce came to Evansville and has since been engaged as supervisor of writing in the High school. He is a self-made man, having earned his way through college and his success has been due in a large measure to his untiring zeal, constant watchfulness and unswerving probity.

At the age of thirteen Mr. Peirce left home against the wishes of his parents to join the army, and his first service was in Kentucky and Tennessee, where he joined the Eighth O. V. C., and was later in service in Virginia and West Virginia. He participated in the campaign of Kewanoh and Shenandoah Valley, and was taken captive at Beverly, West Virginia, January 11, 1865, and for two months was a prisoner, confined in Libby prison. He was one of the youngest captives and enjoys the distinction of having been selected to keep the records for the Confederates, his remuneration consisting of simply double rations and the luxury of a clean bed. He was honorably discharged July, 1865. The plate which bears his name is in a museum at Chicago at the rear end of the first floor.

Mr. Peirce is a member of the Knights of Pythias, Grand Army of the Republic and the Court of Honor. He possesses in a marked degree the attributes of genuine manhood. Honest purposes and laudable conduct have marked his career. His sympathetic nature, the gentleness of his disposition and the worth of his character have won for him the admiration and respect of all who know him.

WILLIAM JOHNSON LOWRY.

IN THE annals of Vanderburgh county no name appears which commands more sincere respect than William Lowry. He came to Evansville after a business career of many years, with strong independence of character and a determination to make his own way among the foremost. He sprang from Irish ancestry that recognized a patriotic duty in rearing large families under wholesome restraint and religious influences. Both of his parents antedated the revolution, and were old enough to remember the stirring events of Concord and Lexington.

William J. Lowry was born in Anne, Arundel county, Maryland, on October 15, 1795, and it was there his mother died. His father moved into Ohio when he was a boy. There were pioneers in Ohio, and the senior Lowry was one in Scioto county. At the age of seventeen years the scholastic attainments and intellectual maturity of young Lowry being quite equal to those of the average young man of twenty-one, he formed the purpose to make his own living and forthwith entered upon the execution of it. Leaving home he was engaged in the river trade for a number of years and performed the venturesome and dan-

gerous feat of walking the whole distance from New Orleans to Louisville, in those days when wolves were more numerous than domestic animals and Indians as common as Caucasians. He returned through what was then known as the Indian nation, and underwent some very thrilling, and to say the least, unpleasant experiences. At one time he found himself in close proximity with the Indians, and it was only by the shrewdest maneuvering that he escaped from them.

He was a manly boy, animated by a noble impulse and fortified by the moral courage which prompted him to accept any honorable employment that offered reasonable remuneration. Prior to 1820 he was employed by the government to assist in surveys of public land in Alabama, Florida and Mississippi. He served in the war with Great Britain, first as adjutant and was afterwards promoted to the rank of major. This was before he had reached his majority.

His father, Thomas Lowry, who married Miss Anne Johnson, removed to Posey county, Indiana, in 1819, and settled near Springfield. In 1820 the son joined him and for eight succeeding years lived in the vicinity of Springfield, then the county seat of Posey county, and became one of the important factors in the history and progress of that county. He was engaged in farming and trading and his efforts were crowned with gratifying success. In 1828 he removed to Mt. Vernon, Indiana, and embarked in mercantile pursuits. For over a quarter of a century he remained in Mt. Vernon and in all of his transactions was eminently successful. In 1855 he followed Mr. N. G. Nettleton, his wife's brother, to Cincinnati and the firm of Nettleton & Lowry was formed to do a banking business in that city. The business grew and prospered until 1861, when Mr. Lowry removed with his family to Evansville. While residing in Evansville where most of his interests centered, he also served as president of the bank at Mt. Vernon from 1861 to 1864. He was the first president of the Evansville National Bank and the founder and senior member of the firm of W. J. Lowry & Company, organized to do a banking business in Evansville. He achieved prominence as a banker by familiarity with the principles of finance and the consistent management of fiscal institutions. He advanced continuously from the ranks of a wage-earner to one of the foremost business men and financiers of Indiana. From the time he left his father's home he made his own way in the world, and achieved success with little financial assistance from any source. He possessed in a high degree those traits of character and disposition that qualify a man for the administration of trusts and endears him to his friends. His personal integrity was never doubted and his honor was unsullied. He was a consistent and faithful member of the Trinity Methodist Episcopal church for more than four decades and he was liberal in dispensing charity, generous towards all. He was a busy man, a man of means and affairs, but also found time to devote to the performance of his religious duties. The characteristics of his religion were exhibited in his domestic, social and business life; gentleness in the rearing of children; kindliness in personal intercourse with others; honesty in dealing with men; thriftiness in accumulating property. His business continued with marked success and unbroken prosperity up to the time of his death, which was brought about by an injury received from a fall in 1872. He became widely known throughout the financial world and was able to amass a comfortable fortune. His life was quiet and unostentatious, but he accomplished much. He was always busy, always economical, always thrifty. He wasted nothing, not even his time. He was large hearted and generous, modest in demeanor and yet quietly relieving the wants and making provision for the unfortunate. His days were devoted to useful employment and his earnings invested so as to yield a good increase. The end justified his sagacity. The present generation of men in the central-western states scarcely realize how much they owe to the sagacity and progressive spirit of the pioneers, who endured the privation imposed upon frontier life to lay the foundation of ample fortune for their children, while building a great and prosperous commonwealth.

W. J. Lowry was united in marriage in 1823 to Miss Sarah Nettleton, of Springfield, Illinois, whose Christian character, womanly sympathy and determination contributed in no small degree to the success of her husband and the happiness of the family.

WILLIAM M. AKIN, JR.,

ONE little expects to find startling incidents in the life of a merchant, but he fails to comprehend the forces which contribute to the advancement of the moral, social and political interests of our people who leaves the careful business man out of his reckonings. No history of Vanderburgh county would be complete that did not mention the part William M. Akin, Jr., has already played in public affairs, to say nothing of the possibilities of the future, even beyond his term of service as mayor of Evansville, which does not expire until April, 1899. His boyhood days were that of a typical Hoosier boy of the present and the immediate past. He was born December 31, 1855, at Carlisle, Indiana, and his elementary education was obtained from the district schools. He was ambitious and determined to seek a higher education than the common schools afforded, and in 1873, he entered the old Asbury College, now DePauw University, and was graduated in 1878.

While earnest and persistent in the prosecution of his studies, his cordiality and social disposition gained him wide popularity among his fellow students. These qualities supported by magnificent physical proportions gained him a leadership in college affairs. At the same time his methods and applications in study, supplemented by his facile comradeship with members of the faculty, furnished him with unusual breadth of qualification for executive work.

In 1865 Mr. Akin came to Evansville and in 1878 became a member of the firm of William Akin & Son, engaged in the pork packing business and the success of the concern, under the guiding hands of his father and himself, has been very gratifying and its operations have extended far and near. The house has a reputation for honesty and fair dealing second to none in the country. Mr. Akin has always affiliated with the democratic party and has been unswerving in his devotion to the interests thereof.

Prior to his election as Mayor of Evansville, he never held public office, with the exception of two terms as school trustee under the administration of Mayor Hawkins, which place he resigned to accept the nomination for mayor. A man of his intelligence and ability could not, however, keep out of public life and he was induced to make the race for mayor of Evansville in the last campaign and was elected by the overwhelming majority of 2,785 votes. His administration has been highly creditable, evincing devotions to the interests of the city and comprehensive knowledge of its wants. He is prompt and untiring in his efforts to serve all with equability and without distinction, and in his daily administration is proving the wisdom of his constituents who placed him at the head of the municipal government of Evansville. Personally Mayor Akin is so genial in his manners, that whenever required to display force and resolution of purpose, he shows so much suavity and tact that he disarms criticism. He seldom offends and

WM. M. AKIN, JR.

H. J. WEISS.

never loses a friendship once formed, socially or politically. His rapid advancement in public life has made no change in that modest, quiet demeanor, which characterized him as a business man before political honors were conferred on him. He is too level-headed to be puffed up by prosperity. His comprehension of human nature and keen incite into motive as the mainspring of human action, and his adaptibility, without surrender of dignity or self-respect, qualify him in a high degree for success as an executive officer. Though strong in his views and independent in action he is careful not to offend others by pushing his opinions upon them.

William Akin, Sr., (father) is a native of Indiana, having been born in 1828. He married Miss Mary Davis, and to them seven children were born, the subject of this sketch being the third. As a business man and public spirited citizen, Mr. William Akin, Sr., has no superior. He is a man of sterling integrity and one who is loved, honored and respected by his fellowmen. Few men have had as successful a career. He is a man of discretion and pronounced virtues. He is well informed, beloved by his friends and respected by the community on account of his generosity, congenial manner and high integrity.

William M. Akin, Jr., is a member of the Knights of Pythias and of the B. P. O. E. His convictions of duty are strong and unyielding. His activity is intense and unremitting whether in the prosecution of his private business or in the discharge of public trust. During the entire period of his residence in town, Mr. Akin has been eminently identified with many of the public enterprises which have affected favorably the growth and improvement of Evansville. He is in all the essentials of good citizenship—a leading and valuable citizen.

He was united in marriage 1886, to Miss Tillie Schlueter, a native of Illinois, but a resident of Evansville since childhood. Their union has been blessed with five children, four of whom survive.

———

HENRY J. WEISS,

A SUCCESSFUL architect and valuable citizen, was born in Evansville July 17, 1860, and is the son of Jacob and Caroline Weiss.

Jacob Weiss, his father, was born in Darmstadt, on the Rhine, Germany, and was engaged in contracting and building. He came to America in 1847 and died in 1889. The mother was born in Berlin, Germany, and came to America in 1852. Their union was blessed with eleven children, of which the subject of this sketch was the second.

Henry J. Weiss obtained his education in the schools of Evansville, and took a course in a commercial college, which prepared him for his active life. After finishing his education he began to do a contracting business, the following being some of the numerous buildings he has erected in Evansville: The city hall, the fire department building at the corner of Third and Walnut streets and he did the wood work in the Orr block, contract for the Eichel block, wood work on the county jail, contract for Gleisige's building, Major Rosencranz's plow works, contract for the Jenner block, F. W. Cook brewery, the Evansville Ice and Storage Co.'s building.

January 1, 1895, he began in the architect business and formed a partnership, which was dissolved June, 1897, since when he has worked alone. He made the plans for the Haynie drug store, residences of Andy Richardt, Ed. Nisbet and Joe Brentano, the Delaware street eight-room, two-story brick school building, addition to the Columbia street school and numerous other public and private buildings in Evansville and in adjoining cities.

Having had many years experience in practical as well as theoretical work, Mr. Weiss is, therefore, in position to serve the public in all forms of modern architecture. His business has prospered beyond expectation, apparently more than keeping pace with the rapid progress of the country. His capacity for work is great, and his dispatch of business rapid. He is an indefatigable worker and always punctual. These characteristics have contributed largely to the successful achievements of his life.

He was united in marriage December 14, 1882, to Miss Ella E. Haskins, a native of Kentucky, and four children have blessed their union, two boys and two girls.

WILLIAM HENRY GILBERT, M. D.

THE citizen of an intelligent community is usually worth the estimate placed upon him by his neighbors. If he is engaged in professional work they appreciate his ability and his honor, his integrity, fidelity and skill. Among the physicians held in high esteem in Evansville is Dr. William H. Gilbert. He started in life with no adventitious aids and has risen to an enviable position in his profession. He was born in Evansville February 8, 1868.

James Gilbert (father) was born in Ireland and came to America with his parents when he was nine years of age. They moved to Canada and remained there until James was thirty years of age, when they removed to Cincinnati, Ohio, where they lived for six years. Then James Gilbert moved his family to Evansville, and he was engaged in the tailoring establishment of J. H. Schrichte & Co., with whom he remained until he retired from business in 1883. He was a man of the highest integrity, loved, honored and respected by all who knew him, and his death, which occurred June 20, 1893, was greatly deplored. James Gilbert married Miss Mary Jane Burrows, a native of Ireland, born August 16, 1829. She came to America when a child with her parents, who located in Canada. Her father, James Burrows, was a representative of the British government at that time. The death of Mary J. Gilbert occurred April 1, 1895.

William H. Gilbert, the youngest of three children, received his elementary

DR. W. H. GILBERT.

training in the common and high schools of Evansville. In 1885 he entered the University of Michigan at Ann Harbor, where he took a classical and preparatory course. Then for two years he attended the Bellevue Hospital of New York, where he studied medicine and was graduated in 1889. In addition to the valuable instruction received in the university he pursued a special course of study in the New York Polyclinic and the Chicago Polyclinic, devoting particular attention to the diseases of women and surgery, taking special course under such able preceptors as Dr. Seen, of Chicago; J. Riddle and James Hawley Burten Shaw, of New York, and is now regarded as being among the more prominent surgeons of southern Indiana. He began the practice of his profession in Evansville March 23, 1889, and has succeeded in building up a most gratifying practice.

Dr. Gilbert is a member and past chancellor commander of Orion lodge No. 35, K. of P., Reed lodge, F. & A. M., LaValette commandery, Knights Templar, and also an Ancient Accepted Scottish Rite thirty-second degree Mason. He is a member of the Vanderburgh Medical Society, the Mississippi Valley Medical Society, the Indiana State Medical Society, the Pan-American Medical Society and American Medical Association. He was visiting physician at St. Mary's hospital from 1889 to 1893 and visiting surgeon to the Deaconess hospital for three years.

His carefully selected library suggests literary taste, and his liberal culture is a result of careful reading. He studies literature as well as medicine. As a general practitioner he has not been less successful than in the special field of surgery, and in all departments of practice he holds a high rank among the physicians of Vanderburgh county.

CAPT. RICHARD T. WILLIAMS,

A PROMINENT citizen of Evansville, and owner and master of the steamer J. C. Kerr, was born April 26, 1833, in Franklin county, Indiana, and is the son of Thomas and Hannah (Evans) Williams, who were natives of Kentucky. His father belonged to that large class of men of worth, who was born to the soil, and he was successfully engaged in farming. Thomas Williams removed with his family from Kentucky to Shelby county, Indiana, at an early day and entered a land claim. He was one of the pioneers of Shelby county and reared a family noted for their honor and true citizenship. He died in 1844, his wife surviving him eight years.

Richard T. Williams was the oldest of six children and his boyhood days were spent in helping his father clear the land and cultivate the farm, which he did in summer, attending the then meagre schools which were in session about three months during the winter. In what was almost a wilderness he grew to manhood, and while his education was limited he was fortified and entrenched with abundant common sense and developed sterling traits of character ere he had reached his majority. The father having died it fell to his lot to maintain the family union and their support naturally devolved upon him. At the death of the mother, the boys, having reached the age of independence, started out to fight life's battles alone and Richard formed the purpose of carving out his own career and learned to be a carpenter. He followed his trade as journeyman until 1870 when, having by hard work and close economy accumulated considerable means, he purchased a saw mill and later built a flour mill, operating both. This continued until 1880 when he disposed of his milling interests and built a grist-mill boat which he operated in the Ohio River for some time. He then purchased the "Little Sandy," a small packet which he run in the trade between Stephensport and Owensboro, Kentucky. His increasing trade demanded a larger boat so he sold the "Little Sandy" and purchased the "Rosa Belle." He became very popular in the trade and his business increased with gratifying success until its proportions were so great as to call for still a larger boat and he sold the "Rosa Belle" and purchased the "Maggie Belle." He continued with the latter in the Ohio River trade until 1889 and then entered Green River. For eight years Capt. Williams has been catering to the transportation wants of the Green River territory. His popularity in that trade and the esteem in which he is held by the shipping and traveling public is amply attested by the fact that he has advanced continually from a smaller

to a larger packet until to-day he owns the elegant steamboat, the J. C. Kerr, which he runs semi-weekly Evansville to Woodbury, Kentucky, and return. Capt. Williams has a strong hold on the people of the Green River country and the confidence which they impose in him is well placed. He has done as much, if not more, than any man to promote the interests of his patrons and to maintain reasonable and indiscriminate transportation rates. He has spent a great deal of money in providing a comfortable and commodious steamer and is certainly deserving of the large patronage which has come to him

Since 1854 Capt. Williams has been an active and helpful member of the Masonic order, and in politics he affiliates with the Republican party. He was united in marriage April 3, 1856, to Miss Patience Suddarth, a native of Perry county, Indiana, daughter of John Suddarth, a prosperous farmer. Their union has been blessed with ten children—five boys and five girls—nine of whom survive, one of the daughters having died in 1896. He is ably assisted in the operation of his steamboat by his five sons, who serve as clerks, pilots and engineers.

Capt. Williams has been a resident of Evansville since 1889 and is deeply interested in all matters pertaining to the welfare of the city. In all the essentials of good citizenship he is a valuable and worthy citizen. He bears up well under the weight of three score and four years and deserves in every way the great popularity which it is his fortune to enjoy.

PHILIP NONWEILER.

PHILIP NONWEILER,

MANAGER of the Evansville Furniture Company, and a prominent citizen of Evansville, was born in Rhine Province, in Prussia, February 11, 1840. He was schooled in his native land, where he obtained a splendid education. Before coming to America in 1857 he served an apprenticeship as salesman and bookkeeper. Upon arriving in New York city he came to Evansville immediately and for several years was employed as clerk with Mr. Henry Stockfleth, who was engaged in the grocery business. When the wolves of war began to howl in 1861, Mr. Nonweiler laid aside his pen and bravely took up his musket in the defense of his country and on August 3, 1861, enlisted in the First Indiana Battery Light Artillery and in September went to Missouri, where he was assigned to General Jefferson C. Davis' brigade. He saw active service at Springfield, Pea Ridge, Helena and also at Milligan's Bend where he was assigned to General Grant's army; was in the Vicksburg, Mississippi, campaign and after the fall of that city participated in the battle of Jackson, Mississippi, and afterwards returned to Vicksburg, where he resigned on account of ill-health, having served for over two years. He entered as quartermaster sergeant and left the service as first lieutenant. He commanded the battery at the battle of Jackson and discharged the duties with dignity and credit.

After he returned from the war he was for a number of years engaged as bookkeeper, first for Keller & White, wholesale druggists, and afterwards for Roelker, Blount & Co. He served in that capacity for five years for Henry F. Blount.

He assumed the management of the Evansville Furniture Company in September, 1870, and thus for over a quarter of a century has been the mainstay of that institution, one of the most important manufactories in the city of Evansville. He is the principal stockholder and is ably assisted in the office by his two sons, Philip, Jr., and Gustave Nonweiler, two young business men of very promising future. Aside from Mr. Nonweiler's extensive duties in the management of the business of which he is the head, he finds time to devote to matters of public import; he is a member of the Business Men's Association and always displays an active interest in any cause intended to advance the welfare of Evansville and her people.

He was a charter member of Lessing lodge No. 464, F. & A. M., and has passed through all the chairs of that lodge. He is also a member of Farragut post No. 27, G. A. R. Mr. Nonweiler does not take an active part in politics, but is always interested in the character of the men who are to fill responsible positions of public trusts. His affiliations are with the republican party.

Mr. Nonweiler was united in marriage July 17, 1867, to Miss Bertha Mueller, who was born in the Rhine Province in 1847. Their union has been blessed with three children, as follows: Philip, Gustave and Berthold.

Evansville is well adapted to the furniture business, and the great trade in this line which she enjoys is a source of gratification to every enterprising citizen, and it is doing more to advertise and make Evansville than probably anything else. Great credit is due the men who have so untiringly pushed the furniture industry to the front, and among those who have, by their energy, honest business methods and strict integrity, been instrumental in accomplishing the coveted results stands Philip Nonweiler. He is a man of rare business ability, and has the furniture business at his finger's end.

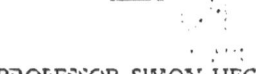

PROFESSOR SIMON HECHT,

INSTRUCTOR of German and Semitic languages, was born March 8, 1828, in Northeim, Bavaria, and is the son of David Hecht, also a native of Bavaria. The early education of Simon Hecht was obtained in his native country. He studied Hebrew and Talmudical literature in Wuerzburg under the direction of Professor and Rabbi S. Bamberger. He passed the state examination at Kaisers Lautern in the Rheinpfalz. He attended the Royal Teacher's Institute in Wuerzburg, Bavaria, 1843 and 1845. Before coming to America in 1866, he taught in Bavaria, Oldenburg and Schwerin. For five years, from 1866 to 1871, he was Rabbi of the Jewish Synagogue Temple and was connected with the Congregational schools as in-structor. Then he was appointed principal of German schools in Henderson and Mt. Vernon, and in that capacity served four years. Then he returned to Evansville and has been engaged up to the present time in the Evansville Public schools. Professor Hecht has written and published several books, notably among them "The Confirmand" which was issued in two editions. It was a worthy effort and was well taken. It is used in the Jewish schools in this country where German is taught. Another production of Professor Hecht is "Jewish Hymns," for Sunday schools and families, published in 1878. It met with deserved popularity and is now published by the Bloch Publishing company, of Cincinnati. He has composed some very beautiful songs, notably among them being one entitled "How Sweet Upon the Sacred Day," and another, "Where Is My Home?" For these songs Professor Cintura, of Evansville composed the music. Professor Hecht has written many poems which have appeared in the past in the Evansville Demokrat and in the Deborah, of Cincinnati. He occasionally corresponds with some of the papers of his native land.

Professor Hecht was united in marriage May 23, 1859, to Miss Regina Heimann, a native of Germany, sister of David and Isaac Heimann, of Evansville. They have two children living. The professor belongs to two Jewish societies in Evansville, and he and his estimable wife are members of the Jewish Temple on Sixth street.

In 1849, Professor Hecht was ap-

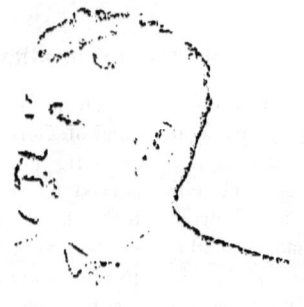

J. H. OSBORNE.

pointed in Bavaria, as supervisor of the Sabbath schools in the District Unterfranken. His father was a teacher and ex-Rabbi of considerable note, and his brother, Emanuel Hecht, was the author of several books. Prominent among the efforts of Professor Hecht should be mentioned an essay which he wrote entitled, "Goethe's Pedagogy, shown in Master's Apprenticeship."

JOHN H. OSBORN,

SUPERINTENDENT of the Evansville Cotton Mills, was born July 20th, 1849, and is a native of Boone county, Illinois. William Osborn (father) was born in Ireland about the year 1822 and now resides in Evansville. Ann (Burrel) Osborn (mother) was a native of Glasgow, Scotland, and died at Cannelton, Indiana, 1872. William Osborn came to America in early childhood and settled in Rhode Island. In 1849 he, with his family, came west seeking a betterment of their condition and temporarily settled in Boone county, Illinois. Three years later they removed to Cannelton, Indiana.

John H. Osborn, who was the second of six children, received his education at Cannelton and there learned the trade of machinist. For about fifteen years he was employed in the Indiana Cotton Mills at Cannelton and for some time at Louisville and Owensboro, Kentucky, in various foundries and machine shops working at his trade.

Coming to Evansville in 1875 he was engaged as master mechanic at the cotton mills, and in 1884 was promoted to the superintendency of the mills. He is entrusted with the supervision of six hundred workmen, and has the care of vast monetary interests. By natural acumen and thorough practical training he is well qualified for the proper discharge of this important trust. His enterprising public spirit, and the general esteem in which he is held, are attested by his selection as a director in the Business Men's Association. Aside from the numerous duties devolving upon him in the way of business, Mr. Osborn manifests an active interest in politics from a Republican standpoint, but he seeks no preferment. He refused in 1895 the nomination for congressman and he has often been solicited to serve in a public office, but with the exception of a short term as water works trustee, has never accepted.

Mr. Osborn is an active and helpful member of the K. of P., the A. O. U. W. and the Elks. He is a director and member of the executive board of the Central Trust and Savings Company and a director in the Union Savings Company. He is a man of means and affairs and owns considerable property in Evansville.

Mr. Osborn was united in marriage, June, 1878, to Miss Mary A. White, who was born in Evansville in 1858, and four children, John W., Charles A., Lillian and Emerson M., bless their union. In all the essentials of good citizenship John H. Osborn is a leading and valuable citizen.

MICHAEL P. WARD.

A PROMINENT and successful farmer living in Center township, Vanderburgh county, was born very near where he now resides and where he has spent his entire life. He first saw the light of day March 21st, 1847, and is the son of Michael Ward, a native of Westmade, Ireland, who came to America in the early thirties and about 1838 located on the farm which adjoins the one which the subject of this sketch owns. Michael Ward was one of the pioneers of the county and at the time he purchased his place there was not another house within three miles of it.

Michael Ward (father) was a prosperous farmer and a public-spirited citizen. He was a school trustee and gave the timber for the first school house in Center township. He married Katherine Leddy, a native of Westmade, Ireland, and their union was blessed with four children. Michael P. being the youngest. The other children were James, Julia and Mary.

Michael Ward, the subject of this sketch, was educated in the school house of which his father was a benefactor. He now owns a fine farm of one hundred acres and operates another as large. He also owns much stock comprising many fine milch cows and he runs a dairy. Mr. Ward's farm is about three miles from Evansville on the Stringtown road. Michael P. Ward was united in marriage, February 4th, 1891, to Miss Eva Saunders, daughter of James D. Saunders, of Evansville. Two children have blessed

their union—a girl, Edith Marie, born June 16th, 1892, and a boy, Michael James, born January 2d, 1895.

In politics Mr. Ward affiliates with the Democratic party but seeks no preferment. His name was once forced on the ticket for Squire but he voted against himself and did all he could to elect the other man. He is a consistent member of the Assumption church, of Evansville. Michael Ward has been successful because he deserved success, and no man in the community is more popular. He is a hard worker, and has by careful management accumulated a considerable fortune. He has a charming wife and two lovely children and his home is known for its generous hospitality.

JAMES J. WARD,

A WELL-TO-DO farmer of Center township, Vanderburgh county, was born about 1839, in Center township, and is the son of Michael Ward, and brother of Michael P. Ward, whose biography appears in this volume. He was educated in the same school with his brother, and grew up on the farm his father had settled. In the early days before Pigeon Creek was numerously bridged the people of Center township had to go around via Stringtown to reach Evansville, a distance three times as far as the present road. It was in the winter of 1847 that Michael Ward, father of Michael P. and James J. Ward, was making the trip via the circuitous route when he met

M. WARD.

his death. He was found hanging to the gearing of his team, and as it was bitter cold, it is supposed he became benumbed and fell asleep and the team became frightened and ran away with the deplorable result of the loss of a noble life.

James J. Ward married Miss Florence Thompson, of Evansville, 1887, and one girl, Florence, born November 18, 1889, is the issue of their union. Mrs. Ward died in 1889. James J. Ward is a straight, forward, honest and upright gentleman, and is held in the highest esteem in his community.

CAPT. WILLIAM REAVIS,

DECEASED, was born in what is now Gibson county, Indiana, August 27, 1815, and died in Evansville, February, 1896. Of his ancestry we have the following written by him some time before his death: "My father was born in North Carolina and my mother in South Carolina. They were the children of revolutionary fathers, who were the descendants of the Huguenots, or at least were in sympathy with and co-operated with that liberty loving people, who left the shores of the old world, and like the Puritans, came to a land where they could worship God according to the dictates of their own consciousness. My mother's maiden name was Strickland. And both my grandfathers, Reavis and Strickland, fought throughout the war of revolution, under the lead of Marion and

Sumter, until liberty was established in all the then states of the union. My grandfather, Strickland was called out of his house by a company of Tories and was shot to death in his own yard, a few days after coming from the army. My grandfather Reavis survived the war for many years and died in Missouri in 1835, aged eighty-seven years, after liberating all of his slaves, some twenty or thirty in number." They were people of the highest integrity, whose lives were characterized by the manner and customs of the early days in this section. When but twenty years of age William Reavis started out to fight life's battles alone, and being of studious habits his aptness soon fitted him for the duties of a teacher, which he followed for some time with very gratifying success. He was elected treasurer of Gibson county in 1846 and was re-elected to the same office three years later by an increased majority. That he was a most efficient officer the county records bear witness. He removed to Benton, Illinois, in 1869, where he engaged in the practice of law until the commencement of the civil war. His loyalty to the union was tested by the active interest which he took in the strife. He was instrumental in raising many troops and served as captain of Company G, Fifty-sixth Illinois infantry. His record as an officer was indeed flattering, showing throughout the most patriotic, unselfish, and soldierly conduct.

He came to Evansville in December, 1862, and returned to the active duties of the legal profession. Captain Reavis was the leading claim agent of southern Indiana, and prosecuted more claims against the government than any other attorney in this section of the state. In 1870, he was appointed register of bankruptcy for the First congressional district, which position he ably filled for many, years.

He was united in marriage in 1836 to Eleanor C. Burton, and to them eight children were born. He was married (second) in 1858 to Mrs. Lathena Damon.

While striving as a professional man in honorable competition for the good things of the world, Captain Reavis was not unmindful of the riches of the next. For many years of his life he was a faithful and consistant member of the General Baptist church. Quiet and unostentatious in his church work as in all other relations, Mr. Reavis was yet a valuable and efficient worker in the church, and was always ready with his personal influence and ample means to cheerfully co-operate in any scheme for the promotion of the moral and religous interests of the community. The moral influence of such a life is incalculable, and it furnishes a valuable example to young men as illustrating how the closest devotion to business is yet not inconsistent with conscientious, punctual performance of his religious duties He died as he had lived, in the clear hope of immortality through Jesus Christ. It is impossible in the limits of such an article as this to give an adequate history of a life like his But it has been attempted to so outline the salient points of his career, that in after years

the student may know something of the life and struggles of one whose name must always stand prominent in the history of the city, and who has contributed largely to lay the foundation of its future greatness.

PETER H. FOLZ,

COUNCILMAN-AT-LARGE of Evansville, was born in Posey county, Indiana, in 1866, and is the son of Jacob Folz, a native of Germany, who married Miss Katherine Weis, also a native of Germany. The subject of this sketch was the fourth of six children born to Jacob and Katherine Folz. Jacob Folz is a man of the highest integrity, a valuable citizen and highly respected by all who know him. He was engaged in farming for a number of years and is now retired from actual business.

Peter Folz received his education in the schools of Evansville and has been a life-long Democrat. He has always manifested a deep interest in the welfare of his party and a man of his calibre could not well avoid getting into politics. He was chosen as a candidate for councilman-at-large in the last campaign and was elected by a good majority. He has been a successful business man, and as a public officer is demonstrating the wisdom of his party in placing him in office. Mr. Folz has charge of a large feed store at 1126 West Franklin street, and for a number of years he had charge of his father's extensive business in West Franklin street. He is a man of means and affairs and a member of one of the oldest and most highly respected German families in Evansville.

Mr. Folz was united in marriage, July 17th, 1894, to Miss Annie Seibert, of Evansville, and one child has blessed their union.

— — —

MATT. G. PERRIN,

A POPULAR constable, was born in Owensburgh, Greene county, Indiana, April 28, 1865, and is the son of Thomas W. and Sibbie (Woody) Perrin. The subject of this sketch was educated in the common schools and at the age of fourteen left home and went to Nebraska with his brother and was employed by the Singer Sewing Machine Co., being at that time their youngest agent in Nebraska. Two years later he returned to Evansville and for a time was variously engaged in the painting business.

In 1885 he went with the Armstrong Furniture Co. and learned the trade of finisher, which he afterwards found he could not follow on account of the severe effect of the turpentine. Then for nearly four years he served as salesman in the Armstrong furniture house on First street. By hard work and economy he managed to accumulate a small capital and leaving the Armstrong Furniture Co. he went in business on his own account, doing a general furniture and stove repair business on Second

18

avenue. He was afterwards variously engaged in Evansville, and in 1894 was appointed constable by the county commissioners and since then has served in that capacity and also as deputy assessor. He has been a faithful and consistent officer, discharging the duties of his office with credit to himself and those who placed him there. He was united in marriage December, 1885, to Miss Mildred Neal, of Morganfield, Kentucky, and three children, two girls and one boy, have blessed their union.

— — —

DUNCAN C. GIVENS,

A TTORNEY at law, city attorney of Evansville, son of M. C. and Kate H. Givens, was born in Madisonville, Kentucky, August 10, 1859.

His father, Judge M. C. Givens, is a native of Kentucky, and resides in Henderson, and is now presiding circuit judge of that district. His mother is also a native of Kentucky.

The early education of Duncan C. Givens was obtained in the country schools in Webster county, Kentucky, his parents having moved to Dixon, Kentucky, when he was five years of age. After completing his literary education he entered his father's law office and under his preceptorship gained valuable knowledge of the law, and was duly admitted to the bar November, 1877. In December of that year he removed to Morganfield, Kentucky, and practiced his profession there until 1880, when he came to Evansville, where he has met with very gratifying success as a lawyer.

In politics Mr. Givens affiliates with the democratic party, and in April, 1897, was appointed by Mayor Akin as city attorney of Evansville. He fills that office with grace and dignity and gives general satisfaction, which is an attestation of the wisdom of his appointment. Mr. Givens owns a large and very fine fruit farm in Missouri.

He was united in marriage February, 1892, to Miss Kate Taylor, of Evansville. He belongs to a number of benevolent orders, including the Masons, Elks and Forresters.

--- --- ---

HENRY WIMBERG,

PRESIDENT of the Evansville Brewing Association, was born in Germany December 31, 1851.

George Wimberg (father) was a native of Germany, where he was prosperously engaged in farming and in the saloon business. He married Lena Lubers, also a native of Germany, and their union was blessed with eight children, Henry being the second.

In 1869 Henry Wimberg, then eighteen years of age, came to Evansville, having received his education in the common schools of his native land. He was a poor boy and did not understand the English language, but he was rich in energy and common sense. He learned the trade of moulder, which he followed four or five years and then for twelve years was engaged in the saloon business. Disposing of his saloon interests he embarked in the livery and team business and is still a member of the firm of Karges & Wimberg, doing a livery, team and fuel business. The business was organized by Mr. Wimberg, who managed it entirely until he became interested in the brewing business at which time he sold a half interest to Mr. Karges.

Henry Wimberg possesses rare ability as a business man, and it was as a brewer that his efforts have met with the most gratifying success. He organized the Evansville Brewing Co., which was incorporated in 1891, he being made president, to which office he has been re-elected each succeeding year. March, 1894, the amalgamation of the three breweries – the Evansville Brewing Co., the Fulton Avenue Brewing Co., and the Hartmetz Brewing Co. occurred, and Mr. Wimberg's services as president became more essential, and under his guiding hand the business has grown and prospered until the operations of the concern extend far and near.

Politically Mr. Wimberg affiliates with the democratic party and has served the people of Evansville three successive terms as councilman. He was for three years police and fire commissioner. In 1884, a year fraught with disaster for all democrats, Mr. Wimberg was a candidate for sheriff of Vanderburgh county, but like others was defeated. Public spirited, energetic and liberal Henry

H. WIMBERG.

Wimberg is a highly honored and respected citizen, and every project having for its object the advancement of the interests of the city of Evansville has always found him a warm friend and supporter. Beginning with little more than his natural endowments as his capital, he has achieved success in all departments of life. Commencing at the bottom of the ladder with no capital he has succeeded in accumulating a considerable fortune. His capacity for work has been great and his dispatch of business rapid. He is in the prime of life, is an indefatigable worker and always punctual. These characteristics have contributed largely to the successful achievements of his life. Henry Wimberg was united in marriage in 1875 to Eliza Enge, and their union has been blessed with four children.

WILLIAM W. IRELAND.

PROMINENTLY engaged in the practice of law in Evansville, was born June 12, 1835, in Gallatin county, Kentucky, and is the son of James B. and Sallie (Lancaster) Ireland. The father is now living in his one hundred and first year and recently celebrated the one hundredth anniversary of his birth, having been born June 4, 1797, in Scott county, Kentucky, and belongs to that large class of men of worth and distinction, who was born to the soil. All his life has been spent in farming and

he is a man loved, honored and respected by all who know him.

William W. Ireland received his early education in the common schools of Gallatin county, and in 1858, entered the old Asbury College, now De Pauw University at Green Castle, Indiana. He was admitted to the bar in 1860, and practiced law in Falmouth county, Kentucky, for a period of fifteen years and for nine years was county and probate judge in that county. In November, 1878, he came to Evansville and has since been engaged in the practice of his profession. He served as county attorney for three years from 1891 to 1894. Originally Judge Ireland was a whig, but he now affiliates with the democratic party and has voted a straight democratic ticket for thirty-five years. For the same number of years he has been an elder in the Christian church in which he an active worker.

He was united in marriage in August, 1859, to Miss America J. Anderson, of Boone county, Kentucky. She died in Evansville, November 12, 1892. Their union was blessed with seven children, five of whom survive.

Judge Ireland has a strong love for the practice of law but detests technicalities in the trials of his cases. He is absolutely fair to all parties concerned; is frank and candid in all of his dealings with every one. Every wise effort to advance the public good finds in him an earnest friend and supporter. He takes an active interest in the work of christianity and the betterment of the moral condition of the community.

His practice has been large and general and his knowledge of the law is not confined to any one branch, but extends through all. He has always been a close student and a hard worker and has upheld the dignity and opinion of the profession in an admirable manner.

JUDGE ROBERT DALE RICHARDSON

WAS born in Spencer county, Indiana, January 13th, 1847, and graduated from the literary department of Indiana University at Bloomington, Indiana, and later from the law department of the same University. He began the practice of law in Evansville in 1868. He was appointed by Governor Gray, in January, 1880, to fill the unexpired term of Hon. William F. Parrett, who resigned to take his seat in Congress, as Judge of the Circuit Court. In the campaign of 1890 he was nominated by the Democratic judicial convention which met in Cannelton as his own successor, and was elected at the ensuing November election by the largest popular majority ever given the candidate for judge in the joint judicial district. His early years were spent upon his father's farm in Spencer county and his first instruction was received in a country school house. In the practice of his profession Judge Richardson had associated with himself Mr. James B. Rucker. The firm of Rucker and Richardson continued about one year.

He afterwards entered into partnership with General James N. Shackelford, which continued seven years. Subsequently he formed a partnership with Mr. James T. Walker, which continued up to the time of his appointment to the circuit bench by Governor Gray. He has been a member of the board of trustees of our common schools and also of the board of trustees of the State University. He is also a trustee of Willard Library and a member of the visiting board of the Indiana State Normal at Terre Haute. He is the father of two sons, both graduates of the State University. Mr. Emmet L. Richardson is at present his father's law partner.

CHRIST. KANZLER,

ONE of the foremost contractors of Evansville, and to whom great credit is due for the building of Evansville, was born in Germany in 1850 and emigrated to America in 1870, locating in Evansville. He is the son of Carl Kanzler, a native of Germany.

When a young man, after receiving his education, Mr. Kanzler learned the carpenters' trade in his native land and followed that vocation in this country up to 1879, when he began to do a contracting and building business. He formed a partnership with Jacob Bippus in 1880, which continued eleven years. Mr. Kanzler has an interest in and is vice president of the Mechanics' Planing

W. W. IRELAND, SR.

Mill. He is a hard worker, and has by careful economic management attained a comfortable competence.

Mr. Kanzler was united in marriage in 1873 to Miss Margaret Singer. She was born in 1854, and their union has been blessed with five children, the oldest of these a boy twenty years of age, has learned his father's business and assists him. Commenting on the life of Mr. Kanzler, one of the leading Evansville papers said: "He is a man of sterling integrity and his honesty has never been questioned by anybody. The builder need not figure on the hiring of a superintendent when Christ. Kanzler has the job. It will be built according to the specifications every time."

E. C. JOHNSON.

PROMINENT business man of Evansville, was born in Woodstock, Illinois, in 1850. He was educated at the Fulton, Illinois, military school and the Lombard University at Galesburg, Illinois, and was graduated from the latter in 1870. In 1872, after two years' study, he was admitted to the bar in Burlington, Iowa, and moving to Canton, Mississippi, practiced law there for two years. In the autumn of 1875 he gave up his profession and came to Evansville to embark in the lead and fluor spar business with Mr. B. Burbank. Upon the death of that gentleman, two years later, he became sole proprietor. He then enlarged his transactions by branching out as a wholesale and retail dealer in paints, oils, varnishes, brushes and such articles as pertain to the painter's trade. At the same time he operated his mines at Mineral City, Illinois, getting out lead and fluor spar, which he shipped all over this continent. In 1890 he sold out his mines to a corporation in St. Louis, known as Mullins' Silicated Iron and Steel Company, and he has been operating as their agent since.

Mr. Johnson has made an enviable record in the commercial world. His success has warranted him in erecting the most handsome paint store in the west. He now occupies a building at the foot of Main street with an eighty foot front, three stories and basement, fitted up with every modern convenience and filled with an enormous stock composed of white lead, zinc, fine colors ground in oil, varnish, ready mixed paint, dry colors, window glass, painter's supplies and all the accessories to this branch of trade, especially brushes. The machinery used in his factory is of the most modern kind and improved pattern. His house is recognized as one of the leading of its kind in the country, as well as in the city, and does a business of $150,000 a year.

Mr. Johnson has always been closely identified with all matters pertaining to the welfare of Evansville. For two years he was an active director of the B. M. A. and an intelligent and able chairman of the committee on commerce in that organization. He was chairman of the committee that started the Tri-State Fair Association, and was instrumental in raising $60.000 for that purpose. He was elected a. director of the Fair Association and subsequently was appointed by the B. M. A. to look after their interests, the B. M. A. being entitled to two directors in the Fair Association, of whom Mr. Johnson was one. Mr. Johnson's executive ability was even more thoroughly recognized when the property owners of Evansville made him chairman of the street improvement committee to obtain outside competition in street improvements. The wisdom of their choice was proven when he obtained bids from contractors in Virginia, Illinois, Ohio and Indiana, saving the city over $40,000.

In April, 1895, he was elected president of the Business Men's Association, and made a good record.

In 1870 he was united in marriage to Miss Clothilde Mills, of Galesburg, Illinois, and he is the head of a delightful family.

INDEX.

www.ingramcontent.com/pod-product-compliance
Lightning Source LLC
Chambersburg PA
CBHW020117030726
47498CB00006B/2146